No Conscience

A Novel

By

Phil M. Williams

Printed in the United States of America.
First Printing, 2017.

Phil W Books.
www.PhilWBooks.com

ISBN: 978-1-943894-24-6

Cover design and interior formatting by Tugboat Design

Contents

Dear Reader,

If you're interested in receiving my novel *Against the Grain* for free, and/or reading my other titles for free or $0.99, go to the following link: http://www.PhilWBooks.com. You're probably thinking, *what's the catch?* There is no catch. I hope you enjoy the book(s).

Sincerely,
Phil M. Williams

1

Wes, Big-Nosed Horse Mouth

"Shit." Wes pounded on his steering wheel. Stuck behind a school bus.

He zipped onto school grounds and swerved into his employee parking spot. Mark Twain Elementary was a one-story beige brick building. He grabbed his laptop bag, his lunch, and did a little run/walk to the side door. He waved his ID badge at the scanner. The door clicked; he yanked it open and fast-walked down the crowded hallway. Artwork and colorful motivational signs hung throughout the hallway.

There's no I *in team.*

Hang in there.

Put your best foot forward.

Kids of varying sizes chattered and carried identical Chromebook cases. Different races intermingled in relative harmony. Self-segregation didn't start until middle school. Public school officials celebrated the diversity. Wealthy white parents sent their kids to private schools.

The boys mostly wore sports attire and goofy T-shirts. One fourth grader wore a shirt that read *I'm not lazy. I'm conserving energy.* The girls dressed for their personalities. The sporty girls wore soccer shorts or sweatpants. The more fashion-conscious emulated the favorite labels of the high schoolers. A handful of sixth grade girls tested teachers with cuffed shorts that could be adjusted to fit the dress code. A few dared to wear the forbidden leggings. They brought a change of clothes for the inevitable.

Wes waded through the crowd and pushed into the faculty lounge. Inside were round tables and chairs, vending machines, a microwave, and a fridge. He headed to the fridge, placing his Snapple and lunch inside. His brown paper bag had *Wes* scrawled across the front in big black Sharpie letters. His Snapple had the same word of warning applied via masking tape.

Wes hustled back to the hallway, finally reaching a door labeled Technology. He shut the door behind him, silencing the cacophony of voices. The narrow room had a long table against the wall with cords plugged into power strips and computers in various stages of setup and repair.

Nick leaned back in his chair at the far end, swiping his thumb across his cell phone.

Wes exhaled as he set his computer bag on the table. "Traffic just gets worse and worse. Is Roy here, or is he at the middle school?"

"He's in a meeting," Nick said, still focused on his phone.

Wes sat down and breathed a sigh of relief. "So, what's on the agenda today?"

Nick shrugged, his massive shoulders threatening to burst through his button-down shirt, like in *The Incredible Hulk*. "Don't know."

"We still have to finish the filter setups for the new Chromebooks. Did you check the tickets yet?"

Nick continued to thumb-swipe.

Wes opened his laptop and logged on to check for pending tickets. "Nothing important," Wes said. "I guess I'll work on finishing the Chromebooks."

Nick continued to thumb-swipe.

"I could use some help," Wes said.

"Relax. It'll get done." Nick set his cell phone on the table. He cracked his neck back and forth. "What are you doin' this weekend?"

"My nephew has a birthday party on Saturday, so Tara and I will probably just watch a movie or something tonight."

"How long you been seein' that chick?"

"Almost four years."

Nick let out a low whistle. "That's a long time. She still givin' it to you on the regular?"

"Uh, that's none of your business."

Nick laughed. "I figured. You always look tense."

Wes's face felt hot. He looked down.

"Don't sweat that shit. Bitches be crazy. You should try bangin' one of the teachers."

Wes stared at the wall and shrugged. "I have my hands full with my girlfriend."

Nick smirked. "Whatever you say. But this weekend, when you're nursin' blue balls, I'll be balls deep in Daisy Bennett."

Wes snapped upright in his chair. "Ms. Bennett has a boyfriend."

Nick exhaled. "Jesus fuckin' Christ, don't you know anything?"

Wes rolled his eyes. *Here come the words of wisdom.*

"Bitches are always lookin' for someone better. Married, boyfriend, doesn't matter. It's a good way to tell if a chick's into you. If she's always talkin' about her man, she's tellin' you that her man's better than you. But, if she never mentions him, it's a green light. And Daisy never says dick to me about a boyfriend. Shit, I didn't even know she had a boyfriend until you just told me." Nick smiled wide. "That should tell you somethin' right there."

"Do you have a date with her?" Wes asked, his voice higher than normal.

"I'm trainin' a class at my Crossfit box on Saturday. She wants to give it a try. You get 'em all hot and sweaty in those tight-ass yoga pants, and it's a done deal. It's all animalistic pheromones and shit."

The door flew open. Nick feigned plugging in a Chromebook. Roy marched into the room wearing a tailored suit. He scanned the room, inspecting Nick with a glare, before turning his attention to Wes.

"Tuck that shirt in," Roy said to Wes. "And why are you sitting there with your thumb up your fourth point of contact?"

Wes stood up, shoving his polo in his khaki pants. "Sorry, sir."

Nick put his fist to his mouth, stifling his laugh.

Wes sat back down.

"We need to have a quick powwow," Roy said.

Wes and Nick swiveled their chairs to face their boss. Roy was fit, with a white-haired buzz cut, a square jaw, and a leathery face.

"I'm gonna give it to you straight," Roy said. "I'm not gonna pussyfoot around the issue. At the meeting this morning, we went over some personnel issues coming down the pike. We don't need two tech guys for this school. Once the one-to-one computers are set up and running, there's not gonna be as much to do. And the rest of the district is in the same boat with extra people. One of you will be furloughed or made into a part-time position. We haven't decided the specifics yet. I wanted to give you guys a heads-up, so it's not out of the blue."

Wes's eyes were wide open. "How do they decide which one of us stays?"

"It's normally tenure, but you two knuckleheads were hired the same day. I'd have to look at the contract to see how they're gonna handle this. I suspect job performance would be the deciding factor."

* * *

Wes looked up from his laptop. "We have an urgent ticket."

Nick glanced at his phone. "Shit, lunch is in fifteen. I'm starvin'. You take it."

"Okay, no problem," Wes answered with a bit too much pep.

Nick narrowed his dark eyes as Wes stood to leave. "Hold on."

But Wes was gone.

Wes stopped short of the windowed door and adjusted his tucked-in polo so it was pulled out just a little and even all around. He ran his hand through his hair, stepped up to the door, and knocked. Daisy's back was to him as she squatted to help a student at his desk. She stood and turned toward the door. Wes held his breath unknowingly. Her shiny brown hair was in a loose ponytail and rested on her right shoulder. She motioned for Wes to enter. He exhaled.

Daisy's classroom was bright, busy, and clean. Purple bean bags were in the corner with a minilibrary. Laminated educational posters filled every nook and cranny.

Wes approached.

"Thank you for coming so soon," she said with a smile that squinted her brown eyes and showed her top teeth—probably a product of good orthodontics. She faced her class. "All right, lovelies, we'll have some SSR time while Mr. Shaw helps me with my computer."

"Yay," a freckled girl said as she lifted her desktop.

"Retrieve your books. If you don't have one, you can procure one from our library but do it quickly. Does everyone remember what *procure* means?"

"Yes," the class replied in unison.

Daisy walked to her desk, her calves bare beneath her gray pencil skirt. Wes followed in a trance. He stared as she logged on to her laptop. She had the type of skin that was radiant in winter and just as beautiful with a tan in the summer. Her facial features were perfectly spaced and perfectly sized.

"The Internet just stops working," she said. "I have no idea why. It doesn't happen all the time but often enough to be disruptive. I have to restart my computer, and then it works again." She looked up at Wes with a frown. "Until it doesn't."

Wes stared blank-faced.

"Mr. Shaw?"

Wes blinked. "Sorry. Umm, have you run a scan for viruses and malware?"

She raised her eyebrows. "Should I have? I'm not much of a techie. Do you think you can fix it? I have a lesson this afternoon that requires the Internet."

“Probably. I’ll make sure your computer is updated and do the scan, and then we’ll see what’s going on.”

“Do I have to do anything?”

“Nope. I’ll handle it.”

She stood and motioned to her chair. “You can sit here.” She flashed another smile and went back to her class.

An hour later, the smell of peanut butter hung in the air as Daisy’s sixth graders chatted softly while eating their lunches.

“How’s it going?” Daisy asked over Wes’s shoulder.

Wes turned. “I think I’ve finally figured it out. I’m sorry it’s taken so long. I’m sure you want your desk back.”

She waved her hand. “I’m the one who should be sorry for causing you so much work.”

“I think it’s this Skype recorder. I uninstalled it, and everything seems to be working fine. I hope you don’t need it.”

“That was for our journalism project last year. Some of the kids had interviews to record.”

“That’s awesome. You do a lot of cool things with your students. Some of the classrooms I go into”—Wes shook his head—“it’s just obvious that they’re here for the pension.”

“That’s nice of you to say, but we have a lot of good teachers here.”

Wes blanched. “Of course.”

“Do you mind if I get into my desk now? I need to grab my lunch.”

Wes stood up abruptly, banging his thighs on the underside of the metal desk. “Sorry,” he said, stepping away.

Daisy slid into her seat. She leaned forward to grab her water bottle, exposing a bit of cleavage. “Did you eat lunch yet?”

Wes smiled and peeked. “I haven’t.”

She glanced at Wes and adjusted her blouse. “Don’t skip lunch. It’s not good for you. I pack my boyfriend’s lunch every day, and sometimes he comes home and says he didn’t have time to eat. Drives me crazy. Anyway, thanks again.” She glanced past Wes toward the door.

Wes’s smile dissolved. “You’re welcome.”

Wes shut Daisy's door behind him and closed his eyes for a moment. *I'm such a fucking dumb-ass. Why did I stare? I'm like a teenager. I can't even control myself. A girl like that would never be into me anyway. With my big-ass horse mouth and big nose. I bet her boyfriend is some big muscly douche like Nick. If she even has a boyfriend. Nick might be her boyfriend soon—or at least fucking her. Fucking Nick. I'd like to bash in his skull with a baseball bat. One of those aluminum ones. It would be hard to get blood out of a wooden one. Daisy would never fuck a loser like me. I'm lucky Tara can even stand to be in the same room as me.*

Wes entered the faculty lounge and shuffled to the fridge. One male teacher and two females sat at a round table, eating and talking. They ignored Wes. He opened the fridge, searching its contents. *Where is my—oh, there it is.* He grabbed his brown paper bag. It felt light. He looked inside to see only trash. He looked back in the fridge. His Snapple was nowhere to be found. Wes slammed the fridge shut. *Motherfucker.*

Wes turned toward the lunching teachers. "Did anyone see someone eating my lunch?"

They continued to talk as if he'd never uttered a word.

Wes clenched his jaw and balled his hands into fists. "Did anyone see someone eating my damn lunch!"

The three teachers looked at Wes, their eyes wide. The male teacher stood, glaring at Wes. "There's no need to talk like that. We didn't hear you the first time."

"Then how did you know there was a first time?"

The male teacher remained standing, now dumbfounded.

"I'm sorry for yelling," Wes said. "I'm starving, and someone ate my lunch. Did you guys see someone eating it? This isn't the first time."

"We didn't see anyone," the male teacher said.

"What did you have in your lunch?" one of the females asked.

Wes exhaled. "A turkey sandwich with cut-up apples and a granola bar, and a Snapple to drink."

"Sorry, no, we didn't see anyone eating that," she said.

"It happens all the time," the other female teacher added. "People were using my honey. I keep it in my room now. That stuff's expensive."

"Right, happens all the time. For unlabeled condiments maybe," Wes mumbled as he trudged to the vending machines.

2

Wes, the Jerk

Wes parked his car—an eight-year-old Hyundai—and surveyed his aging apartment complex. It was a sunny, cloudless sky with a light breeze, temps in the low eighties—perfect. The playground in the center of the complex was devoid of children. They preferred indoor activities, regardless of the weather. The apartments were a cluster of four-story vinyl-sided buildings that housed sixteen units each. Wes slogged up the steps to his third-floor apartment. He jammed his key into the dead bolt. The third floor was the worst. He had to walk up lots of stairs, but he still had people above him stomping on the ceiling, and people below him making noise.

Wes set his laptop bag on the coffee table in the family room. *Family room. More like TV room.* The walls were barren, the couch brown and worn. He did have a plasma-screen television. He went to the tiny kitchen and made himself another turkey sandwich and a glass of milk. He sat at the small round table for two next to the kitchen. His iPad was on the table. He turned it on while he munched on his sandwich.

He touched the Netflix app. Under the header Continue Watching for Wes, he tapped *The Walking Dead.* He continued to eat as zombies had their brains pierced with bullets, arrows, swords, and knives. The carnage wasn't one-sided. Human beings were gang-eaten alive.

Wes rinsed his plate and glass and put them in the dishwasher with the zombies growling in the background. He grabbed his iPad and lay on the couch. The screen was propped up, resting on his chest. He watched the women. They were hot, even covered in blood, even wearing zombie battle gear. Their mannerisms, their voices, their faces, their curves, their cleavage. He replayed his earlier interaction with Daisy in his mind. He removed the kids. Just the two of them in her colorful classroom. He ordered her to stand up. He reached under her skirt. She was warm. She jerked at his touch and gasped. He slid her panties down her legs. No, he ripped them off, and she had a look of terror on her face. He bent her over her desk and took her from behind. She was somewhere between ecstasy and agony. Her top was off. *Wait, when did I do that? Shut up. I took it off before.* Her breasts were firm. The same light tan as the rest of her body.

The iPad screen jostled as Wes touched himself. He set the screen on the coffee table, and pulled his pants and boxer briefs to his knees. His skinny legs were covered in dark hair. His penis pulsed as if it had a heartbeat. He grabbed the iPad and typed in his favorite porn site. He looked for the scene, the perfect scene to come to. He scrolled through endless images and videos, still touching himself. She had to look like Daisy, and it had to be dirty. It had to be standing from behind. And she had to be in agony. He was about to explode when he finally found the video, the one he had used last time. He pressed Play and grabbed his penis. *Shit, tissues.* He looked around. *Fuck.* He pressed Pause.

Wes stood and pulled up his pants and boxer briefs, holding them at midthigh, his erection pointing at the ceiling. He hustled to the kitchen and grabbed the tissue box. *Shit.* It was empty. He grabbed some paper towels and headed back to the couch. He settled into position and pressed Play. She really did look like Daisy, except for the huge implants. And it was a school scene. What were the chances he'd find a Daisy lookalike being violated in a school? It was thrilling. Well, it wasn't a real school, but a desk and papers were involved. He could pretend there wasn't cheesy wood paneling in the background. He was more bothered by the fact that the Daisy lookalike had pigtails and a Catholic school uniform. He didn't wanna bang the kids. He tried not to think about it.

She was bent over the desk. He was hurting her. She screamed. Wes grabbed the paper towels, put them over his penis, and continued to stroke. *Shit.* The paper towels were too coarse. Wes paused the video. *Toilet paper? No, dumb-ass, you buy that cheap shit that makes your asshole hurt.* He scanned the room and looked at his feet. He reached down and pulled a sock off his foot. It was black, but it was an athletic sock. He inserted his penis, imagining entering Daisy. He pressed Play on the video and went back to work. He had to slow down to manage it. Wes wanted to time his orgasm to the muscled horse-cock guy in the video. He wanted to *be* the muscled horse-cock guy, making her cry and begging for him to stop. There was no doubt who was in charge.

The muscled man pounded harder and started to grunt. He was almost there. Wes was almost there, on the brink. Wes heard a click, or did he? He was in a haze, so close. The point of no return. He had tunnel vision. The man gasped, and the woman turned around for the shot to the face. He heard a door slam. It had to be outside. A car door. Wes's penis spasmed in the sock, in perfect synchronicity with the muscled horse-cock guy. Wes gasped and moaned in ecstasy as the Daisy lookalike was covered in semen.

"What the *fuck* are you doing?"

Laughter filled the apartment as Wes came down from his high, suddenly very aware of his surroundings. His heartbeat raced as his eyes met hers—Tara's hazel eyes. She stood a few feet away, with one side of her mouth raised in contempt. She wore a tight skirt and a tight T-shirt. His hand still held his sock-covered penis, and the Daisy lookalike was eating the semen with a smile. Tara moved closer, shaking her head, her flip-flops snapping. She looked at the screen and winced.

"Ohmigod!"

Wes tapped buttons, frantically trying to turn off the damn thing. Finally the video stopped.

"What is *wrong* with you?" she asked. "That's fucking gross. Is this what you do when I'm not here?"

"What are you—"

A popup appeared of a woman asking for a private video chat. Wes powered off the iPad, his face hot. He dropped the iPad on the carpet and yanked up his pants and underwear. The soiled sock remained on his penis.

"You're pathetic," she said.

Wes sat up. "I'm sorry. It just … happened."

"Seriously?" She shook her head. "I hope you don't think I would ever let you do that to me."

"No, no. … God, no. Of course not. I would never do that to you."

"Damn right you wouldn't."

Wes took a deep breath. "I'm sorry. It doesn't mean anything."

She scowled with one hand on her hip, the other gripping her tiny purse. "Is that what you want? Some skank with big tits?"

"No, of course not. I want you. I just wish we were … together more."

She let out a quick breath and rolled her eyes. "I'm supposed to swoon after this?"

Wes hung his head.

"Craig offered to buy them for me," she said.

Wes looked up. Tara's face was all sharp edges, perfectly made up. Her brown hair was long and straight, with a few blond highlights. She was thin, like a model. She was what women thought men wanted.

"To buy what?" Wes asked.

"Breast implants." She had a crooked grin.

Wes's eyebrows rose. "Why would your boss do that?"

She shrugged. "Maybe he likes me. I think he thinks I'm a nine, and, with breast implants, I'd be a ten. He has tons of money. It's not a big deal to him."

Tara walked away, toward the kitchen. Wes stood, zipped up his khakis, and followed. She dropped her purse on the counter and moved toward the fridge.

"Are you gonna do it?" Wes asked.

She lifted one shoulder and opened the fridge. She retrieved a Chobani Greek yogurt.

"What does that mean?" Wes asked.

Tara lifted one shoulder again, opened a drawer, and fished out a spoon. She removed her phone from her purse. Wes followed her to the table. She sat and pulled the lid off her yogurt, her phone flat in front of her. She tapped on her screen and absently sucked yogurt off her spoon. She giggled at her phone.

"What?" Wes asked.

"Nothing," she replied without looking up.

"Why are you home so early?"

"Craig let me off early."

"But why?"

She frowned and looked up from her phone. "Next time should I text you? I wouldn't wanna interrupt your sock-fucking session."

"I was just wondering, Jesus."

She went back to her phone, now typing with her thumbs.

"Who are you texting?" Wes asked.

She kept texting, unresponsive.

"Tara."

She glowered at Wes. "What? I have to tell you everything, but you can have secret jerk-off time." She shook her head. "I'm texting Katie and Jess. We're going out tonight." She focused back on her thumbs. "I left work early to get ready."

"Where are you going?"

She sighed. "Don't know yet. We're figuring it out."

"Please don't take a cab to DC this time. It's really expensive."

She looked up. "How are we supposed to get there then? You gonna take us? Oh, that's right. You're afraid to drive in the city."

Bitch. "Maybe someone else could drive, or you guys could go out in Virginia."

"We live in this dump to save money. The least you could do is not give me shit about having a good time."

Wes rubbed his temples. "It could be better here if you would help me fix it up. We've been here almost two years, and it still looks like we just moved in."

"You said this would be temporary. Why would I waste my time?"

"I thought it *was* temporary. I've been looking for a better job. Everyone's outsourcing. They're even laying off tech people at school."

"If the job market's so bad around here, why is it that everyone drives a BMW or a Mercedes, and fucking mansions are everywhere?"

He exhaled. "Those people have better jobs than me."

"Your own mother lives in a mansion. Her job's not *that* great. Your brother and sister live in nice houses. Maybe not mansions but at least they live in houses."

"That doesn't have anything to do with me."

She pursed her lips. "Don't you think it's weird that you're the oldest and you live in the shittiest place?"

Wes looked down. "I don't know."

"Obviously. You know, I actually thought you'd be an internet millionaire by now. Remember that phone app? The internet security company?" She shook her head. "I should've known better." She went back to her phone.

They sat in silence, Tara enjoying her yogurt and her phone, Wes sitting and thinking of a way back into her good graces. Well, maybe not *good graces*. But *tolerance* would be nice.

Tara stood, clutching her phone, leaving the yogurt container on the table.

"Where are you going?" Wes asked.

"To shower. Do you have to be up my ass all the time?"

Wes stood from the table. "Don't forget. We have Connor's birthday party tomorrow."

She put her hand on her hip. "I'm not going over there early."

"It's not until two."

"And I'm not staying there all day."

Wes held out his palms. "Everyone's gonna be there. We can't leave early."

"It's not my fault your mom hates me."

"She doesn't hate you. She's never said anything mean about you."

"That's right. She's *so* nice. Her and Allison, so fucking perfect. It gets old. I mean, be real for once."

"What did Allison do?"

"It's not *what* she does. It's *how* she is. Turns up her nose at everybody, like she's perfect. Your mom's the same way."

"But neither of them have ever done anything to you."

"You don't know how women are."

Wes rubbed his temples. "If you go into it thinking that they don't like you, you're gonna act standoffish."

"Why do you always take your family's side?"

"I don't. I just—"

"Whatever." She walked away.

3

Mary and Connor's Birthday

Mary squeezed the icing dispenser and finished the "nor" on "Connor." Writing *Happy Birthday, Connor* on the hood of the police car cake was the easiest part. She covered her masterpiece with the Tupperware lid and turned her attention to the side dishes. The kitchen was open with a center island and built-in grill. She had a double oven, stainless steel appliances, granite counters, the works. She checked the roasted vegetables and the baked chicken in the ovens. Rosemary wafted into the air as she cut into a chicken breast. Still pink inside. She put it back in the oven. *Just a little longer.*

The screech of sneakers on her hardwood floor made her turn. It was Rich, the baby of the family. He was already six feet tall, blond, muscular. He was sweaty, with acne on his face and shoulders.

"How was practice?" Mary asked.

"Okay," Rich replied.

"Are you going to shower?" Mary asked.

Rich raised the front of his sweaty tank top to his nose. "Do I smell?"

"I would rather not know the answer to that."

Rich grinned and walked toward his mother with his wingspan wide open. "Can I have a hug?"

Mary screeched and ran away from her son with a giggle. She was at the far end of the kitchen with Rich still coming. "I have a knife in my hand," she said. "Don't make me run. It's dangerous."

He relented, dropped his arms, and kissed Mary on the cheek. "Is that okay?"

Mary beamed. "Of course."

They walked back toward the food. Rich grabbed the orange juice carton from the fridge and guzzled directly from it.

Mary shook her head. "How about a glass, young man?"

Rich replaced the carton in the fridge. "I just wanted a sip."

"Is Brandi coming today?"

"Yeah, I have to pick her up."

"That's nice." She pointed with her knife toward the basement steps. "You need to get your butt in the shower."

"I'm going," he said with his hands up.

The doorbell chimed, and the front door opened. Mary set the knife and fork on the counter.

"Hey, Mom. We're here," Matt, her middle son, called out.

"I'm in the kitchen, honey," Mary called back.

The pitter-patter of little feet ran through the foyer, then the dining room, then the kitchen, followed by the *click-clack* of nails on the hardwood.

"Nana!" Kyle said as he ran into Mary's legs.

A black Lab trotted toward them, his tail wagging and his tongue hanging out. Mary bent down and hugged the little blond boy, her eye on the dog who wanted to jump on them.

"You're getting so big," Mary said to Kyle. "I'm not sure I can pick you up anymore."

"You prob'ly can't," Kyle said. "I'm the biggest in pre-K."

"Hey, Mom," Matt said, as he walked into the kitchen. Allison and the birthday boy were behind him.

"Hi, honey," Mary said as she hugged her son, her head just below his neck.

His arms and chest were solid, like they were carved from stone. He always was a solid boy, now a solid man.

"I put Connor's gifts on the dining room table with the others," Matt said.

"That's perfect," Mary replied. "I thought we'd have his cake and presents in there." She glanced at the panting dog. "I really wish you would tie up Rocky outside. He'll scratch my hardwood."

Rocky sniffed the counters, near the food. The black Lab stood on his hind legs, putting his front paws on the counter.

"Get down," Matt said, knocking the dog's paws off the granite.

Rocky still wagged his tail, his tongue hanging out, as if it were a game.

"I'll take him out," Matt said, grabbing the dog by the collar.

"No," Kyle said, scowling, with crossed arms. "Rocky's invited to the party."

"Don't you show me that sour puss," Mary said, as she tickled Kyle, making him laugh.

"Hi, Mary," Allison said. "Thank you so much for hosting. Our place is just too small for everyone."

Mary let go of Kyle and stood up. "Anytime—you know that." Mary moved gracefully to hug her daughter-in-law. They embraced, barely touching. Mary stepped back, looking her over. "You look positively beautiful."

Allison blushed.

She *was* striking. Allison looked Swedish. Her hair was platinum blonde, without artificial coloring. Her eyes, bright blue. Her cheekbones, high. Matt was also a blond but not platinum. He kept his hair cut very short, all the same length. Matt was six feet tall, Allison five eight or so. It was no wonder Kyle was a beautiful blond boy who towered over his classmates. Connor on the other hand was different.

Connor hid behind his mother. Allison turned around. "Are you going to give Nana a hug?"

Connor shook his head and grabbed the back of Allison's knee, just beneath her loose skirt. Connor had dark hair and almost olive skin. He was a little guy, slightly below average size for a newly minted three-year-old.

"Do you have any treats?" Kyle asked, tugging on Mary's calf-length floral dress.

"Let's see what I have for you," Mary replied, opening a drawer and pulling out two full-size Hershey's chocolate bars.

"Whoa, can I have the whole thing?"

Allison's eyes bulged. "Kyle, I don't want you ruining your appetite."

"Nana said it was okay," Kyle said.

"One's for your brother," Mary said, handing the chocolate bars to Kyle.

"Can we go to the playroom and eat them?"

"Can you be careful not to get chocolate on my carpet?"

Kyle nodded with a grin.

"Okay then," Mary said with a smile.

"Yes," Kyle said, as he threw his fist upward in triumph. "Can we go into the doll room?"

"Maybe another time, honey. The doll room's locked."

Matt walked back into the kitchen without Rocky.

Kyle approached Allison and Connor. He handed one of the chocolate bars to his brother, but Allison intercepted it.

"Why don't you two share the one?" Allison said.

"Aw, I want my own," Kyle replied.

"Kyle." Allison bent down and raised one eyebrow to her son.

Depriving them only makes them want it more.

Kyle frowned. "Come on. Let's go." Kyle grabbed Connor's hand. The boys climbed the white-carpeted stairs to the playroom.

"What can I do to help?" Allison asked.

"Oh, just relax. Most everything's done," Mary replied. "So, what's new with you two?"

"I was giving this—" Matt started.

"Where are my manners? Would you two like something to drink?"

"We'll get what we need," Matt said. "You don't need to wait on us."

"What were you saying, honey? I interrupted you."

"I pulled this lady over last week, and she tried to give me her number."

"Like for a date," Allison interjected.

Mary laughed.

"I think she just wanted to get out of the ticket," Matt said. "She was doing forty-five in a twenty-five."

"I don't know about that," Mary said. "You're very handsome. You're quite the catch."

Allison sucked in her lower lip.

"Where's Nana?" Matt asked.

"She's in the family room, watching television," Mary replied.

"I don't hear the TV."

"I turned down the volume. Once it gets into the afternoon, she's not very lucid. She just watches the images. I put on the Discovery Channel for her. She seems to like that."

"I'm sorry to hear that," Allison said.

"I should see how she's doing," Matt said, leaving the kitchen.

"And I should check on the boys." Allison went upstairs.

The doorbell chimed, then chimed again.

Mary sighed. *It's probably Ed and Sheryl.* Her ex-husband rang the doorbell with gusto since Warren had told Ed that he couldn't just walk in anymore. Mary pressed her dress with her hands, and checked her hair and makeup in the microwave window. Her blond hair was cut to chin length, although it was going white. Her hair stylist made sure they were the only ones who knew it. Her makeup was still intact, covering her crow's-feet and forehead wrinkles. She pressed her dress one more time, running her hands over her flat stomach. She took a deep breath and stepped to the front door.

The doorbell chimed again as Mary opened one of the double doors. Ed stood with a wide grin and a large present but no Sheryl.

"Hey, good-lookin'," Ed said.

"Where's Sheryl?" Mary asked.

"She's not feelin' too well." He leaned forward and kissed Mary on the cheek. "Thanks for invitin' me."

"Of course. You know you're always welcome."

Ed dropped off his gift in the dining room as they made their way to the kitchen. He opened the refrigerator and helped himself to one of Warren's beers. Mary glanced out the kitchen window. Matt stood on the deck, talking on his phone. She turned to Ed. He peeked inside the covered dishes on the center island burners.

Mary tapped his hand with a grin. "Keep your grubby hands out of there."

He smiled, his mustache stretching across his face. "It smells good. I never could resist your … cooking."

Mary giggled. "Stop it."

His smile receded. "You look pretty, Mary."

"You look good too."

And he did. His blond and white hair thinned a little at the back, but he was still in great shape. No small feat for a man in his early fifties.

The front door opened. Mary listened to see who it was this time.

"Can you at least hold the door?" Colleen asked in a hushed whisper that carried to the kitchen.

"I have the gift," Greg replied and swaggered into the kitchen, the gift probably left with the others.

"Gregory," Mary said, as she approached the muscled man with dark skin, leaving Ed in her wake.

She hugged him and stepped back. Greg had a broad grin with bright white teeth. "Hi, Mom," he said.

Mary loved that Colleen's husband called her *Mom*.

Colleen ambled behind him, clutching an infant carrier in one hand with a diaper bag on her shoulder.

"How do you keep yourself in such great shape?" Mary asked Greg.

He laughed, a deep masculine laugh. "Not much. Some lifting. I play basketball three times a week."

"Well, whatever it is, it's working." She turned to her daughter. "How's my favorite new mom?"

Colleen exhaled with a frown toward Greg. She set the baby and carrier on the center island away from the food and burners.

"Let me get that for you," Mary said, taking the diaper bag. She placed it on the counter opposite the food and appliances.

Ed approached Colleen. "Lookin' good, babe."

Colleen hugged Ed. "Thanks, Dad."

Mary walked over to the carrier, a mobile bassinet that attached to the baby's car seat. The curly-headed beauty with the café-au-lait skin was fast asleep.

"Oh, she's so adorable," Mary whispered with her hands clasped. "I just love her."

"She's adorable, … when she's sleeping," Colleen said.

"Colleen," Mary said with a frown.

"I love her, Mom, but I'm like a slave to her every whim." Colleen exhaled. "I'm just tired."

Colleen wore a purple flowing short-sleeve dress. Even the loose dress couldn't cover her meaty arms, thick hips, and bubble butt.

"Oh, honey," Mary said as she embraced her daughter and disengaged. "You should let Gregory help you with an exercise program. It'll give you more energy."

"I don't even have time to sleep, much less work out."

"I tried," Greg interjected. "She doesn't listen to me."

"It'll get better," Mary said to her only daughter. "But, when it comes to fitness, you should take Gregory's advice."

Colleen rolled her eyes.

"Greg," Ed said.

Greg's jaw tensed. "Sir."

"It's good to see you." They shook hands.

"Sir," Greg repeated, expressionless.

"Would you two like something to drink?" Mary asked.

"I'm good with beer," Ed said as he raised his bottle.

Mary smirked. "I was talking to Gregory and Colleen."

"I'll have a beer," Greg replied.

Colleen glared at Greg, then turned to Mary. "He can get it himself."

Mary waved her hand. "Oh, nonsense." She grabbed a beer bottle from the fridge and handed it to Greg.

He twisted off the top and took a drink.

Matt walked inside from the deck. He shoved his phone in his pocket and joined everyone in the kitchen.

Ed smiled at his son. "Matt."

"Sir," Matt replied, as they shook hands.

"What's up, Greg?" Matt said, turning his attention to his brother-in-law. They shook hands and gave each other a manly half embrace.

"Not much. How you doin'?" Greg asked.

"Same bullshit, different day."

"I hear that."

"Matthew, language," Mary said. "I can hear you from over here."

Matt put his hands up. "You're right. Sorry, Mom."

"That's one of the things you pick up in the infantry," Ed said. "Like coffee and hot sauce."

Heavy footsteps descended the stairs.

"Pick up what in the army?" Warren asked, as he exited the staircase.

"Profanity," Ed said.

Warren's smile disappeared at the sight of Ed. He turned his attention to Matt and Greg, his smile reappearing. "I knew quite a few foul-mouthed soldiers," Warren said.

Despite his hefty presence, Warren was ignored.

"You ever put hot sauce on an MRE?" Matt asked Greg.

Greg laughed. "Shit, that's the only way I could eat some of 'em."

Mary crossed her arms. "You too now?"

Greg grinned. "Sorry."

"I did that," Warren said, moving closer to the young men. "We used to get free samples in supply all the time. I actually liked them."

Ed marched over to the men. "MREs taste different in the field, when you're filthy and sleep-deprived."

Warren clenched his jaw and dipped his head. His gray hair was feathered and thinning on top.

"I brought a volleyball net," Ed said. "I thought we'd have a friendly game, and, by *friendly*, I mean fight to the death." He grinned.

Greg and Matt gave each other a look.

Ed pointed to the young men. "You two, help me set up the net."

"Is that an order?" Matt asked.

Ed smirked. "I outrank both of you."

The men went outside. Warren stayed in the kitchen.

"Look at this little cutie," Warren said, his face inches from the baby.

Abby started to cry.

"Warren," Mary said. "Abby was sleeping."

Warren stood upright as Colleen hustled to the baby. Once the mother picked up her daughter, she quieted.

"Sorry about that," Warren said to Colleen.

"You're like a bull in a china shop," Mary said as Warren stomped toward her.

He smiled wide, his beady eyes shrinking as his face tightened around his smile. "That's why you love me, cuddle cakes," he said.

Colleen let out a giggle. "Cuddle cakes?"

Mary's face felt hot.

Warren turned to Colleen with a crooked grin. "Because your mom is the best cake maker and the cuddly part, … well, that's private."

Colleen laughed.

"Why don't you make yourself useful and get the grill started?" Mary said to her husband.

Warren sighed and yanked up his jeans, resting his belt on a more comfortable position above his gut. "I know when I'm not wanted."

Mary handed Warren the burgers from the fridge. He left the kitchen with the meat.

The front door opened once more. Footsteps moved from the foyer, through the dining room, to the kitchen.

"Hi, Mom," Wes said.

"Hi, honey," Mary said, walking around the center island to give her eldest son a quick hug. "Hi, Tara dear." Mary moved in for the hug, but Tara offered her hand.

Wes was darker than his siblings. His hair was dark brown, his arm hair also dark. His eyes were too small and too close together. His face was all nose and mouth and pointy chin. He looked better from afar, like a Monet. Up close it got a little chaotic.

"Hey, Colleen," Wes said, as he hugged his sister.

"Hi, Tara," Colleen said, as she let go of Wes.

"Hi," Tara replied, only to sit down at the round kitchen table and to fish her phone from her purse. Like a bored teenager, she tapped away at the miniature screen.

"Did you know Warren calls Mom *cuddle cakes*?" Colleen asked Wes.

Wes laughed. "Cuddle cakes?"

Mary shook her head with a crooked smile. "After all I've done for you kids."

The door from the deck opened, and Ed spilled inside.

"All right, gang, volleyball net's up," Ed said. "And everyone's playing." Ed noticed Wes and approached with a grin. "Wes, I'm glad you're here. You can be on my team."

Wes shook his head. "Dad, you know I'm terrible at sports."

Ed smacked Wes on the back. "That's not true. Let's go, everyone. Game starts in two minutes."

"Not me," Mary said.

"Me neither," Colleen said.

Ed looked at Colleen. "You're playing."

Colleen played her trump card. "I have to watch the baby."

Ed blew out a breath, his hands on his hips. "Where's Rich?"

"He's picking up Brandi," Mary replied.

Ed glanced at Tara, sitting at the table. "You too, Tara."

"No thanks," she said, glancing up from her phone.

"Come on anyway," Ed replied. "You can be a cheerleader. You sure are built like one."

Tara blushed and grinned.

"The food will be ready in about fifteen minutes," Mary said.

"Enough time for a game," Ed replied.

Wes and Tara followed Ed outside.

"I should check on the burgers," Mary said to Colleen.

Mary walked from the kitchen, through the sunroom, and onto the massive deck—complete with built-in benches, a Weber grill, and steps down to the backyard, where the volleyball game was underway.

Warren tended the grill with slumped shoulders.

"How are the burgers?" Mary asked.

"They're burgers," Warren replied. "If I mess 'em up, add cheese and ketchup."

"Are you okay?"

Warren worked the spatula. "I don't like it when he's here. No matter how I try, I can't forget what he did to you."

Mary stroked his forearm, held at his side. "I know, honey, but you can't keep doing this to yourself. I don't want you to be angry. It was a long time ago."

"I'm a nice person—"

"That's why I love you."

"But, when he's here, I wanna kill 'im. Then he acts like he owns the place. It's our house, not his. You're *my* wife, not his. Not anymore."

"I know. And I'm so much happier with you."

Warren clenched his jaw. "Then why do you still have his name?"

Mary pursed her lips. "We've been through this. I don't think now is the time or the place to rehash it."

Warren shook his head with a scowl.

"Be the bigger man. He is their father."

"He's a sick, disgusting human being. He's a God damn—"

"Warren, you're spiraling." Mary frowned. "Focus on the kids and grandkids."

“Did you hear what he said about MREs tasting better in the field?”

Mary held up her palms. “I would think they would taste the same anywhere. What difference does it make?”

Warren pressed hard on a burger, causing a sizzle. “He was making fun of me. I knew guys like him in the army. Cocky assholes who think they’re so tough because they’re in the infantry. Everyone else is just some wimp, some POG.”

“POG?”

“*Person other than grunt.* That’s what they called us. So what? I was supply. I had to go through basic just like them.”

“I know you did, honey. It doesn’t matter now.”

“I’m too old to be dealing with guys like him.”

Mary kissed him on the cheek. “I’m with you. Only you.”

4

Mary and the Seed of Lucifer

Mary leaned on the deck railing, watching the volleyball game below. Matt and Greg dominated Ed and Wes. Tara wasn't much of a cheerleader, but at least she wasn't staring into her phone. Actually she stared at something else—someone else. And it wasn't Wes, who was too painful to watch. Mary felt embarrassed for him at his awkward attempts to return Greg's or Matt's spikes. It was obvious that he was afraid of the ball.

"Burgers are ready," Warren said to Mary.

Mary turned toward her husband at the grill, then back toward the volleyball players below. "Food's ready! It's time to eat!"

The guys and Tara headed for the deck steps. Rocky whimpered as the players walked by. They left him tied to the deck post with a bowl of water. Mary held the door for Warren as he carried the burgers inside on a platter and set them on the center island. Mary added a stack of plates, silverware, and glasses. Everyone spilled into the kitchen. Wes sneezed and washed his hands in the kitchen sink.

"We can prepare our plates in here and eat in the dining room," Mary said. "Oh, shoot, the table's covered in presents. Could someone set them on the floor next to the hutch?"

"I got it," Wes said.

"Would you like me to get drinks for everyone?" Matt asked Mary.

"Thank you, honey. That would be really helpful."

Matt grabbed the glasses from the center island and filled them with filtered water from the fridge. He glanced over his shoulder. "You're all getting water. If you want something different, make it yourself."

"I have a bottle of white in the fridge, and red on the rack, if anyone wants wine," Mary said.

"I'll have a glass of red," Colleen said.

Mary raised her eyebrows. "You're breastfeeding, aren't you?"

Colleen frowned. "It's one glass of wine."

"We also have beer," Warren added. "Matt, Greg, Wes, you guys want a beer?"

"I'll have one," Greg said.

"Me too, thanks," Matt said.

"Wes?" Warren asked.

"I'm just gonna have water," Wes replied.

"Can someone please go upstairs and tell Allison and the boys that we're ready to eat?" Mary asked.

Nobody moved.

"Matthew, can you please let Allison and the boys know we're about to eat?"

"Okay." Matt finished filling a water glass. He walked to the steps leading upstairs. "Allison, it's time to eat!"

Mary shook her head.

Matt grinned and returned to filling water glasses.

Allison and the boys descended the steps to the kitchen. The family arranged themselves, their plates, and their drinks in the dining room.

Mary tapped *Richard* on her phone, wondering when her youngest would arrive home.

The recorded voice said, "This mailbox is full and cannot accept any messages."

Mary blew out a breath and ended the call. She sent a text.

Mary: Where are you? We are eating now. Please come back as soon as possible.

Mary set her phone on the counter. She watched Wes, the last one in the kitchen, shovel food onto his plate.

Wes looked up from his full plate. His face was red and puffy. "You're not gonna eat?"

Mary narrowed her eyes. "Your allergies acting up?"

"Yeah, the dog. Matt let him off the leash, and he jumped on me."

"I have Claritin."

"He does it on purpose, you know. He was laughing."

Mary frowned. "Let me get you some medicine."

She gave Wes the tablet. He swallowed it with a gulp of water.

"Is Nana gonna eat?" Wes asked.

"I'll make her a plate after I'm done. I may have to feed her. She gets mixed up in the afternoon."

"The Alzheimer's?"

Mary nodded.

"I didn't know she was that bad." Wes sniffed and wiped his nose with a tissue.

Mary sighed. "The last few months she's really gone downhill. It breaks my heart, but she is eighty."

"I'm sorry, Mom," Wes replied.

Mary kissed Wes on the cheek. "Thank you."

Mary placed a skinless chicken breast on her plate and a small salad. Wes and Mary walked into the dining room lit by a chandelier and dominated by a linen-covered table that sat ten. Matching hutches displaying fine china sat at opposite ends of the room. Every seat was already taken. People talked and ate. Abby was in her carrier, asleep against the wall. Connor and Kyle sat in their own seats. Kyle was tall enough to sit in the big-boy chairs, but Connor was unhappy, curled up in his chair, uninterested in his food. Allison sat between them, making sure they ate and didn't make a mess on the Oriental rug.

Mary watched as Wes surveyed the scene. He looked at Tara sitting between Ed and Matt. She whispered something to Matt, and he burst out laughing, a laugh he stifled at the sight of Wes. Wes went to the family room.

"I can move the boys," Allison said, "to make room for you and Wes."

"That's okay," Mary said, "I should probably tend to Nana. The boys are doing such a good job in the big-boy chairs."

Kyle smiled with slightly chewed burger in his mouth. Connor curled into a tighter ball.

"Sit up and eat your food, Connor," Allison said. "You can't have cake if you don't eat some healthy food."

In the family room, Mary sat in the upright recliner, Wes at the opposite end of the couch from Nana. The Discovery Channel was muted on the television.

Nana stared at the screen, slack-jawed. Her hair was white, short, and thinning. Her eyebrows were painted on in a permanently surprised expression. She sat, wrinkly and sun-spotted, in her light-blue bathrobe with the remote next to her.

"Are you hungry, Mom?" Mary asked and took a bite of chicken.

Nana did not respond.

Wes set his plate on the coffee table. He sneezed three times into a soggy tissue, a spray of clear mucus dotting the table and his food.

He sniffed back mucus. "Sorry. They come in threes." He went to the kitchen and returned with a handful of tissues. He wiped the mucus from the table.

Mary and Wes ate in silence, watching bearded men in hard hats working on a drilling platform.

Wes turned to his grandmother. "Would you like me to turn it up, Nana?"

She remained unresponsive.

"Nana?"

Nana narrowed her eyes at Wes. "Shh, I'm listening."

"But you could hear better if we turned up the sound." Wes reached across the couch, grabbing the remote.

Nana smacked his hand. "No."

Wes pulled his hand back as if it were burned.

"Mom, do not hit Wesley," Mary said. "He was being nice to you."

Nana ignored Mary and glared at Wes, her veiny finger pointing. "You shouldn't be here. Seed of Lucifer."

Wes's eyes opened wider.

"Mom, you stop that this instant," Mary said.

Nana's gaze settled back on the screen, her jaw loosening and drool puddling in the corner of her bottom lip.

"Did I do something wrong?" Wes asked Mary.

Mary sighed. "No, honey, she's just not herself after a certain hour. She doesn't know what she's saying."

After the late lunch, the family settled in the dining room for cake and presents. Mary sent another unrequited text to Rich. They sang to Connor, who buried his head in Allison's chest. Everyone oohed and aahed at the police car cake.

"It looks just like mine," Matt said. "Lemme take a picture before you cut it. The guys'll get a kick outta this."

Matt snapped a few photos with his phone, and Mary cut the cake. Everyone sat and ate cake, except Mary, always aware of her figure. Colleen held Abby. Connor sat in Allison's lap and Kyle in Matt's. Matt and Allison smiled at each other, and he leaned in for a cake-filled kiss. Allison giggled but accepted his offer.

"Can I open the presents now?" Kyle asked.

"Kyle, sweetie, it's Connor's birthday," Allison replied.

"But he's not gonna open 'em."

"You can help, but everyone has to finish their cake first."

The doorbell chimed. Mary stood from the table. "That must be Grace."

"I can get it," Matt said, but he made no physical gesture to actually answer the door.

"Finish your cake, honey."

Mary opened the door to see her sister Grace, taking a deep drag on a cigarette.

"You can't smoke inside," Mary said.

Grace blew smoke in Mary's face and dropped the cigarette on the brick stoop. Mary waved her hand to deflect the smoke.

"Relax. I wasn't going to dirty up your perfect house," Grace said, crushing the cigarette with her heel.

Grace was forty-five, a couple years younger than Mary but looked older. Her darkened skin was leathery from too many trips to the tanning bed. Her hair was bleached blonde, stringy. Her legs were bare under her tight skirt, and her implants burst from her low-cut blouse.

She stepped inside past Mary. Grace looked down on her sister. It was partly due to her heels, but she was taller, five foot eight, and beefier, now that age and neglect had overcome good genetics.

"We've already eaten, but we haven't opened presents yet." Mary glanced at Grace's empty hands. "You did bring a present, didn't you?" Mary whispered.

"Shit, I left it at home," Grace said. "Put my name on one of yours. I'll pay you back."

Grace walked into the dining room without waiting for a reply from Mary. She took a deep breath as everyone greeted fun Aunt Grace.

* * *

"You don't want to give Nana a hug good-bye?" Allison asked.

Connor shook his head, hiding behind his mother.

"She had such a nice birthday party for you."

Connor buried his face in the back of Allison's skirt.

"He's so shy," Allison said. "I don't know where he gets it."

"It's okay, Connor," Mary said. "I was a shy little girl once. Happy birthday. Nana loves you."

"Thank you for everything," Allison said, as she hugged Mary.

Mary smiled. “It was my pleasure.”

“It was great, Mom,” Matt added and hugged his mother. “I left Rocky for you. He’s in the backyard.”

“Better not be.”

Matt grinned. “He’s in the car.”

“Thank you, Warren,” Allison said.

“Yeah, thanks, Warren,” Matt said, as he shook Warren’s hand.

“Until next time,” Warren said with a broad smile.

Mary shut the door after them, and, with that, they had their house back. Warren gave Mary a big hug that she wriggled out of after a moment.

“It’s time to clean up,” Mary said.

“We can do it tomorrow,” Warren replied.

Mary laughed. “We? Are you planning to help me clean tomorrow?”

“I have an early tee time. Leave it until Monday. Isn’t Rosa here then?”

“I can’t leave this big mess for her.”

“Just pay her a little more. Come sit down with me. Let’s watch a movie.”

“The house is filthy. I am *not* leaving it like this for her. It’s not about the money.”

Warren shook his head. “You’re the only person I know who cleans before the housekeeper comes. I’m gonna watch TV.”

“Can you put Nana to bed first?”

Warren sighed. “Sure.”

Mary went to the kitchen and started on the dishes. She heard the rumble of an engine. Mary hurried into the garage, pressed the garage door opener on the wall and ducked under the door as it rose. Rich and Brandi giggled and headed for the basement entrance.

“What do you think you’re doing, young man?” Mary asked.

Rich and Brandi turned around, lit by the garage lights. Brandi was a diminutive girl with dangerous curves. She wore cut-off jean shorts, cowboy boots, and a low-cut tank top.

"We're going to my room," Rich said, his hair jelled in a faux hawk.

"You missed your nephew's birthday party," Mary said, her hands on her hips.

"I'm sorry about that. We got caught up."

Brandi flipped her hair off her shoulders, a frown on her face.

Mary furrowed her brow. "You got *caught up*?"

"Chill, Mom," Rich said. "It's not like Connor even noticed."

"And how would you know that?"

Rich smirked. "Because he's two."

"He's three," Mary said. "You would know that if you were here for his birthday."

"I'm sorry, okay? Can we just drop it?"

"Next time I expect you here."

"Okay."

Mary returned to the kitchen.

Warren stomped down the stairs and entered the kitchen. "Was that Rich?"

Mary frowned. "He had no excuse for missing Connor's birthday. That kid is driving me crazy. If he keeps it up, I'll send him to Ed."

"He's just being a teenager."

Mary nodded. "Well, thankfully he's the last one. How's Nana?"

"She seems more out of it than usual."

"Is she okay?" Mary asked.

Warren held up his palms. "She said something like, 'He's the seed of Lucifer.' I thought maybe she was quoting something from the Bible. She kept repeating it, so I asked her who she was talking about, and she said, 'Wes,' but she said it in a deep voice. It was strange."

"She's been acting peculiar. It's the Alzheimer's."

"Wes *is* different," Warren said. "Did you see his expression when he came in to eat and all the seats were taken?"

"I didn't."

"It looked like he was about to snap. Allison was gonna move the boys, but he just left without a word."

Mary sighed. "He has some issues, but, deep down, he's a good person." She glanced at the kitchen table. "I need to sit down for a minute. My feet are killing me."

Warren sat next to Mary at the round kitchen table.

"You think Wes could have done something to Nana?" Warren asked.

"Like what?"

Warren shrugged. "I don't know. Something to make Nana think he's the devil's kid? I mean, I like Wes and all, but something is off about him."

"What does that even mean, something off?"

"He's a lot different than his brothers—and Colleen for that matter. He just doesn't fit in exactly. I can't put my finger on it. You said Tony was a nice guy, but what about his family? Did anyone have problems?"

"His parents were nice, but it was an awful thing to deal with. When Tony died, his parents took it really hard." Mary's mouth turned down. "I took it hard. I had no idea how to raise a child at seventeen by myself. I love my mother, but she was no help. She was too busy making sure I felt that Catholic guilt. I was in a terrible no-win situation. I worry that I didn't do a good job with Wesley when he was a baby. Maybe I wasn't a good mother to him, and that's why he's different." Mary hung her head.

Warren leaned closer and lifted Mary's chin. "I don't buy that for a second. If there's one thing I'm sure about, it's that you're an excellent mother."

Mary leaned forward and kissed Warren on the cheek. "You're sweet, you know that?"

Warren half smiled. "What happened to Wes's paternal grandparents? Did they spend much time with him?"

"A little when he was young, but they were never around much. After Tony died, their marriage fell apart. They divorced and went their separate ways. Wes's grandmother moved to California. His grandfather died when Wes was six, and his grandmother when he was thirteen or fourteen."

"How did Wes take it?"

"It didn't seem to bother him."

Warren raised his eyebrows. "That sounds callous."

"But he really didn't spend much time with them."

Warren nodded. "He was a kid without a father. That could have messed him up."

"Ed's his father. He adopted Wes."

"I know, but he didn't have his biological father."

"Other things worried me about him. I don't think they had anything to do with his father."

"Like what?"

"He used to have accidents, and he would bury his dirty underwear in the yard."

"That's strange. How old was he?"

"He did it until he was nine or so. He refused to move his bowels. He would just hold it in, and then it would come out at night. He had the worst stomach cramps."

"I'm surprised you never told me that before."

"I didn't want to embarrass Wesley." Mary placed her hand on Warren's forearm and raised her eyebrows. "So please don't repeat this."

"I won't. You said there were other things, *things* plural."

Mary exhaled. "I shouldn't even tell you this because nothing happened. It probably doesn't mean anything."

"Now you have to tell me."

"Colleen developed early for a girl. When she was in her early teens, I'd see Wesley staring at her sometimes. He never did anything, but I know that look."

"That's not good. Did he ever do anything violent?"

"He tried to pick on Matthew when they were young, but that stopped pretty quick because Matthew was such a strong kid. I remember Wesley taunting Matthew, and he hauled off and popped Wes in the nose. Wesley cried and cried. He stopped teasing his little brother after that. But that was just the normal fighting that happens with brothers."

"Well, he's an adult now. No longer your problem."

Mary frowned. "He'll always be my son. I don't care how old he is."

"I just don't know why your mother would say something like that. It has to come from somewhere."

"It could be her Catholicism mixing with her Alzheimer's."

5

Wes, Be a Man

"I have to update the servers this weekend," Wes said, his hands on the steering wheel.

When he received no response, he glanced at Tara. She had her arms crossed, staring out the car window.

"Did you hear me?"

She turned her head for a moment, her jaw set tight. She turned back to the window.

Why does she always get to be a bitch? Because I'm her bitch. I need to show her that I'm the man. "Why were you and Matt laughing at me?"

Tara turned from the window again with a scowl. "When?"

"At the table, when we were eating and I had to go to the other room."

"Get over yourself. We weren't laughing at you. And you could've stayed."

"Then who were you laughing at?"

"We weren't laughing at anyone."

"Then what were you laughing about?"

"What's with all the questions?"

Wes gripped the steering wheel—hard. "Why can't you just tell me?"

"Allison, okay? We were laughing at how Allison listens to the gayest music."

"I don't see how that's funny."

"It's funny because Allison's a fucking bitch."

Wes looked at Tara, his eyes wide, then refocused on the road. "Why do you seem so pissed at her?"

"You wouldn't understand."

"Try me."

"It's just how she looks at me, like she's better than me. Then she acts like she has this perfect family with Matt. It's such bullshit. They're not so perfect. Like, be real for once in your life. I just can't stand fake people."

"Maybe she doesn't want people to know her problems, so she pretends she doesn't have any. Or maybe she wants to avoid them."

Tara let out a breath. "Then why look down on me? She's not prettier than me. I mean, everyone thinks she's so hot, but remember last summer at the beach? She has stretch marks."

"I don't know about—"

"And your mother kisses her ass so bad. It's so blatant. I'm surprised Colleen doesn't get mad. It's so obvious she likes Allison better than her own daughter."

"Colleen doesn't feel that way. She would tell me."

"Whatever. She's in denial."

Wes rubbed his eyes with his thumb and index finger. "That's their problem. We can't worry about that."

"Your mother hardly said one thing to me. Neither did Colleen. The women in your family are so stuck-up."

"We don't see them that often."

"It's too often." She faced the window yet again.

They drove in silence to the apartment complex and trudged up the steps to their third-floor apartment. Wes held the door for Tara, who entered without a word. The apartment smelled like garbage. The offending trash bag sat next to the front door. Wes placed his keys on the kitchen counter.

"I'll take out the trash," Wes said.

Tara stared at him, unresponsive.

"I'll be right back."

"Do you think I'm prettier than Allison?"

Wes jumped, not expecting her to speak. "Uh, of course. You're the most beautiful girl … in the world."

Tara narrowed her eyes at Wes. "Do you like her?"

"Allison?"

"No, the fucking Queen of England."

"Not really."

"Your brother can do better."

"He made his choice."

Tara nodded and stepped into Wes's personal space. She grabbed the crotch of his jeans. He sucked in a breath.

"She's a fucking cunt," Tara whispered.

Wes nodded.

She undid his belt, his jeans, and unzipped his fly. She moved slow at first and then fast as she plunged her hand in his pants, grabbing his penis. His erection grew. She squeezed hard and jerked her hand up and down.

"Is this how you like it?" she asked.

He groaned. She let go and kicked off her chunky heels. She and Wes were no longer equal height. She undid her white shorts, and slid her thong and shorts down her legs at the same time. She stood in her tight blouse, no pants—everything freshly shaven, except a small strip. She bit the corner of her lower lip.

"Who's hotter?" she asked.

Wes breathed heavily. "You. You are."

"Then man up and show me."

She turned around and bent over the counter, exposing her vagina.

Wes's heart beat rapidly; his stomach turned. He pulled his pants and underwear beneath his penis. *Be a man.* His erection softened. He touched her from behind, moving two fingers in and out. She moaned.

After a minute, she turned her head toward him. "Fuck me. Hard."

He pulled out his fingers; they glistened in the fluorescent light of the kitchen. Wes touched himself, trying to revive his erection. He rubbed the head of his penis against her vagina. *It's working. Be a man. Make her scream.* With a semierect penis, he wedged himself inside her. She didn't react to his insertion. He hardened inside. She moaned and pushed back on him. Almost immediately he came. He stopped moving to control the spasms, but they were too powerful. Wes grunted and softened. He tried to continue, but he fell out, soft and impotent.

Tara spun around and shoved him.

Wes staggered back, almost falling with his jeans around his knees.

"You fucking came, didn't you?" she said.

Wes looked down. "I'm sorry. I, uh, I can go again soon."

Tara shook her head with a smirk. "You're pathetic." She stomped to the bathroom.

Wes pulled up his pants and underwear, refastening his belt. He smacked the counter with both hands. *Fucking bitch.* He thought of smashing her face into the counter, bright red blood pouring from her nose down her neck and between her tits.

He grabbed his keys, his laptop, the bag of trash by the door, and left the apartment. He put his laptop in the front seat of his car and the trash in the trunk. He drove to the back of the complex. The Dumpster was full. It always was on the weekends. He opened the side doors, but garbage bags were already jammed too tight to wedge another bag inside. The top lid was open because the Dumpster overflowed. He tossed his bag on top of the heap. It rolled off the pile and fell to the asphalt, splitting the bag. Trash spilled out—a few takeout containers with brown stinky sauce spreading across the asphalt. *Shit.* Wes kicked the bag, spreading more trash on the pavement. *Fucking idiot.* Wes cleaned up the mess and placed the bag precariously on top of the heap.

Wes drove across town. The school parking lot was deserted. He parked and scanned himself into the school. The hallways were dark so he used the flashlight on his phone to navigate. He stopped at Daisy's classroom door. He tried the knob. It was locked. He shone his phone light in the window. He imagined holding her, kissing her. He imagined her happy to see him. He imagined her telling him everything would be okay. A tear slid down his face. *Tara's right. I am pathetic.* He continued to the technology office.

Wes turned on the lights and the work station connected to the server. He logged on to the server and started the updates. With the updates running, he had some time to kill, so he turned on his laptop. He scrolled through his Facebook newsfeed. He saw pictures of the police car cake posted by Matt. A bunch of his work buddies had already "liked" the pictures. He saw a handful of pictures of Abby, taken by Colleen. An army of women had "liked" the pictures, and commented and "liked" the comments. Wes typed, *Beautiful baby. I'm proud that she's my niece.* He hovered over the Enter key. He held down the Backspace key, eliminating his sentiment. He scrolled down the feed. Ed had posted a meme that read *Rangers Lead the Way* and showed soldiers jumping from an airplane. Nick had posted pictures of a group of people wearing workout gear, jumping on boxes and throwing medicine balls high up on a wall. He had written *Great class today.* Wes clicked on the pictures and searched them for any sign of Daisy. He smiled. *She didn't go.*

He typed *Daisy Bennett, Alexandria, Virginia,* in the Facebook search bar. Three Daisy Bennetts appeared. Two were obviously not her. He clicked on the third, but the profile was private. Wes checked the server. It was still working. He returned to his laptop and typed his favorite porn site into the browser. He found the video—the one with the woman who looked like Daisy. This time he was the man.

6

Mary, Charity Starts at Home

Mary parked her BMW X5. Her gray skirt rode up as she slid from the driver's seat. She shut the door with a solid thud. She straightened her skirt suit, and did a quick check of her hair and makeup in the window. *Perfect.* The concrete office building had sixteen floors and tinted windows.

Mary marched inside, her purse on her shoulder. The floors were marble, the elevators stainless steel. A security guard sat at the marble desk in front of the elevator, wearing a crisp rent-a-cop uniform.

She was greeted by a familiar smile. "Good morning, Mom," Greg said.

Mary smiled. "Good morning, honey."

His dark hands rested on the desktop, folded as if he were praying. Mary covered his hands for a moment and gave them a squeeze.

"Have a good day," she said as she let go, headed for the elevator.

"You too. Don't work too hard," he replied over his shoulder.

She rode the elevator to the ninth floor. She stepped from the elevator and marched past a law firm on the way to We Heart Children. The glass door sported the logo synonymous with the charity. It read *We* in big letters. Underneath was the centerpiece, a large red heart, followed by the word *Children.* Mary entered the charity, striding toward her corner office, her toned calves flexing with each high-heeled step. She smiled and greeted underlings in the bullpen—the cluster of cubicles in the middle of the room—as she strutted past.

Mary stopped at the desk in front of her office. An overweight woman with a young face pressed buttons on the desktop phone. At the sight of Mary, she hung up the receiver.

"Good mornin', Mary," she said.

"Good morning, Patti," Mary replied. "Any messages?"

"I was just gettin' to 'em. I'll have 'em in a few minutes."

"How was your weekend? Did you see the cherry blossoms with your parents?"

She shook her head with a frown. "They're mostly done. Luckily I checked before we went to DC. Would've been a waste."

Mary sighed. "Well, that's too bad. They really are spectacular. There's always next year."

Patti smiled and looked past Mary, motioning with her eyes and head. "Looks like someone had a bad mornin'."

Mary turned around and saw an attractive blonde, her hair wild, holding a broken high heel in her hand, a laptop bag on her shoulder. She walked with a slight limp, one bare foot on her toes, the other in an unbroken high heel.

Mary turned to Patti. "Could you please call Megan to my office? Give her five minutes to settle in."

"Yep."

"Thank you, Patti." Mary marched past her administrative assistant to her office.

Mary's office was like a fishbowl, windows all around. She had a view of the beltway, the office building next door, Dan's office, and the cubicles. She turned on her laptop and scrolled through her email, looking for fires to put out.

Mary saw Megan through the glass as she approached Patti. The desktop phone rang. Mary pressed the blinking extension and put the phone to her ear.

"Megan's here," Patti said.

"Send her in," Mary replied.

The door opened. Megan stood on one heel, her other foot in the broken one. Her hair was brushed now, loose waves, parted in the middle. She wore a pencil skirt and a button-down shirt, her feminine curves too much to hide completely.

"Shut the door, please," Mary said.

Megan bit her plump lower lip and complied.

"Have a seat." Mary gestured to the two wooden chairs in front of her desk.

Megan settled into a seat, silent, her face expressionless.

"Are you okay?" Mary asked.

"I'm fine," Megan replied.

"You were late this morning."

"I know." Megan looked down for a moment. She had catlike facial features: a small mouth, button nose, small chin, and high cheekbones. "I don't have an excuse other than traffic and a wardrobe malfunction. I know they aren't valid excuses."

Mary nodded. "It seems to happen a lot on Mondays, like your job is taking a backseat to your social life."

Megan looked up. "But I'm here later than anyone, and I'm doing a good job."

Mary sighed. "I was young once too. I understand. I really do. I see so much potential in you. So much potential to do good work for children. Do you want to be here?"

Megan's eyes watered. "I do. I really do."

"You could be late every day for all I care. I don't like to nitpick. But you can't be late *and* short of your contribution goals."

A tear streamed down Megan's face. "The goals are impossible in my territory. There's no money in Pennsylvania. The person before me did even worse. I looked it up."

"That person is no longer with us, so I doubt they make a good role model."

Fresh tears rolled down Megan's cheeks.

Mary opened a desk drawer, removed a box of tissues, and handed the box to Megan.

"Thank you," Megan said, as she wiped her face.

"The reality is, if your numbers don't come up, you will be let go. I'm very sorry, and it gives me no pleasure to tell you this. I can defend you to Mr. Nelson if there's improvement, but, if things continue as they are, he won't keep you on."

Megan nodded, clutching her tissues.

Mary pushed a single piece of paper and a pen across the desk. "This document is for you to sign. By signing, you acknowledge that you've been counseled for the second time in regard to your job performance. No action will be taken against you at this time, but, if your job performance does not improve, the next meeting will result in your termination pursuant to the employee handbook that you signed when you were hired. Do you understand?"

Megan nodded, blotting the fresh tears before they made new pathways through her makeup. She signed the document and sniffed a wet sniff, the snot pulled back into her sinuses before they leaked from her nose.

"I really like you, Megan. I see a lot of myself in you. I want you to succeed. If I can do anything to help you reach your goals and the company goals, please let me know." Mary stood from her chair.

Megan stood a few second later, not sure if they were done. "What should I do to raise my numbers?"

"You have to get on the phone," Mary said. "You have to be tenacious. It's not glamourous, asking for money. Just remember that you're not asking for yourself but for very sick children."

Megan nodded and exited the office. Employees in the cubicles stared at Megan's puffy eyes and blotchy face as she rushed to the bathroom. A couple men stood, making unreturned eye contact, hoping to save the damsel in distress.

Mary sat down with a sigh. She grabbed a tissue and dabbed at the corners of her eyes.

Dan tapped on the glass wall between their offices. He said, "I'm coming over." His voice was muffled by the glass.

A few seconds later Dan was in her office, with a sympathetic smile. He sat in one of the wooden chairs with a groan. Dan was a big man—tall, with a gut. He wore an off-the-rack suit that was too big in the shoulders and too small in the midsection.

"Tough morning?" he asked, pushing his wire-rimmed glasses up his nose.

Mary exhaled. "You could say that. I had another counseling with Megan."

"I saw that. How'd it go?"

"I really hate this part of the job."

"I know. That's why you're the perfect person for it. That's why God sent you here. Because you care. This is why we've never been sued by a former employee, because you handle these delicate situations with compassion."

"Thanks, Dan." Mary dabbed her eyes with her tissue.

"You're welcome."

Mary looked down for a moment, then at Dan. "I don't think she'll make it."

Dan took a deep breath. "She's such a nice Christian girl."

"She is." Mary nodded. "Can I be frank with you, as your friend, not your employee?"

Dan smiled wide, accentuating his scrunched-up facial features. "You know we're friends first."

"I'm strong in my faith. Almost as strong as you are."

Dan nodded.

"But that faith can also cloud our judgment. I'm your VP of HR, yet you hired Megan yourself—against my recommendation, if you remember."

"I do. You're right."

"There's also the matter of how it looks to the other employees. A few have complained to me that they think she gets special treatment because her family goes to your church."

Dan raised his eyebrows, his close-set eyes bulging. "Who told them that?"

"I don't know. She probably mentioned it. You know how gossip spreads."

"Is it still a problem?"

"Don't worry. I handled it. And, after her running from my office in tears today, I'm pretty sure nobody thinks she's getting special treatment."

"That's good."

"It's not that Megan doesn't mean well. She's a wonderful person, but our job is to raise money for kids with congenital heart disease. It takes tenacity to do that, not compassion. It takes hard work, not faith. It takes a thick skin to make call after call when you're hung up on and told to f-off."

"And you think Megan doesn't have that tenacity."

"I don't."

"Will you at least try to help her?"

"I will do everything I can, short of doing her job for her."

"Thanks, Mary."

"On one condition."

"There's always a catch."

"Let me do the hiring. That's what you pay me for."

"Will do, boss."

Mary smirked.

Dan grinned. "How about a lighter topic? How was little Kyle's birthday party this weekend?"

"It was Kyle's little brother, Connor, with the birthday."

Dan snapped his fingers. "Connor, that's right. How'd it go?"

Mary beamed. "It was wonderful. All my kids were there. My grandkids. It was such a beautiful day. The boys played volleyball. We had burgers and cake and presents. Simple but really nice."

"Sounds nice."

"How about you and Rebecca?"

He took a deep breath, his gut visibly rising and falling. "I really do envy you, having your kids so close. With Mark in Texas and Angela in Oregon, we rarely see them or the grandkids. It's been so busy here, but I need to find a way to take some time off for a visit."

"How long has it been?"

"Since last Christmas."

"Oh, Dan. You really do need to take some time off. I'd be happy to help, take some of your workload."

Dan shook his head. "I couldn't. I'd be taking advantage. You're already working so hard."

"We're here for the kids, but we have to be there for our kids first."

7

Wes and Brotherly Love

Wes lay on the couch, watching *Pay It Forward* on his television, and eating a Slim Jim. His iPad rested on his stomach. He scanned his Facebook newsfeed during the frequent TV commercial breaks.

Tara entered the front door like a whirlwind. She slammed the door behind her, and dropped her keys and purse on the kitchen counter.

"Hey, Tara," Wes called out.

No response.

She hurried to the bathroom. Wes set his iPad on the coffee table and hustled after her.

He knocked on the bathroom door. "Did you wanna watch a movie?"

"I'm going out with Jess and Katie," Tara replied through the door. "I'm late. I have to hurry."

The *whoosh* of the shower started.

"What time are you gonna be home?" Wes asked through the door.

No answer.

When is she ever in a hurry for anything?

He returned to the depressed spot on the couch. A commercial was still on—some manly guy with a superclose shave. Wes went back to his newsfeed. Everyone on Facebook was happier and more successful than him. They were living their lives. The pictures and videos were from places they went, places they enjoyed. He wasn't living; he was watching people live. And he wasn't even watching in real time, in real life. He was watching the artificial representations of life presented by people who only showed what they wanted the world to see. He thought about what he would show if he ever posted anything. He didn't even have a profile picture. *I don't even have a life I can lie about. I know. I'll take a picture of Tara when she leaves. I can post a caption that says; There goes my girlfriend on a Friday night. Out without me again. Doesn't she look hot!*

Wes closed Facebook and set his iPad on the coffee table again. *Pay It Forward* returned with Jon Bon Jovi telling Helen Hunt how he had changed. Tara's phone buzzed and chimed a text notification from the kitchen. *That chime is annoying.* The phone buzzed and chimed again. He sat up. The shower was still on. The phone buzzed and chimed again.

He stood up and walked to the kitchen. He picked up her purse, red leather with a little metal horse and buggy and a label that read Coach. He turned the silver clasp and opened it. He stepped from the kitchen and listened. The shower still ran. He returned to the kitchen and looked inside her purse. Keys, a couple tampons, a packet of tissues, lipstick, a hairbrush, a red leather wallet, and her phone. He grabbed the phone, pressed the button on the side, and thumb-swiped the screen. It asked for a password.

Wes exited the kitchen, holding the phone. He listened. The shower was off. He went back to the kitchen and typed *1234*. Nope. Second try, *password*. No. *Wes*. Of course not. *Tara*. No. *Tara1*. No. Then *0000*. Nope. *1111*. The apps appeared on the screen. Wes's heart pounded. He peeked his head around the corner. The bathroom door was shut, and a sliver of light emanated from the bottom of the door.

He tapped the text history. The latest was from someone named Matt. *What the fuck?* He set Tara's phone on the counter, ran to the coffee table, and snagged *his* phone. The bathroom door opened.

"What are you doing?" Tara called out. She stood by the bathroom, a towel wrapped around her body and another one on her head. Wes stepped toward the bathroom, trying to restrain his breath.

"Nothing," he said, his voice higher than normal.

She scowled, without makeup to blunt the effect. "Sounds like you were jumping up and down."

Wes shrugged. "Must be the people upstairs."

She went into the bedroom and shut the door. The lock clicked in place.

Wes went back to the kitchen. He cross-checked his brother's phone number with the Matt in Tara's phone. His stomach turned. He read the texts:

Tara: r we still on

Matt: same spot at nine

Tara: see u soon love u

Matt: me too

Matt: wear pink thong and skirt and don't be late. I don't have much time

The bedroom door creaked open. Wes backed out of Tara's text history. He pressed the button on the side, putting the phone to sleep, and shoved the phone back in her purse. Tara's steps slapped the floor as she transitioned from the carpeted living room to the linoleum floor of the kitchen. Wes opened the refrigerator, bumping into Tara as she turned the corner. Her hair was damp, and she still wore a towel.

She narrowed her eyes. "God, you're always in the way."

Wes shut the fridge and stepped aside, allowing Tara to pass in the tiny kitchen. She snatched her purse. It was open. She glared at Wes.

"What?" Wes said.

She shook her head and grabbed her phone. She pressed the button on the side and swiped. It asked for her password. She padded back to the bedroom. Wes exhaled. He grabbed his keys and wallet from the counter, and shoved them into the pockets of his sweatpants. He returned to the couch and the endless stream of commercials between snippets of *Pay It Forward*. He waited, watching TV, his heart pounding and his palms sweating.

Tara emerged from the bedroom, her makeup flawless, her hair straight and shiny. She wore a tight skirt. *And I bet a pink thong.*

"What time will you be back?" Wes asked.

She ignored the question, checked her phone, and placed it in her purse.

"Where are you going?" Wes asked.

"Out with the girls," she replied without making eye contact.

And she was gone.

Wes bolted from the couch to the door. He slipped into his sneakers, without untying them. He cracked open the front door and peered outside. Tara hurried down the steps. Wes followed at a safe distance. She strutted to her car—a Volkswagen Jetta. Not exactly a Mercedes but much closer than Wes's Hyundai. She had parked near his car, so he hid behind a tall holly bush on the corner of the building. The prickly leaves scratched him every time he moved. The streetlights cast circular beams of light throughout the parking lot. She sped from the parking lot, and Wes sprinted to his car. He cranked the engine and motored after her. The suspension creaked as he drove too fast over the speed bumps of the apartment complex. He saw her white Volkswagen, turning right onto Route 1.

He followed, gunning the engine as cars and trucks zipped past on the four-lane highway. Wes couldn't see her. Too many cars separated them. He weaved in and out of traffic to catch up. She was up ahead in the left-hand turn lane. He pulled up behind her, half-a-dozen cars back. The green arrow displayed on the traffic light, and the line of cars moved. Some jackass in front was slow to go. The light went yellow a couple cars ahead of Wes. An Acura gunned through the light, but the minivan in front of him stopped. Wes checked over his right shoulder and smashed on the accelerator, driving around the minivan through the red light. A couple horns blared.

Wes was through the intersection, driving north on Telegraph Road. He followed a car or two behind Tara, unconcerned about detection. She'd be on her phone, barely paying attention to the road. They passed half-a-million-dollar townhouses that would cost a hundred grand in another locale. They passed an industrial park, one of the few sanctuaries for landscapers and construction companies this close to Alexandria. Massive McMansions dotted the roadside. The older communities were in transition, with ramblers and split-levels torn down in favor of brand-new behemoths on their priceless patches of ground. It did seem like everyone had a mansion. Or at least everyone made payments on one.

She turned into a park on a tree-lined drive that snaked away from the hustle and bustle of Telegraph Road. Wes cut his headlights as he followed her, then parked off to the side, concealed by trees. He exited his car and hiked along the woods for a closer look. She had parked next to Matt's police cruiser. There was enough moonlight for a clear picture. She had a blanket in hand. They embraced and kissed. It was long, their mouths open. He didn't wear his duty belt. Matt spread out the blanket in the backseat of his cruiser. They laughed as they climbed into the backseat, out of sight, concealed by the tinted windows of the cruiser.

Wes felt rage course through his veins, like a shot of heroin. He fantasized about sneaking up to the cruiser and grabbing the gun from Matt's duty belt. It had to be in the front seat. He could shoot them both and throw the gun in the Potomac. *What about the tire iron in my trunk? I could bash in their fucking skulls.* He imagined being covered in their blood. He thought about the childhood slights, about Matt always being better than him, always making sure he and everyone else knew it. He thought of them laughing at him. Just last weekend. At dinner. *They were laughing at me. I bet she told him how she caught me. Fucking bitch. Does she think Matt never masturbated? In high school, his room was disgusting. It smelled like sweat and bleach. He did have plenty of girls in there. My younger brother was getting laid while I wasted my life surfing the Internet.*

He thought about how he had tried to pick up women at bars with his friends from college. It always went horribly wrong. It wasn't that he was totally ugly. From a distance, he looked okay. He wasn't fat. He wasn't muscular either. He was so awkward and not near good-looking enough to be the cute shy guy. He was the weird awkward guy who liked computers. The funny thing was, he didn't even like computers that much. He just wasn't good at anything else.

His rage subsided, replaced with sickness. He doubled over and heaved. Half-digested chunks of Slim Jim mixed with a frothy red bile splashed on the grass. He heaved again and again and again, until his stomach was empty. He groaned, spat, and wiped his mouth with his sweatshirt sleeve. He stared across the parking lot at the cruiser with its foggy windows. He turned and staggered back to his Hyundai. *I'm a fucking coward. A little bitch beta male. This is what I get. This is what I deserve.*

Back at his apartment complex, Wes sat in his car, catatonic, staring out the front windshield. His phone rang, making him jump. He swiped right and pressed the phone to his ear.

"Wes," Colleen said.

He didn't respond at first.

"Wes."

"Hi, Colleen," he said, barely audible.

"Are you okay? You sound sick."

Wes cleared his throat and sat up. His throat burned from the puke. "What do you want?"

"That's rude. I don't want anything."

"Sorry."

"I just called to see when you were coming to see Abby."

"Soon. I have to check my schedule."

She let out a sharp breath. “She's your niece, and you haven't been by once.”

Wes hung his head. “I know.”

“If you know, do something about it. How about tomorrow?”

“I don't know.”

“What do you mean, you don't know?”

“Is Greg gonna be there?”

“Is that why you haven't been by? You don't like Greg?”

“I like Greg. I don't think he likes me. He doesn't talk to me, and he's always looking at me like he wants to kick my ass.”

Colleen sighed. “Really? That's not what Greg says.”

“What does he say?”

“You sure you want to know? You won't like it.”

“If I did something to offend Greg, I'd like to know—”

“He thinks you're a racist.”

“What?” Wes's voice was high. “I'm not a racist.”

“You sure about that?”

“What the hell is that supposed to mean?”

“It means, you've said some racist things.”

“Greg said that?”

“No, I'm saying it.”

Wes exhaled and shook his head. “I have no idea what you're talking about.”

“Well, let me give you an example. Last year, when we told everyone we were pregnant, you asked if the baby would have problems fitting in because the baby wouldn't be all black or all white.”

“It was a legitimate concern. I *was* worried about the baby fitting in. If you're different, you get picked on.”

“Seriously, Wes, you're defending that?”

“I, uh—”

“And a few weeks ago, remember when we were talking on the phone, and I was complaining about the weight I've put on since having Abby. I said something about being worried about Greg still finding me attractive. And you said something dumb about black men liking heavier women."

"Sorry. I didn't mean it to be racist. I was trying to be … It doesn't matter what I was trying to do. I'm sorry."

"That's why he thinks you're a racist."

"I don't understand. He only heard the one comment, but Greg's been standoffish with me even before that."

"I don't know every stupid thing you've ever said to him. We have no idea what it's like to be black. I'm sure he knows racism when he sees it."

"I'm really sorry. I'll watch what I say from now on. Do you still want me to come over?"

"Yes. I wouldn't be bugging you if I didn't."

"Now it'll be even weirder with Greg."

A pause ensued. "He'll be playing basketball on Sunday from two to five. Come then if you're too much of a coward to face him. Jesus."

"Sorry. See you Sunday."

She hung up without saying good-bye.

8

Mary, the Matriarch

Mary cruised through her wooded neighborhood, soft music on the radio, sounds from the outside silenced by German engineering. Redbuds were blooming purple in the understory of the hardwood forest. Estates were separated by at least five acres, and rings of mature trees maintained a buffer of privacy. Each mansion was custom built, no McMansions. Those were for the wannabe wealthy on the other side of Ox Road. Mary drove toward her classic redbrick colonial. The three-car garage was on the side of the house. She pressed the garage door opener attached to the visor and drove her SUV inside.

Mary hauled groceries from the car to the kitchen in cloth Whole Foods bags. The house was quiet. She placed the bags on the center island with a sigh. She put the organic milk in the fridge, along with the cage-free eggs. When her cell phone rang, she glanced at the ID and picked up.

"Hi, honey," she said.

"I really need to talk to you," Wes said, his speech rapid.

"Are you okay? You sound stressed."

"I have a really big problem, and I don't know what to do about it."

"Slow down, honey. Take a breath."

Wes took a deep breath. “I don’t know what to do.” His voice quivered.

“Whatever it is, I’m here for you. Why don’t you tell me what’s bothering you?”

“Matt’s been sleeping with Tara.”

Mary gasped. “Your brother?”

“I don’t know any other Matt.”

Mary sat at the kitchen table. “My God. Honey, I am so sorry. Are you okay?”

“I guess. I don’t know.”

“How did you find out? If you don’t want to tell me, it’s okay.”

“I looked at her phone, and she had texts from Matt. They were texting back and forth. Arranging meetups and stuff like that.”

“That doesn’t necessarily mean—”

“It was obvious. They were explicit, like Matt asking Tara to wear her pink thong.”

Mary winced. “God damn him. I’m so sorry.”

“I followed Tara. They met in some park and had sex in his police car.”

“Have you thought about what you might want to do?”

“What difference does it make?”

“It’s not just you and Tara and Matthew. There’s Allison and Kyle and Connor. Like you, they’re innocent.”

“Are you saying I should let it go?” Wes asked, his voice elevated.

“Of course not. I’m just saying you should consider how this comes out and to whom. This could destroy the family.”

“It’s not my fault. Matt should have thought about that before he started fucking my girlfriend.”

“I’m on your side, honey. There’s no need for that kind of language.”

“Sorry.”

“I know this isn’t your fault. You’re 100 percent the victim here, but you have the chance to be the selfless, wonderful person who I know you are.”

"What does that mean?"

"It means, this stays between us. Let me deal with Matthew. I'll handle it discreetly. He will not be seeing Tara anymore."

"I'm just supposed to let my mom handle all my problems?"

"No, I'm afraid you'll have to handle Tara on your own."

Wes swallowed. "What am I supposed to do? I love her." He paused. "Or I used to. Things used to be good. Fucking Matt—Sorry."

"That's the thing about the past. For better or worse we can't go back to it."

"Matt's always been better than me at everything. Even my girlfriend likes him better."

"Oh, Wesley, you must not be seeing what I see. Your brother's used to getting whatever he wants. He's always had girls throwing themselves at him—"

"Is that supposed to make me feel better?"

"Let me finish. What I'm trying to say is, he's had it easy compared to you. I know things haven't always worked out in your favor, but that makes you a more empathetic, compassionate person in the end."

"I guess."

"I know I'm just your mom, but I would much rather be married to someone as kind as you."

"Thanks." He paused. "What am I supposed to do when the family gets together? How can I even be in the same room with him?"

Mary sighed. "We'll cross that bridge when we come to it. One thing at a time, sweetheart."

"Okay."

"If you need a place to think, you're welcome to stay here for a while."

"Thanks, Mom. I'll let you know."

"I love you, honey."

"I love you too, Mom."

Mary ended the call and placed her phone on the table. She shook her head. *Damn you, Matthew.* She picked up her phone and pressed

Matthew from her contacts.

"Hey, Mom. What's up?" Matt asked.

"I have something to discuss with you that's very sensitive. I suggest you find a private place."

"I'm in my truck on the way back from the gym. What's wrong?"

"I know about you and Tara."

"What do you mean, me and Tara?"

"I know you've been sleeping with her."

"That's crazy. I never touched—"

"Enough, Matthew. You will not play me for a fool."

The line went silent.

"Keep up the lying and I'll go straight to Allison."

The line remained silent.

"How did you find out?" he asked.

"I have eyes. I saw you two interacting at Connor's birthday. But I didn't know for sure until just now."

Matt blew out a breath. "Dammit, Mom. Don't manipulate me."

"I think you've lost the moral high ground."

"It's none of your business."

"It is my business. Allison and those boys are dear to me. Wesley is dear to me."

"What about me? I'm not dear to you?"

"Of course you are. That's why I'm telling you to end it."

"All's fair in love and war, right? Allison was fucking around on me when I was deployed. You said so yourself."

"Two wrongs do *not* make a right. And I did not tell you that she was having an affair."

"You might as well have. She was leaving Kyle with you, going out looking like a fucking whore, and coming back smelling like cologne. What am I supposed to think?"

"I told you that in confidence."

"Is that what you care about? You know I never said anything."

"I can't be at odds with Allison if you want my help."

"At odds with Allison? Jesus, Mom. Do you have any idea how it feels when someone comments about how different Connor and Kyle are? Do you have any fucking idea?"

"He's yours. I see pieces of you in his face from when you were his age."

"You can't be sure."

"Get a paternity test if it bothers you so much. Otherwise let it go, and be a man."

Matt sniffed. "I'm not even sure I wanna know."

"Beautiful women have their secrets, but Allison loves you. You need to find a way to let go of the past."

"It used to be that we were all over each other. Now, she … I don't know."

"Marriage is hard, honey. Couples go through rough patches. Being away was hard on both of you."

"She barely touches me. With Tara, it's different."

"What about your brother?"

"She doesn't love Wes. I'm doing him a favor."

"You think you're the right person for this favor?"

"She's gonna leave him as soon as she gets enough money for a place of her own."

"You cannot continue to see her. Period."

He half laughed. "Are you serious? I'm an adult. You can't tell me who I can and can't see."

Mary shut her eyes tight for a moment and opened them. "You're right, Matthew. I can't make you do anything. But I can stop that monthly check to Chase Bank."

"You're the one who wanted us to live so close to you! I told you how we couldn't afford it."

Mary sighed. "Maybe I wouldn't have wanted you to live so close if I knew you'd be involved in this … this debauchery."

"And the will?"

"What do you think?"

Matt didn't respond.

Mary waited.

"I'll end it," he said and hung up.

Mary shook her head and set her phone on the table. She heard the garage door open. *Warren.* She returned to the groceries. Warren walked into the kitchen, with a wide smile, his keys in hand. He approached Mary with outstretched arms, sweat rings on his golf shirt.

"Hey, cuddle cakes. Give papa bear a hug."

Mary grinned, holding her arms in front of her. "Not until you take a shower."

He laughed and dropped his arms to his sides. "How's your day been?"

"Uneventful."

9

Wes and a Tangled Web

Wes paced in the living room before the blank television screen. He wore jeans and a T-shirt. The carpet was matted in his path. The dead bolt turned, and there she was, her face vapid. Tara held a shopping bag labeled White House Black Market.

Wes stared, his fists clenched.

"What's your problem?" she said.

"We need to talk."

"I don't have time. I need to get ready." She marched past him with tunnel vision.

"Where are you going?"

Tara stepped into the bedroom and shut the door.

Wes followed. "Where are you going?" he asked through the door.

"Out."

"I know about Matt." He grabbed the doorknob. It was locked.

No response.

"I know you heard me. Let me in."

Still he heard nothing.

Wes clenched his jaw. "Let me in."

Nothing. Again.

He pounded on the door. The particle board buckled but held.

She giggled.

Wes felt hot, his rage building. He hit the door again. Harder, faster.

She laughed, like a fucking hyena.

Wes kicked the door in a frenzy. The jamb cracked, and Wes stumbled forward into the room. The laughing stopped. Tara raised one side of her mouth in contempt. She held her phone, tapping the screen. Wes stalked closer and smacked the phone from her hand. She slapped him across the face. Wes grabbed her by the upper arms and squeezed. She struggled, but his grasp tightened.

Her gaze was wild-eyed. "You're hurting me."

He squeezed tighter. "You hear me now, don't you?"

"Stop." Her voice quivered.

Wes gritted his teeth. "Why. Did. You. Do. It?" He shook her with each syllable.

"Let go."

Wes shoved her to the ground. She fell to the carpet, her skirt riding up and her shoulder banging against the bedside table. She rubbed her shoulder.

"Ow. You asshole. Don't you ever put your hands on me." Her eyes were still wide, and she stayed down even as she gave the command.

Wes looked at his hands, the rage dissipating, the tide already turning. "I'm sorry. I … I—"

"You what?"

Wes looked down. "Nothing. … I'm sorry. I didn't mean to hurt you. Please don't tell anyone."

"What? That you're an abusive, pathetic piece of shit?" Her voice was unwavering now.

Wes rubbed his eyes.

She stood up and cackled. "I'll tell whoever I damn well please. My brother's gonna beat your ass."

"Tara, I'm sorry."

"I know a lot of guys who would gladly kick your ass. Your own brother included. I'd watch your back."

"Tara." He held up his palms.

She pointed to the bedroom door. "Get the fuck out."

Wes stood, frozen.

"Leave me the fuck alone!"

Wes shuffled from the room, his head hanging.

"Don't you ever talk to me again," she said over his shoulder. "Don't you even look at me."

The door slammed behind him but bounced open because of its broken jamb. Wes wiped his fresh tears with balled-up fists like a baby. He grabbed his keys, phone, and wallet from the kitchen. He slipped on his sneakers and headed for his car.

It was sunny, in the upper sixties. Two black men talked in the parking lot in front of Wes's car. One had cornrows. The muscular men talked loudly, laughing and gesticulating. Wes walked to the mailbox, a big metal cube near the curb. He opened his box. It was empty, but he knew that. He locked it with the little copper-colored key.

Wes glanced at the men again. They were still there, almost directly in front of his Hyundai. He'd have to say something. And they'd probably give him a dirty look, call him a white boy, and stay there even longer just out of spite. If he tried to pull out and make them move with his car, ... well, that would be bad. They'd probably pull him from the car and beat his ass. Then they'd say Wes tried to hit them with his car. So he'd get his ass kicked, and he'd go to jail for attempted vehicular manslaughter.

Wes thought about the time in college when he had stopped his car at a light a little too fast, and a black man was crossing the street. The man glared at Wes and called him a motherfucker. Wes shook for days after that.

Wes looped around the edge of the parking lot, entering his car from the rear, so he didn't have to pass the men. One of the men glanced at Wes as he opened the car door. Wes forced a smile and waved.

"How you doin'?" the man asked.

"Good," Wes mumbled and hurried into his car.

The men stepped aside, continuing to talk as if Wes wasn't there. His hands were shaky as he started the Hyundai. Wes pulled out slowly, giving the men a wide berth. He waved again, but the men ignored him. The time on the radio read 4:20.

He drove along Lorton Road. Traffic backed up near the exit for 95 South, but he stayed on Lorton Road, bypassing the Sunday interstate traffic. He turned right on Silver Brook, by the Shell station. Silver Brook bordered endless rows of massive townhomes and single-family homes with tiny plots of land. Those tiny plots made the owners feel superior to the townhouse dwellers, even if the difference was only one thousand square feet of land. He turned into a neighborhood of vinyl-sided townhomes with brick facing and luxury cars in the driveways. He parked behind Colleen's SUV. The clock now read 4:28.

He trudged up the sidewalk to the front stoop of the middle-unit townhouse with its small square of grass and six-foot-tall twig of a tree. The tree still had supports, like training wheels. He pressed the doorbell. Colleen answered the door with Abby on her ample hip. She wore loose purple sweatpants, an oversize T-shirt, and a towel over her shoulder.

"I didn't think you'd make it. It's almost five," she said with a smirk.

"Sorry, I, uh …" Wes looked down.

"You're here now, so come in."

Wes stepped inside, and Colleen guided him to the family room. There was a playpen, a brown leather sectional and a recliner. A sixty-inch plasma television hung on the wall flanked by framed prints from The National Gallery of Art.

"Sit down," she said. "I need to get her bottle."

Wes sat on the far end of the sectional. Colleen and Abby disappeared to the kitchen. His sister reappeared with a bottle in hand and sat on the corner of the sectional, facing Wes. She adjusted Abby, who grunted and cooed, eyeing the milk. Colleen gave Abby the bottle, and she guzzled it.

"It's breast milk," Colleen said. "I pump."

Wes shrugged. "Okay."

"I didn't want you to think I give Abby formula. I'm a big proponent of breast-feeding."

Wes nodded.

Colleen's left eye was a little misshapen, a little lazy, but her face was attractive. She had Mary's high cheekbones and perfect skin. People often said she had a pretty face. What they really meant was, she'd be pretty if she just lost some weight.

"Well, I'm glad you're here," she said.

Wes forced a tight smile.

"I feel like I never see you anymore, since I took maternity leave. No more having lunch at school. I miss that."

"Me too."

"I'll be back in September," Colleen said.

Wes nodded.

"So, how's everything at school? Nick the dick still being Nick the dick?"

"You could say that. I think he eats my lunch sometimes."

Colleen cackled for a moment, then stopped when she noticed Wes's blank expression. "Seriously? Why would he do that?"

Wes shrugged. "To be a dick, I guess."

"Did you tell him to stop?"

Wes shook his head. "I'm not even 100 percent sure it's him. And they're cutting technology people anyway. One of us'll be gone soon."

Colleen's eyes widened. "Do you think you'll lose your job?"

"I don't know. Maybe. It's based on tenure, but Nick and I were hired together. Roy said it would probably come down to job performance."

Colleen frowned. "If they keep Nick, everyone'll finally figure out how incompetent he really is."

"Roy seems to like him." Wes paused. "More than me anyway."

"We'll see if he likes him without you doing all the work."

"I don't really care."

"What's going on with you?" Colleen asked, her eyebrows arching.

Wes lifted one shoulder and looked away, toward a Monet reprint.

"I know when something's bothering you. It's written all over your face. Is it the cutbacks?"

Wes kept silent.

"It's Tara, isn't it?"

Wes looked at his sister, his eyes red.

"I thought so," she said. "You want to tell me what happened?"

"If I tell you, you have to promise me that you won't tell anyone."

"I won't."

"Not even Greg or Mom."

"Okay."

Wes narrowed his eyes at his sister.

"You have my word," she said.

Wes took a deep breath.

Colleen leaned forward, holding Abby. She set the bottle on the coffee table, sat up straight, and burped Abby over her shoulder–the one with the towel.

"I'm listening," Colleen said.

"Matt's been sleeping with Tara."

Colleen was slack-jawed, her eyes like saucers. "Holy shit."

"Exactly."

"How did you find out?"

"I looked in her phone."

She shook her head. "It's always the phone." Abby burped. "Good girl."

"Then I followed her and I saw them together."

"Jesus. Where?"

"A park. They were in his police car."

"Gross." She scowled. "I never did like that bitch. And Matt, I know he can be selfish, but this is low, even for him." Abby burped again.

"It is what it is."

"Are you okay?"

Wes shrugged. "I'm still processing."

"I can't believe he'd cheat on Allison. She's perfect. And with Tara of all people. She has the personality of this couch."

"I don't think Matt's there for the personality."

Colleen stifled her laugh. "Sorry."

"It's okay. My life's one big joke."

"Aw, come on. That's not true. She was wrong for you anyway. Trust me." Colleen sat back with Abby, cradling her.

"How do you know that?"

"Because I know women like her. They treat people like shit because they're pretty. And nobody calls them on it *because* they're pretty. So they go through life thinking it's perfectly fine to treat people like shit."

"I treated her like shit too."

Colleen raised her eyebrows.

Wes bit the inside of his cheek. "I hit her."

She glared at Wes. "You what?"

"I didn't hit her exactly. I mean, I grabbed her and shook her and pushed her down."

Colleen's mouth hung open.

"I don't think she was hurt," Wes said. "It's more likely I'll be hurt. She said that her brother's gonna beat me up."

"Jesus, Wes, you can't do that."

Wes hung his head. "I know. I feel bad. It's just … she was laughing at me. She made me so mad. It was like I couldn't control myself. I literally wanted to kill her."

"This is bad. I understand your frustration, but you can't put your hands on a woman like that."

"I know."

"She could go to the police and file assault charges."

Wes's heart raced. "Shit."

"Matt would probably tell her not to. If anything, just for him to avoid the embarrassment."

Wes relaxed.

"What are you going to do?" she asked.

"I don't know. Tara and I are done. I'm gonna tell her to leave. It's my apartment. I pay for everything. She might be packing now, after what happened."

"Do you want to stay here for a few days?"

"Thanks for the offer, but Mom said I could stay at her house."

"You sure you want to stay there? I hear Rich is out of control. I went downstairs at Connor's party, and the whole basement smelled like pot."

"I'll be staying upstairs."

"With Nana creeping around? I know I'll be old one day too, but, seriously, kill me if I ever get like that."

"At Connor's birthday, Nana told me that I was the seed of Lucifer."

Colleen laughed. "She *is* crazy."

"You don't think it means anything?"

"Like you're the son of the devil?"

Wes frowned.

"No, it doesn't mean anything," Colleen said with a laugh.

Wes pulled his phone from the front pocket of his jeans, checked the time, and shoved it back. "I should get going. I'm blocking the driveway. Greg'll be home soon."

Colleen frowned. "So soon? You haven't even had a chance to hold Abby." She stood with Abby cradled in her arms. "Sit back," she said.

"I should go," Wes said.

"Sit *back*," she said, coming closer.

Wes leaned back, and Colleen handed Abby to him. He cradled her, a grin forming on his face. Wes stared into Abby's dark brown eyes, mesmerized by her cherub face. She had chubby cheeks, a button nose, and plump little lips. Abby cooed and yawned. She shut her eyes.

"I think she's going back to sleep," Wes said.

"Do you think she's fat?" Colleen asked.

Wes scowled at his sister. "She's a baby."

Colleen sighed. "She's a little overweight for her age and length."

"She looks perfect to me."

The front door opened, and Greg stomped into the family room. Wes's heart rate increased; his stomach churned. Greg wore long basketball shorts and a T-shirt. His jaw was set tight, his arms veiny and muscular.

"I need you to move your car," Greg said.

Abby began to cry.

"Sorry," Wes said.

Colleen leaned over Wes to take Abby. Wes handed her off, and she quieted. Greg went outside to his car. Wes rose from the couch.

"Park in one of the visitor's spots and come right back," Colleen said.

"I should get going," Wes replied.

"You need to come by more often. Abby likes you."

"I will."

Wes hurried outside. He waved at Greg before he entered his car. Greg didn't wave back. Wes left, and Greg took his rightful space.

Wes took Silver Brook to Ox Road. He crossed Ox into Roseland Estates with its massive mansions, checkerboard lawns, and fresh mulch. He pulled into his mother's driveway at the end of the cul-de-sac.

He exited his car and peered into the garage. Mary's SUV was there but not Warren's car or Rich's pickup. He called Mary's cell phone, but it went to voice mail. Wes walked around to the front door and rang the doorbell. He waited and peered through the sidelight windows. Nobody answered. He grabbed the ornate handle and squeezed. It was locked. He walked back to the garage and typed the code into the keypad–1225—Mary's favorite holiday. The right-hand door opened. Inside the garage, the door to the house was unlocked.

Wes walked past the laundry room to the kitchen.

"Mom," he called out.

Nothing.

He walked past the kitchen dining area and the sunroom on the way to the family room. Nana sat on the couch, the remote next to her, the Discovery Channel on mute.

"Hey, Nana," Wes said.

She didn't react to his presence. Her skin sagged, giving her a perpetual scowl. On the television, a naked man and woman were making a fire in the jungle. Their private parts were covered with satchels.

"How about some sound?" Wes asked.

She remained unresponsive. He approached, slow and deliberate. He grabbed the remote.

She looked up at him; her eyes narrowed. "You shouldn't be here." Her voice was gravelly.

Wes turned his attention from the remote to his grandmother. "I tried to call my mother–"

"No. You shouldn't be alive." Her eyes were unblinking, her drawn-on eyebrows raised.

Wes clenched his jaw. "That's a terrible thing to say."

Nana turned back to her show. "Your father did a terrible thing. The devil's inside him, and he's in you." She said this as if she were rattling off some inane fact or statistic.

Wes was shaky. He sat down on the couch, dropped the remote, and turned to face Nana. "What did he do?"

"A terrible thing."

"I know, but what did he do … exactly?"

She didn't reply.

"Nana?"

Her face went blank.

Wes scooted closer on the couch.

"Nana?"

Nothing.

He reached out and put his hand on top of hers.

"No!" she said, yanking her hand from beneath his. "Rape, rape, rape."

Wes scrambled to his feet and backed away.

She continued to chant, "Rape, rape, rape, rape, rape."

"What is going on in here?" Mary said, her hands on her hips.

10

Mary and Love Taken Too Soon

Mary pumped her arms back and forth as she power-walked through her neighborhood. She wore yoga pants and a T-shirt that only partially covered her ass. Even at her age, she could still pull it off. It was sunny, warm, quiet. She hadn't seen one car, yet she had spotted a deer bounding in the woods, and a flock of turkeys. *What other neighborhood is this secluded, only thirty minutes from DC?*

She returned to her redbrick colonial. Wes's Hyundai was in the driveway. The garage was left open. *What a mess this is.*

Mary entered the kitchen, hearing Wes's voice coming from the family room. She moved through the kitchen and dining areas. Nana said, "Rape, rape, rape, rape, rape."

"What is going on in here?" Mary asked, her hands on her hips.

Nana grew quiet.

Wes held up his hands. "I don't know. I didn't touch her."

Mary walked over to Nana. "What's wrong, Mom?"

She remained unresponsive.

Wes said, "She was telling me that my father did something terrible and how I shouldn't be alive. Then she started saying *rape* over and over again."

Mary looked at Wes and sighed. "She gets like this in the afternoon.

Why don't we go to the kitchen?" On the way to the kitchen Mary said, "It's nice to see you, honey."

"Why would she say that to me?" Wes asked, ignoring her greeting.

"Would you like something to drink?" Mary asked, as she stepped to the fridge.

Wes stood by the center island, frowning. "No. Why would she say that?"

Mary shut the fridge and stepped toward Wes. She stood across from him at the center island. She twisted the top off her bottled water and took a sip.

"Mom, seriously. Nana seemed like she knew exactly what she was saying."

Mary set the plastic water bottle on the counter. "I know it's weird, but she says awful things to me all the time. It doesn't mean anything. It's the disease."

Wes shook his head. "It's really messed up, Mom." His speech was rapid. "She told me that I'm the seed of the devil at Connor's birthday, and now she says my father did a terrible thing, and she's saying *rape* over and over again. Was my father some kind of rapist?"

"Wesley! Of course not. That's an awful thing to say. Your father was a wonderful man who I loved very much. If it wasn't for the ..." Mary's voice quivered, her eyes watered.

"Mom, it's just what she said."

Mary turned around and snatched two tissues from the box on the counter. "I know what she said." Her back was to Wes. She turned to Wes, blotting her eyes with the tissues.

"I'm sorry. I'm not trying to upset you. It's just been a bad couple days."

Mary sniffed. "It's been a long time since we've talked about your father. Would you like to talk about him?"

Wes nodded.

Mary guided her son to the kitchen table. She sat next to him.

"What would you like to talk about?" Mary asked.

"Everything. Whatever comes to mind."

"Is it okay if we don't talk about the accident?"

Wes nodded.

Mary took a sip of her water. "He was Italian."

Wes smiled for a moment.

"That's where you get your coloring and your dark hair. He was Catholic. We had that Catholic guilt in common. We were very much in love. He was a good athlete. He played baseball. He had a good sense of humor." Mary smiled at Wes. "He laughed a lot. … We laughed a lot."

Wes grinned. "Can you tell me the story about how you met?"

"We met our sophomore year in Biology. I was his lab partner. We were dissecting a frog, and he was so freaked out by it." Mary laughed, which made Wes laugh. "I did everything and told the teacher that Tony helped so he would get a good grade. I joked that he owed me a movie.

"So, he took me to the movies. He didn't have his license yet, so he had one of his friends drop us off and pick us up. He wanted to see *Rocky III*. I wanted to see *Tootsie*. We went to see *Tootsie*. He watched *me* more than the movie. It took him about halfway through the movie to muster the courage to hold my hand, but, when he did, he didn't let go, not once."

Wes listened to his mother, spellbound.

"We were inseparable after that. His parents thought we were too young to be so serious. Nana wasn't very happy about it either. Granddad was too busy to offer much of an opinion. We stayed together even though our parents tried their best to keep us apart."

"What did they do?" Wes asked.

"Curfews, chores that had to be done every time we had plans. They even tried to send him to baseball camp. Nana tried to send me on some summer art thing in Paris. Your dad and I never took the bribes. We were going to be together forever. We both knew it.

"By the time we were seniors, our parents had given up on keeping us apart. I think they just hoped that I wouldn't get pregnant. Of course I did, and I was really scared. But your dad wasn't. He said that we would have had kids anyway. Our parents were upset, but they got over it, especially when we told them that we wanted to get married. Tony's dad owned a construction company."

"Do you remember the name of the company?" Wes asked.

Mary shook her head. "No. Sorry, honey. It was a long time ago. Tony would work for his dad after high school to support us. We were a bit naive, but we weren't delusional. We knew it would be hard. But we would have made it. I'm sure of that."

Wes smiled. "How do you know that?"

Mary's eyes were wet. "Because we made it without him." Her voice quivered. "But there's not a day that goes by that I don't think of him. I love him still. And your father loved you before you were born. I know he would have adored you."

"Thanks, Mom."

"You're welcome, sweetheart." Mary sighed and blotted her eyes with a balled-up tissue. "Do you want to tell me why you stopped by?"

Wes frowned.

"I'm guessing this isn't a happy visit?"

"Tara and I are done."

Mary pressed out her bottom lip. "I'm sorry, honey."

"I guess it's for the best."

"I think you're right."

"I was wondering if it was still okay if I stayed here."

"Of course. You know we have two guest bedrooms upstairs. Whichever one you want."

"It'll probably only be for a week or so. I wanna give Tara a chance to find a new place. It's gonna be really awkward if I'm there."

"I understand, honey. It's no trouble."

"I just need to go grab some clothes and stuff."

11

Wes and the Aftermath

The sun set behind the apartment complex. Wes's building cast a shadow that covered the parking area. *Shit, her car's still here.* He thought about leaving, maybe buying a toothbrush and toothpaste at the grocery store. But he needed clothes for work tomorrow. He couldn't show up in jeans. Like a dead man walking, he trudged up the steps. He stood in front of the apartment door and took a deep breath. He unlocked the door and pushed inside.

It was almost quiet. A faint whimpering came from the bedroom. The door was ajar, unable to shut after he had broken the jamb earlier. *Man up. She's the one fucking your brother.* He knocked soft enough not to move the door.

"Go away." She sniffled.

She's crying. She realized what a mistake she made. "We can talk about it. Maybe we can work it out."

"Go away."

"Come on, Tara. We both messed up. We both made mistakes. We can figure it out."

"It wasn't a mistake, but, if you wanna *figure it out*, call your brother and ask him why he broke it off."

Wes hung his head.

"I bet it was your *fucking* mother. She controls everyone like a puppet."

Wes massaged his temples. "It's puppeteer. The puppets don't do the controlling."

"What the fuck are you talking about?"

"Nothing."

She went back to blubbering.

"I need to get some clothes," Wes said.

She didn't answer.

Wes pushed into the room. Tara lay on the bed in the fetal position, her phone next to her. Her face was puffy, her eyes red. There was a trail of mascara down the side of her face. Wes opened the closet and grabbed his gym bag—the one he never used. He had a small section of the closet for his clothes. Everywhere else was packed to the gills with women's clothing and accessories. He grabbed a few button-down shirts, a polo, some pants, and his dress shoes. He stuffed everything in his gym bag.

He opened the bottom drawer of the four-drawer dresser. She had the top three. He grabbed some socks, underwear, and a few T-shirts. He snuck a wary peek, like she was Medusa, and a single glare from her could turn him to stone. She sniffled and stared at her phone in a trance. The mistress waiting for the married man to call.

Wes went to the bathroom and took his toothbrush, toothpaste, mouthwash, shaving cream, disposable razors, shampoo, and his hairbrush. He thought about how she wouldn't have any toothpaste and mouthwash. Her breath was wretched in the morning as it was. He thought about Tara showing up at Matt's house with a serious case of halitosis. He smiled to himself.

Wes had everything he needed for the next week or two. He stepped into the bedroom, staying close to the door.

"I'm gonna stay at my mom's for a week," he said.

She pulled her knees tighter to her chest.

"I thought it would be a good idea, so you can pack your stuff and leave without me here."

"Go away," she said, without looking at Wes.

Wes's voice was shaky. "You can't, umm, be here when I get back."

Tara sat up with her eyes narrowed. "What the fuck does that mean?"

"It's, uh, over. We can't continue to live here … together."

"No shit. *I'm the one* who decided it was over. You think I wanna be here?"

"Can you leave in the next week?" Wes winced.

"I'll leave when I find another place. I don't know when that'll be."

"But that's not—"

"Just stay at your mother's until I find a place. Jesus. It's not that fucking complicated."

"So, when do you think—"

"How the fuck should I know? I'll leave when I leave. Do you have any idea how hard this is for me?"

"But … how will I know when you find a place?"

She raised one side of her mouth in contempt. "I'll send you a text when it happens. Don't be coming here either. I need my space."

"But—"

"Leave me alone."

12

Wes and Internet Gold

Wes sat at Mary's kitchen table, eating granola cereal. He wore khakis and a light-blue button-down shirt. His laptop bag was on the floor, leaning against the leg of his chair. Mary came from Rich's room in the basement, headed directly for the coffeepot.

"He wouldn't get up for school if it wasn't for me," Mary said.

"He has an alarm on his phone," Wes replied.

Mary shook her head as she poured a cup of coffee. "He doesn't even care enough to set it. And Brandi needs to get up too. It takes her forever to get ready."

"Brandi lives here?"

"No, she just stays when her dad's flying overnight." Mary took a sip of her coffee.

Wes glanced at the time on his phone. "They're gonna be late."

"He has some sort of teacher-assistant thing first period. He says it's with Coach Williams, and he doesn't have to go. I don't know about Brandi."

"She doesn't seem like the studious type."

Mary nodded with a frown.

After breakfast, Wes drove to school.

Early in the day, Wes was on his laptop, replying to tickets opened by staff members. Most of the tickets came from older school employees. Two-thirds of the problems could be solved without leaving the technology office. Nick was on the opposite end of the long table, with the ticket window open on his laptop, but he tapped his phone instead. Roy was in the small office beyond the work stations. From his vantage point, Roy could see Wes but not Nick.

Wes stood and stretched his arms back and forth. He left the office for the bathroom. He returned a few minutes later. His laptop was asleep. He hit the space bar. Three men grunted, the volume on his computer turned up to 100 percent. They were naked, having anal, oral, and manual sex—a mishmash of bodies and parts and excretions. Wes hit Stop on the video, then the *X* on the corner of the browser. Underneath was another video of a man masturbating. Some of the grunting came from this guy. He was all hair. Wes closed the video and glared at Nick, standing behind him, with his phone pointed at him and his monitor.

Roy emerged from his office. Nick retreated to his seat.

"What are you two doing in here?" Roy said, alternating his glare from Wes to Nick and back to Wes.

"Uh, nothing," Wes replied. "Just working on the tickets."

Roy raised his white eyebrows. "Didn't sound like nothing."

"Nick sent me some weightlifting video."

Roy turned to Nick, who held his phone discreetly, still recording the interaction. "My fault, sir. I've been tryin' to help Wes get into shape. I sent it yesterday. I didn't think he'd open it on school time."

Roy glared at Wes. "It seems you have too much time on your hands. Don't worry, that'll be fixed soon enough." Roy returned to his office.

Wes balled his hands into fists and glowered at Nick, still pointing his phone at Wes.

"Why would you do that?" Wes asked.

Nick laughed but said nothing.

"You're an asshole." Wes turned back to his laptop. He could feel the camera on him and the tears welling in his eyes. He knew it was

Internet gold, but he couldn't help it. A tear spilled out, but it was on the opposite side of his face. He couldn't wipe it away; that would be too obvious. He had a lump in his throat. The dam broke, and tears flooded both sides of his face. He imagined the close-up on Nick's phone. He stood and hurried to the bathroom.

In the hallway, he wiped his face with his sleeve. His head was down as he approached the faculty bathroom. It had a single toilet and a locking door. Wes and Daisy arrived at the bathroom in perfect synchronicity. He saw her feet, stopped, looked up, and looked away.

"You go ahead," she said.

He squeegeed his eyes with his thumb and index finger, and looked at her. She smiled, her upper teeth showing. She wore a flowing blue dress with a white cardigan. Her face fell as she caught a glimpse of him.

"Are you okay?" she asked.

Wes felt the lump returning to his throat, the tears filling his eyes. He did the only thing he could to avoid breaking down in front of her. He turned and walked away.

* * *

Wes trudged across the asphalt, his head down, his laptop bag over his shoulder. The lot was mostly empty. He wanted to leave earlier, right at contract time, but he had an appointment at 4:30. It was right around the corner. It didn't make sense to go to Mary's then drive back in traffic.

"Mr. Shaw," Daisy called out.

He heard hurried footsteps behind him. He turned, and Daisy had that perfect smile. Her face was oval but more round when she smiled. Her eyes squinted but grew big and brown as her smile dissipated. Her tiny frame was loaded down with a huge backpack on her back, laptop bag in one hand, and her keys in the other.

"I'm sorry to bother you again," she said, as she approached.

"You're no bother," Wes replied.

"Sometimes I stick my nose into things I shouldn't. I just wanted to tell you how I was sorry about earlier."

"I don't know …" He trailed off.

"I'm sorry if I upset you."

"I'm not upset."

"I mean earlier."

"I wasn't. I'm sorry."

"Oh, no, it's okay. I was just making sure."

Wes forced a smile. "Can I help with your stuff?"

"I got it," she said. "You should see me in the morning. My boyfriend says I'm a Sherpa. I'll see you, Mr. Shaw." She smiled once more and started toward her car.

"You can call me Wes," he said to her back.

She turned with a giggle. "Okay, Wes."

13

Wes in Treatment

Wes sat in a padded armchair opposite a middle-aged woman in a matching padded armchair. Judy was thin, short, her face young for her age. Her blue eyes were a bit too small and her nose a bit too big. She looked up from her notepad, pen in hand. Her auburn hair was cut to chin length.

"How are you feeling now?" she asked.

"Like I wanna kill my brother," Wes replied. "Like really kill him."

"Is this something you're seriously considering?"

Wes frowned. "No, and I know why you're asking."

"You do?"

"Don't you have some rules about having to call the police if you think someone might get hurt?"

"Yes."

"Well, I won't, so don't worry. Even if I tried, he'd probably kill me instead."

"Do you think Matt might hurt you?"

Wes sighed. "No, so don't call the police on him either."

Judy didn't say anything.

"Can we talk about something else?" Wes asked. "It's just … Tara. … It's all I've been thinking about. I need a break from it."

"We can talk about anything you want."

"My grandmother told me that I'm the seed of the devil and that my dad was a rapist."

Judy raised her eyebrows. "How did that make you feel?"

Wes shrugged. "It was weird. My mother said it doesn't mean anything. I guess my grandmother says weird stuff because of the Alzheimer's. But I don't know. It felt like …"

"What did it feel like?" Judy asked.

Wes exhaled. "I don't know. I mean, I've always felt something wasn't right about my father and his family."

"For example?"

"My mom said that I saw my grandparents when I was young, but I have no recollection of it."

"How old were you?"

"She said I was four or five the last time I saw them, and then they got a divorce and moved away."

"Many people don't have memories from that age."

"And she said my father didn't have any brothers or sisters. That seems strange for someone who came from an Italian Catholic background, don't you think?"

"It doesn't conform to the stereotype, but many people don't conform to the stereotypes of their religion and ethnicity. Your mother only has one sibling. She's Catholic."

Wes sighed. "I just wish that I could talk to someone besides my mother who knew my father or even his family."

"Do you think your mother's being untruthful?"

"No, I don't think so. I just think it hurts her to talk about him. It must have been hard on her, stuck with me, without him."

"Is that what you think? She was stuck with you?"

Wes pursed his lips. "Maybe."

"It was a tough situation. A situation that you didn't cause."

"I guess."

She smiled. "You don't sound convinced."

Wes shrugged.

"Do you think a baby who cries in the middle of the night is to blame for the parents' lack of sleep?"

"Maybe not to blame but the baby's responsible."

Judy mock-frowned. "If the baby is responsible, then the baby should have to pay reparations to the parents to make up for the sleep they lost. Do you think people should have to pay their parents for the hardships of raising them?"

"I don't know."

"For all the hardships, raising children is the greatest joy of a parents' life. There are no debts to be repaid in a loving relationship."

Wes nodded.

"You could talk to someone else who knew your mother when you were very young. Maybe they might know something about your father or your paternal grandparents."

"My grandmother's too out of it, but my aunt Grace might know or even my stepfather."

They sat in silence.

Wes fidgeted in his seat. "Nick put gay porn on my computer today at work."

"This is the same Nick who you think is stealing your lunch?" Judy asked.

"One and the same. He likes messing with me. I can tell he enjoys it. I just don't understand how someone can enjoy causing problems like that. A mistake or an accident I can understand. But I don't understand someone who gets pleasure from the pain of others."

"What makes you think he enjoys messing with you, as you say?"

"He always has this … this grin on his face. Why do people have to do stuff like that?"

"A sadist derives pleasure from the pain of others."

"Do you think Nick's a sadist?"

"I'm not sure. He could be sociopathic. You might be more familiar with the term psychopathic."

Wes's eyes opened wide. "Like a serial killer?"

"A sociopath or psychopath is someone without a conscience."

"What's the difference?"

"It's simply terminology in my opinion. Some psychologists classify the psychopaths as more cunning, smarter, their crimes better planned, and the sociopaths as having lower intelligence, their crimes being more spontaneous. I classify anyone without a conscience as sociopathic, and, like all people, they come in different shapes and sizes and with varying intelligence levels. It's the lack of a conscience that makes them unique and destructive."

"How many of them are serial killers?"

"Very few. The FBI believes there to be twenty-five to fifty serial killers operating in the United States right now. Sociopathology is very prevalent in comparison."

"How prevalent?"

"We don't know for sure exactly how many of them are out there, but I've seen estimates of about four percent of the population."

Wes's mouth hung open. "That's like one in twenty-five."

"Yes. There are 330 million people in the U.S., so approximately thirteen million sociopaths wreaking havoc in people's lives."

"What types of things do they do?"

"If you and I hurt someone, generally we feel bad, but a sociopath isn't held back by a conscience. They'll often do things that would seem illogical to us. They often prey on the sympathy of others, by playing the victim. To them, we are simply pawns on a chessboard to be manipulated for their personal gain and sometimes simply for their amusement."

"So they themselves have no empathy, but they manipulate the empathy of others?"

Judy nodded.

"That's twisted."

"It is."

"Do you have sociopathic patients?"

"Yes."

"How do you treat a sociopath?"

"Unfortunately you can't. They spend our sessions trying to manipulate me."

"How do you deal with someone who doesn't have a conscience? Outside of here, like in the real world."

"They tend to create problems wherever they go, so avoidance is often the best strategy."

"But I work with Nick. I can't avoid him."

"I don't know for sure if he's sociopathic, but he is a bully, and, at his age, that shows a lack of empathy and emotional maturity. I would stay away from him as best you can. You may want to document his bullying behavior, especially if it's creating a hostile work environment."

Wes nodded. "The whole thing today with the gay porn, I almost got busted by my boss. I could have been fired. Nick filmed the whole thing on his phone, with that f-ing grin on his face."

"How did that make you feel?"

"Mad … upset. I was mad at myself."

Judy nodded and scribbled something on her notepad. "Why would you be mad at yourself?"

"Because I allowed myself to be bullied. I always have. Ever since I can remember."

"Do you think you could have avoided this somehow?"

"If I was someone worthy of respect, he wouldn't do this shit to me."

"You don't think you're worthy of respect?"

"No."

"Why not?"

Wes hung his head, looking at the carpet. "Because I'm a loser."

"What is it that makes you a loser in your opinion?"

Wes's eyes filled with tears. He grabbed two tissues from the side table next to his chair. He wiped his eyes. "Because I'm unsuccessful at everything I do. I made a phone app. I spent thousands of hours writing code. It was a flop, just like my internet security business. I'm not good at anything. That's what a loser is."

"What about a young man who works a minimum-wage job, with no girlfriend, no family, but he tries hard at his job, and he's kind to others? Would that person be a loser? Would he deserve to be bullied?"

"Of course not. Maybe he hasn't found success yet. But, if he's nice to people and tries hard ..." He trailed off. "I know what you're doing."

"You do?"

"You're gonna tell me that I have it way better than this guy, and he's not a loser, so neither am I."

"Do you think that logic makes sense?"

He frowned. "Yes."

"Do you think you're to blame for the bullying at work?"

"I guess not."

"Bullies often pick on people who have been abused in their childhood."

Wes nodded.

"Last time you told me how your stepfather hit you when you were a kid."

"I guarantee you nobody bullies my brothers."

"But you said your stepfather never hit your brothers. Is that not true?"

Wes hung his head and closed his eyes. "It's true," he said, barely audible.

"Why do you think he hit you and not your brothers?"

"My mother said my stepfather was young and didn't know any better. Since I'm the oldest, I guess he was learning on me."

"You don't sound convinced."

"I'm only the oldest by two years. He hit me until I was fifteen, but he never touched Matt. At least I didn't see it."

"Did Matt see you being physically abused?"

Wes swallowed. "Sometimes."

"How did Matt react to the abuse?"

Wes fidgeted in his seat. "He just watched."

"Why do you think your stepfather hit you and not Matt?"

Wes shrugged, tears spilling down his face. He wiped the tears and shrugged again. "Because I'm not … his real son."

14

Mary, Better Late Than Never

Mary sat at a traffic light, humming to the soft music on her car radio. The afternoon sun was still high in the sky. Her phone rang. It was Warren.

"Hey, honey—"

"You need to come home, right now," Warren said. "I just got off the phone with 9-1-1. It's your mother."

Mary's heart pounded. "I'm close. Is she okay?"

"I don't know. She fell."

"I'll be there in two minutes."

Mary hung up and sped through the traffic light to Roseland Estates. She pulled into the garage and hurried from her SUV to the kitchen.

Nana lay on her back in the kitchen, moaning. "It hurts. It hurts."

Nana smelled like urine. Warren had put a pillow under her head. Her sweatpants were soaked.

"What hurts?" Mary asked, acknowledging Warren with her eyes, before turning her attention to Nana.

Nana groaned.

"I didn't wanna move her," Warren said. "I didn't know if that would cause more damage."

Mary nodded, a siren audible in the background. "I think they're coming. Why don't you go outside and wait for the ambulance?"

Warren nodded and left.

The siren grew louder, then went silent. A diesel motor idled. Doors opened and shut. Commanding voices spoke with Warren. They came in from the front, through the double doors, pushing their gurney. Two men and a woman. The woman was small and thin, her chin-length hair tucked behind her ears. The men were fit with military-style haircuts. They were all uniformed and competent—professional.

"Mrs. Sullivan, can you tell me where it hurts?" one of the male EMTs asked.

"Head hurts," Nana replied.

The female EMT spoke to Mary a safe distance away from Nana.

"Mrs. Shaw," the female EMT said, "I'm Linda." She held out her hand.

They shook hands.

"We'll be taking your mother to the Inova Healthplex in Lorton. It's on Sanger Street, just off Lorton Road–"

"I know where it is," Mary said.

The two men stabilized Nana and lifted her onto the gurney.

"You and your husband can meet us there. Enter through Emergency. We'll be there."

The two men wheeled Nana outside. The ambulance exited the driveway, lights flashing and siren wailing.

Mary backed from the garage in her SUV with Warren in the passenger seat. She drove on Ox Road toward Lorton.

"I should call the kids," Mary said.

"Why don't we wait until we get settled at the hospital?" Warren said. "Once we have some downtime."

Mary nodded, her face sagging.

"You okay?" Warren asked.

She sighed. "She's getting worse. We can't leave her alone anymore. I should have been there."

"Mary, don't. Do not start blaming yourself—"

"How long was she on the floor by herself?"

Warren sucked in a breath.

“Long enough that she couldn’t hold her bladder,” Mary said.

They parked at the Inova Healthplex. The lot was mostly empty. It was a new building—a modern design with concrete and glass. They fast-walked through the automatic doors of the Emergency Room. They told the woman at the front desk who they were and why they were there. They spoke with the triage nurse.

“The doctor’s with her now,” the nurse said. “We’ll call you when you can see her.”

Warren settled into a seat in the waiting room. His girth spilled onto the adjacent seats. He tapped on his phone, probably surfing the internet. Mary stood, her purse hanging from her shoulder. She called Colleen first.

“Hi, Mom,” Colleen said.

“Honey, Nana’s had an accident. She fell in the kitchen,” Mary said.

Colleen gasped.

“I’m at the hospital. The doctor’s with her now.”

“Will she be okay?”

“I hope so. We’re waiting to hear from the doctor.”

“Should I come to the hospital?” Colleen asked.

“We can’t see her right now. No need to rush over here just to wait, especially when you have Abby. I’ll call you as soon as we know anything.”

“Are you okay, Mom?”

“I should’ve been there. I feel responsible.”

“It was an accident. It wasn’t your fault.”

Mary sighed.

“I’m worried about you,” Colleen said. “You’re too hard on yourself. I can come to the hospital now if you need me.”

“I’ll be fine.”

After Colleen, Mary called Matt, then Wes, then Grace. She tried Richard, but it went straight to a useless voice mail with a full mailbox. She texted him. No reply.

Mary shoved her phone in her purse and paced, her heels hurting her feet. A doctor approached. He was Indian and short, with a paunch.

"I'm looking for Mary Shaw," the doctor said.

"I'm Mary Shaw," she replied.

"I'm Dr. Jindal. I wanted to let you know that your mother is okay. She has a bruised hip and a mild concussion, but she'll be fine."

Mary exhaled, her hand over her chest. "That's a relief. When will she be released?"

"I'd like to keep her overnight to be on the safe side, but, if all goes well, you should be able to take her home tomorrow. Will someone be at home to take care of her?"

"I work, but I could take some time off."

"She should be up and around in a couple weeks, but someone should be with her until then."

Mary nodded. "Okay, I can do that."

* * *

Mary sat in a chair next to Nana's hospital bed while Nana slept. Warren watched TV, his neck craning back to see the screen that hung from the upper corner of the room. Wes walked into the hospital room. Mary stood and hugged her son. Warren stayed seated as he shook Wes's hand. Wes was still dressed in his khakis and button-down from work. He glanced at Nana and sat in the empty chair along the wall. Mary sat back down.

"Thank you for coming," Mary said.

"How's she doing?" Wes asked.

"She was complaining of a headache, but she's fine now. She's knocked out on pain meds."

"The good stuff," Warren said.

"Has anyone else been by?" Wes asked.

"Colleen left a little while ago," Mary replied. "Matt and Aunt Grace are on their way, but I wouldn't hold my breath on Grace's arrival." Mary frowned. "You know how my sister operates."

Mary heard Allison from the hall. "Because you'll ruin your dinner."

"I never get to do anything," Kyle said. The little blond boy burst into the hospital room. "Nana."

"Not so loud, buddy," Matt said, right behind him.

Allison and Connor entered the room.

Wes stood. "I should get going." He started for the door, avoiding eye contact with Matt.

"Okay, honey, thanks for stopping by," Mary called after him.

"Hi, Wes," Allison said as he passed, but it fell on deaf ears.

Matt, Allison, and the boys were dressed casually in jeans but yuppie stylish, like a J. Crew ad.

"Hey, guys," Warren said with a wave.

Matt nodded at Warren.

"Hi, Warren," Allison said.

Mary hugged Kyle from her seat next to Nana.

Kyle let go of Mary and asked, "Is she dead?"

"Kyle, don't be rude," Allison said.

Kyle shrugged. "She looks dead."

"Thank you for coming," Mary said to Matt and Allison. She stood, hugged Matt and then Allison. Connor lurked behind the scene, avoiding contact with Mary.

"How's she doing? It's a concussion, right?" Matt asked.

"A mild one," Mary replied, "and a bruised hip. She had a headache, but she's sleeping like a baby with the pain meds."

"They gave her the good stuff," Warren said, recycling his joke.

"Is Wes okay?" Allison asked. "He seemed upset."

Matt looked away.

"He's fine, as far as I know," Mary said.

"Nana, can I have some change?" Kyle asked.

Mary smiled.

"Kyle, I said no. We haven't had dinner yet," Allison said.

Kyle grunted. "I'm hungry now."

"I have change. It's no problem," Mary said, as she dug in her purse and pulled out a handful of quarters.

"Not too much junk," Allison said.

Kyle flashed a crooked grin at his mother. Mary handed over the change, and Kyle ran from the room.

"Wait for me," Allison called out.

Kyle didn't wait.

Allison sighed. "That boy is addicted to sugar."

Connor tapped on the back of Allison's leg. She turned around.

"Can we go home now?" Connor asked.

"We'll be here for a little while, sweetie," Allison replied. She looked at Mary. "I should check on Kyle." Then back to Connor. "Come on, sweetie. Let's go check on your brother."

Allison and Connor left the hospital room.

Warren stood with a groan. "I'll be back. I'm gonna hit the vending machines myself."

Matt watched Warren leave. He glanced at Nana and whispered to Mary, "Does Wes know?"

"I have no idea," Mary replied. "Did you break it off?"

Matt was stone-faced. "It's over."

Mary nodded. "You're much better off. She's—"

"I said it was over. You don't need to sell it."

"Fine."

* * *

Mary still sat in the chair next to Nana's hospital bed. Nana was still asleep, the kids long gone. Richard and Grace never showed. Warren dozed. Mary stood and tiptoed to Warren. She tapped him on the shoulder. His eyes opened, and he sat up.

"We should get going," Mary said. "Visiting hours are over at ten."

Warren stifled a groan as he stood. He rolled his neck.

They left the hospital room, headed down the hall, past the nurses' station to the elevators. The stainless steel elevator doors opened, and there she was. Over six-feet tall in wedged heels. Her legs were bare under her tight skirt.

"Grace," Mary said, her eyes narrowed, her mouth slightly open.

"Mary, Warren," Grace replied, glancing at each of them, before settling on Mary. "How's she doing?"

"She'll be fine," Mary said.

Grace pursed her lips. "Is there anything I can do?"

"She'll need care for the next couple weeks. You could take care of her."

Grace's eyes opened wide. "My place is too small."

"You can stay with us. That way we don't have to move her. Otherwise I'll have to take off work."

"I would, but I just started a new job."

Mary frowned. "Really? Where?"

"The Charthouse in Alexandria. I'm tending bar."

"We're going home. Visiting hours are over in five minutes. We've been here for six hours." Mary pressed the button for the elevator.

Grace shrugged. "They won't give a shit if I look in on her."

"She's sleeping, Grace. Why are you even here?"

"She's my mother too."

The elevator doors opened. "Good-bye, Grace."

Warren gave her a wave as the elevator shut. Mary pressed *L*. "I can't believe her. The gall to show up now."

Warren yawned. "She's a mess. She'll never change. I don't know why you get yourself so worked up."

"You don't know her like I do. She needs money. Did you see that disappointed look on her face, when I told her that Mom was fine?"

The elevator doors opened.

Warren raised his eyebrows. "You said that she's not in the will."

"She's not."

Mary stepped out; Warren followed, catching up. They walked through the main lobby.

"If she's not in the will, why would she be disappointed?" Warren asked.

"She doesn't know that. And neither does anyone else, so do *not* spread that information. If she knew, she'd spend all her time trying to manipulate our mother into changing the will."

They were in the parking lot now.

"That's kinda cold, don't you think?" Warren asked. "I know Grace is a wreck, but she's still her daughter."

"I told Mom to include Grace, but you know how judgmental she is. She told Grace many times that, if she didn't get her act together, she'd be cut out of the will."

Mary pressed the unlock button on her key fob. They climbed into the SUV. She started the BMW.

Mary continued, "Ultimately it wasn't my decision, nor should it be. And now Mom's in no condition to make these types of decisions."

15

Wes's Hard Work Pays Off

Wes entered the technology office. He set his laptop bag on his desk and checked the analog clock on the wall. *Seventeen minutes early*. He removed his laptop from his bag and turned on his computer.

Roy emerged from his back office. His weathered face was blank. "I need to speak with you."

"Yes, sir," Wes said and followed Roy to his office.

In his Spartan office, Roy gestured to the chair in front of his wooden desk. "Have a seat."

Wes sat across from his white-haired boss. Wes swallowed, his Adam's apple bobbing up and down.

Roy glared, his jaw set tight. "Some people come to work to work, and some people come to work to convince others that they're necessary. You come to work to work. I told Principal Taylor that I'd like to keep you on next year."

Wes smiled. "Thank you, sir."

"Don't thank me. You earned it. Keep up the good work."

"Thank you."

Wes sat in the chair, basking in his glory.

Roy frowned. "Go on. Get back to work."

Wes stood abruptly. "Right, of course. Thank you, sir."

"When Nick gets here, tell him that I need to speak to him."

"Yes, sir."

Wes returned to his desk, a grin plastered on his face. He logged into the ticket system and checked for anything urgent. Daisy had opened a ticket, and it was a teacher's workday. *No kids to interrupt us. This day just keeps getting better.* Nick entered the office, earbuds in his ears, and his laptop bag slung over his shoulder. He set his bag on his desk at the opposite end of the long table—the dead spot that Roy couldn't see from his office. Wes stared. The swivel chair creaked as Nick sat. He scowled at Wes and removed his earbuds.

"What are you lookin' at?" Nick said.

"Roy wants to see you in his office," Wes replied, stifling a smile.

"What for?"

Wes shrugged. "He didn't say."

"Now?"

"Yeah."

Nick exhaled and rose to his feet. He disappeared into the back office. Wes practically skipped to Daisy's classroom. The halls were quiet. He knocked on her open door. She looked up from her desk and smiled, her brown eyes squinting. She stood from her desk. Wes approached. She wore jeans and sneakers—casual and cute.

"I'm so glad you're here," she said.

Wes smiled wide. He tried to restrain it, to keep his horse teeth covered, but he was too happy.

She looked at him, her head cocked, as if she were figuring something out.

Wes reined in his grin, but it still tugged at the corners of his mouth. "So your printer's not working?"

She narrowed her eyes, not unkind. "What's so funny?"

"Nothing," Wes replied, shaking his head.

"You seem different today." She looked him in the eyes. "Happy. I like it."

He smiled again. "I am having a good day today. I guess it's been a while."

She nodded. "Well, I'm glad."

"So, what's going on with your printer?"

She sighed. "I can't get my computer to connect, so I can't print anything, and I need some things for tomorrow."

"Do you mind if I get in here?" he asked, motioning to her laptop.

"Be my guest."

Wes restarted her computer. He scanned for viruses and malware. Ultimately he had to uninstall the printer and reinstall it.

The printer began to spit out pages.

Daisy stood from a student desk. "You fixed it."

Wes stood from Daisy's desk, and approached her. "I think you're all set. I uninstalled the printer and reinstalled it. That seemed to do the trick."

"Thank you. And thank you for responding to my tickets so quickly. You must be getting tired of them. I feel like I've sent so many lately."

Wes shook his head. "You haven't sent that many. Besides, I like to help. It gets me out of the technology office."

She smiled.

"Well, I'll let you get back to work."

"Before you go," she said, "I wanted to ask you something, but I was hoping you could keep it between us."

Wes raised his eyebrows, his heart pounding. "Sure."

"Is there a way that, if I open a ticket in the future, only you can take it?"

"I take a lot of the tickets, but it just depends on who gets to it first. So, sometimes you get me, and sometimes you get Nick."

She took a deep breath. "That's kind of the problem. Please don't repeat this."

"Okay."

"Nick is sometimes inappropriate. It's nothing really bad, but he does flirt, and it makes me uncomfortable. Even if I didn't have a boyfriend, it's unprofessional, especially with the kids around. So, I was hoping that I could just deal with you, without making a big thing out of it."

"Instead of opening a ticket, you can email me directly. That way Nick won't see it, and I can take care of the problem."

She nodded. "Thank you, Wes. I hope you don't think I dislike Nick—"

"Daisy, he's a jerk. I understand completely."

16

Wes and Pandora's Box

Wes ran in a forest, his breathing labored, leaves crunching under his feet. Nick gained ground, the knife glistening in the moonlight. Wes pushed faster, his heavy breathing escalating to wheezing. He turned to look. Nick was closer, a grin on his face. Wes tripped on a fallen branch, banging his knee on the ground. He couldn't get up, now held down by a dark figure.

"Take it like a man," the figure said, as Nick approached.

Wes looked up at the figure to find Ed glaring back. Nick squatted next to Wes and raised the knife with both hands. Wes thrashed, trying to loosen Ed's grip, but Ed wouldn't budge. Nick plunged the knife into Wes's chest.

Wes thrashed in the bed, the covers swirled and chaotic. He awoke with a sheen of sweat covering his body. The room was dark; his breathing was rapid. He was disoriented. His eyes adjusted to the darkness. He remembered that he was in Mary's guest room. *It was only a dream. Just a dream. Jesus.* His heartbeat slowed. He was breathing normal now.

Now awake, he heard groaning and whimpering. He stood from the bed in his boxer briefs. He slipped on his sweatpants and T-shirt from the floor. His bedroom door creaked as he pushed it open. The whimpering was louder as he padded into the carpeted hallway. It was Nana. He passed a converted bedroom, the door open. Hundreds of eyes stared at him from the darkness. Wes caught a glimpse of the eyes in his peripheral vision. He sucked in a breath, his hand over his heart. Then he remembered. *Those fucking dolls are so creepy.* Hundreds of antique dolls were arranged in the room just for them. Different colors, genders, shapes, and sizes. A few were the size of real children. There were dolls that looked perfect, like they'd never been played with, and others ragged, either expensive rare dolls or expensive because they came from famous owners.

Wes continued toward the whimpering. Nana's door was shut. He listened at the door. No way was he going in there. She'd probably start screaming rape. How would that look? Him in her room in the middle of the night. She mumbled. It was barely audible. Wes cupped his hand over his ear and leaned against the door.

"Too young." More whimpering. "She's too young. It's …" Nana groaned. "Unholy. Abomination."

* * *

Wes padded down the stairs to the kitchen toward the smell of bacon. He was in sweatpants and a T-shirt, his dark hair disheveled.

"Hey, sleepyhead," Mary said.

She stood over a burner on the center island, pushing scrambled eggs around with a spatula. She was in yoga pants and a long sweatshirt. Bacon strips cooled on paper towels. Warren sat at the round kitchen table, reading the Saturday paper and sipping his coffee.

"Morning, Wes," he said.

"Good morning," Wes replied. "Smells good."

"I was getting worried," Mary said. "It's after nine. You're usually an early riser."

"I had trouble sleeping."

"I'm sorry, honey." Mary removed the pan of scrambled eggs from the burner and set it on the granite. "I have some melatonin. Works great for insomnia. It's all natural. Remind me tonight, and I'll give you some."

"Thanks, Mom."

"You hungry?"

"Starving."

Mary smiled. "Grab a plate then."

Wes picked up a plate from the stack of four on the counter.

"What about Rich?"

Mary sighed. "We won't see him until lunch."

"Nana?"

"I'll take her plate upstairs."

"I can take it," Wes said.

"Are you sure?"

"She doesn't need to be fed, does she?"

"She's usually okay in the morning," Mary replied. "You just need to set the tray in her lap. She likes to have breakfast in bed."

"It seems like she's gotten a lot better in only a week."

Mary prepared Nana's plate and some orange juice. Wes carried the breakfast upstairs on a wicker tray. Nana's door was shut. The television was on. He knocked.

"Come in," Nana said.

Wes balanced the tray with one hand, turned the knob, and pushed into the room. "Good morning, Nana. I have your breakfast."

She sat up straight in the bed, wearing her blue robe, covers over her legs. "Wesley."

Wes had both hands on the tray now. "Where do you want this?"

"Set it in my lap."

She was alert, her face less saggy. Wes set the tray on her lap. On the television, a diver splashed into the Bering Sea. Nana took a bite of her bacon.

"You were talking in your sleep last night," Wes said.

Nana scowled. "You stay out of my room. You kids are always into everything."

"I heard you from my room."

Her face softened. She went back to her bacon, her eyes on the television.

"You said, 'She's too young,' and, 'It's unholy and an abomination.'"

She looked at Wes. "Who's too young?"

"I don't know. That's what you said."

"Your mother swears I say a lot of things. I don't remember saying them." She looked back at the TV.

"A few weeks ago you told me how my father did a terrible thing."

She balled her veiny hand into a fist, the other still holding the bacon. Her jaw clenched, but she was silent, still watching the show.

"Nana, did you hear me?"

She didn't respond.

"My father. What did he do?"

She started chewing, her jaw relaxed now.

"Nana, I know you hear me."

"Ask your mother," she said, her eyes still on the TV.

"I did. She said she loved him. She still does."

Nana coughed and looked at Wes. "It might be in you. You have that look."

"What might be in me?" Wes's voice was high. "What look?"

"Ask your mother." She turned back to the TV.

"Did my father rape my mother?"

She blinked, her free hand clenching again.

"Nana, please, I tried asking her. I know something's not right."

She ignored Wes.

"Nana, please."

"Everything okay?" Mary called from the bottom of the steps.

"Everything's fine," Wes called back.

"Your breakfast is getting cold."

"I'm coming."

"Ask Ed," Nana whispered.

* * *

Wes parked in front of the two-story brick box. The Shaws lived in this house when Wes was a preteen. Ed's parents' rental house. The childhood memories flooded back. The 6:00 a.m. wake up for the leaf-removal extravaganza. No brown-skinned workers with blowers attached to their backs. Just disgruntled little white boys with rakes and plastic bags. The knockout punch for sneaking a beer. Another for teaching Colleen how to say *fuck*.

Wes hiked up the driveway. The carport was for one. Sheryl had her little Honda there. Ed's truck was parked along the curb. Wes knocked on the front door. Ed appeared. He wore jeans, no shoes or socks, and a T-shirt. His feet were gnarled, his toenails yellow with fungus. *Jungle rot*, he'd say.

"Come on in," Ed said, patting Wes on the back as he entered.

The front door opened to the living room with its glass coffee table, worn couch, and armchairs.

"Sit down, sit down." Ed gestured to the couch. "Did you want something to drink?"

"I'm good. Thanks, Dad," Wes replied, as he sat down.

Ed sat on the armchair opposite the couch. An open thriller novel rested on one arm, the cover faceup. The big bold title gave it away. No doubt a book of military heroism.

"This is a surprise," Ed said. "I don't think you've been here since Sheryl and I moved in."

"Not since I was fourteen," Wes replied.

"Well, not much's changed, but Sheryl's given me quite the honey-do list. I don't know when I'll get to it."

"How's work going?"

"I'm an infantry officer. That's all I know." Ed shook his head. "DOD contracting—I do it for the paycheck." He laughed.

Wes forced a smile.

"If it were up to me, I'd quit and live in some little cabin in the middle of nowhere."

"When can Sheryl retire?"

"She has another five years before early retirement."

"You could quit then," Wes said. "Go live in that cabin."

"Sheryl's kids still need her help financially." He frowned, throwing up air quotes when he had said *kids*.

"Cut them off. That's what you'd do to us."

Ed laughed. "Sink or swim, that's my motto. You gotta let kids fail and feel some pain. That's why you kids are all doing so well. You know, Matt's up for a promotion."

Wes clenched his jaw, his face expressionless.

After a beat, Ed said, "What did you wanna talk to me about?"

"My grandparents on my biological father's side."

"I don't know much about them."

"Were my grandparents around when I was a kid?"

Ed paused, brushing his mustache with his thumb and index finger. "A few times, when you were young."

"I know about my biological father. Nana told me all about it."

Ed blew out a breath. "Then you know your grandparents were never around."

Wes nodded. *I do now.*

"I'm sorry for repeating the party line. I told your mother it would come out eventually. Have you talked to her?"

"No."

Ed's face was rigid. "Don't. It was hard enough for her to do it once. Don't make her relive it."

"Can you tell me what happened, from your point of view?"

"You ever hear the saying, let sleeping dogs lie?"

"Yes."

"Here's another one. Don't go opening Pandora's box."

Wes frowned. "It's already open. Nana gave me an earful, but she's not always reliable, especially with the Alzheimer's, so I'm just trying to get the facts."

Ed paused for a moment. "If I tell you what I know, you gotta keep it to yourself. Don't go upsetting your mother."

"Okay."

"When I met your mother, I was stationed at Belvoir. You were barely one at the time. We had been dating for a month before she told me about you."

"Were you mad at her for not telling you?" Wes interjected.

Ed nodded and drew in a breath. "I was pissed. But, after she told me the circumstances, I understood. We were married six months later."

"Did the … circumstances cause you guys any problems?"

"We tried to put it behind us. She was in the middle of the civil suit. That dredged up some things."

"What did you think of the civil suit?"

"What he did was even more despicable than the other two. Seventeen—or younger for that matter—I don't give a shit. He belonged in prison. It was a consolation prize, but at least she made that bastard's family pay."

"Were you mad at the guy?"

"I was furious. I would have killed him if I ever came across him in a dark alley. Hell, I would have killed all of 'em. They were lucky they were behind bars."

"What about my biological father?"

Ed looked down, then to Wes, his jaw set tight. "For all the heartache it caused, your mother always said it was worth it because of you."

"Thanks, Dad."

Ed nodded.

"What happened to the men? Are they still in prison?"

"I don't know what happened to the youngest one, but the other guys were out in 2000. We were notified of their release by the Department of Corrections. I remember the year because I thought that it's a helluva way to start the new millennium."

"How did Mom deal with it?"

"Not well. We tried our best to maintain a happy front for you kids, but she was a wreck for a while. Paranoid that they'd come looking for revenge."

"What happened?"

"Nothing. As time went on, and nothing happened, she got better."

"But then you guys got divorced."

"A few years later, but we were having problems that had nothing to do with that situation."

Wes nodded, his mouth turned down, his eyes droopy.

"You do understand why she lied, don't you?" Ed asked.

"I guess."

"She didn't want you to ever associate yourself with either of those pieces of shit. It was a no-win situation for her. She wanted to protect you from all of it."

"What do you mean, either of those?"

"Paternity was never determined. She didn't want one of 'em to weasel their way into our lives."

17

Mary and XTC

There was a buzzing noise. Mary was in a haze, in limbo between sleep and awake. More buzzing. Mary blinked, the red of her alarm clock blurry. She blinked again, the numbers coming into focus. It was 2:11 a.m. Her phone buzzed on the night table. She reached for it, her hand fumbling in the dark.

"Hello," Mary said, still waking up.

"Mom, I'm sorry to bother you at this hour," Matt said. "Rich got picked up."

Mary sat up in bed, her eyes widening. "What do you mean, picked up?"

Warren rustled next to her.

"He was at a party that got busted," Matt said. "He had MDMA on him."

"MDMA?"

"Ecstasy."

Mary shook her head. "I can't believe him. Where is he now?"

"In the back of my cruiser, … making out with Brandi."

"What is wrong with him?"

"He's still high. They both are. I'm bringing them home."

"Is he in trouble?"

"I took care of it."

Mary let out a sigh of relief. "Thank you, Matthew."

"I can't do it again, Mom. Next time he's on his own."

"I understand. Is he okay … medically?"

"Yeah. They need to sleep it off. And give them some water before bed. MDMA can cause dehydration."

Mary nodded to herself. "Can you bring them in through the basement? I'll meet you down there."

"See you in a few minutes."

Mary sat her phone on the night table.

"What happened?" Warren asked. He had turned on his side, facing Mary.

"Richard was at a party. The police showed up. He's fine. Go back to sleep."

"Is he in trouble?"

"He's with Matthew."

Warren yawned. "It's good to know a cop. Must've been a helluva party."

"Not helpful." Mary swung her legs out of bed and dropped her feet to the carpet. The four-poster bed sat tall in the room. She wore bikini underwear and a T-shirt, no bra.

"Lookin' good over there," Warren said.

Mary frowned and stepped to her dresser.

"You need any help?" Warren asked.

"No," she said, a bit too quick and a bit too loud.

"*Sorrr-ree.*" Warren rolled over.

Mary put on a pair of sweatpants and a sweatshirt. She went to the bathroom and turned on the light, illuminating a shower with two showerheads, a Jacuzzi tub, a water closet, and his and her sinks. She looked in the mirror over her sink. She had bags under her eyes, crow's-feet, forehead wrinkles, and deep creases where she once had smooth lines. She frowned. *My face looks so … old. When was the last time I was carded? Three years ago maybe. Forty-five, that's when I hit the wall.* She brushed her blond hair, a bit of white showing at the roots. She held her hair back with her hand and leaned into the mirror, inspecting the roots.

"Damn it," she said to herself.

She applied a bit of foundation and eye makeup, and hurried to the basement. Mary flicked the light at the top of the basement steps. The smell hit her as she descended. Like skunk roadkill. *Pot. Poor-quality pot.* She entered the bathroom at the bottom of the steps. It was relatively clean. A few pubic hairs on the bowl. *God only knows what it would look like without Rosa. That poor woman.* She turned on the bath fan, hoping to remove the smell. Richard's bedroom was next to the bathroom. The double doors were open. She flipped on the light and peered inside. The bed was a mess. The comforter was swirled, and the fitted sheet was off one corner, exposing the mattress. Clothes were in haphazard piles. A faint smell hung in the air. *Sweat and sex.*

Mary fixed the sheet and straightened the bedspread. It had been a long time since she'd been downstairs. Richard had wanted his own space, "like an apartment." He said he wanted the space to be an adult. *An adult.* She shook her head. *I'd like to be a seventeen-year-old adult with no responsibilities too.* She walked down the hall away from his room and bathroom. To her left was a small square room. A punching bag hung from the ceiling, and a speed bag was in the corner. A crate held a handful of boxing gloves. Mary wondered if impromptu matches were held here. The white walls were marked up and one had a hole in it. With writing around it. Mary stepped to the hole. She frowned. *Damn him. God damn him.* The hole was at crotch height with what looked like black circular markings around the opening. An arrow pointed to the hole with the words *Fuck me.* Pink insulation had been arranged against the hole, soft and inviting. She wondered if anyone was stupid enough to try it.

At the end of the hall, the basement opened up to a full-size gym offering free weights, a squat rack, bench press, incline press, and a handful of other machines. All twenty-seven recessed lights in the high ceiling were left on. The bar on the bench bent slightly from the plates on either end. Weights were more likely to be on the floor than on the racks. A plasma television was built into the wall over a gas fireplace. A few dark stains showed on the white carpet.

Next to the gym was a full kitchen. Two pizza boxes were on the counter plus a few Gatorade bottles, with varying amounts of orange liquid inside. The sink was filled with dirty dishes. *No doubt awaiting Rosa.* Beyond the kitchen was an octagon-shaped room. She flicked on the lights. Inside, the walls and ceiling were black. A sixty-inch television was built into the wall. An open bag of chips was on the couch. Crumbs were scattered, obvious against the black fabric.

She saw movement from the corner of her eye. She turned her head toward the floor and shrieked, jumping back, her hand over her chest. A mouse. Mary scurried from the theater.

She thought about all the people she'd have to call. Exterminator, painter, carpet cleaners, Rosa. She'd pay Rosa handsomely. Mary went to the kitchen and opened the cabinet, finding a couple plastic McDonald's cups that were probably clean. She added some crushed ice from the icemaker on the fridge and filled the cups with water. She put her hands on the counters and pulled them back. Something sticky. She washed her hands, with barely enough room to fit her hands between the pile of dishes and the spigot. She glanced around for a towel—none found. The paper towel dispenser contained an empty cardboard roll. She flicked the water from her hands onto the dishes and then wiped them on her sweatpants.

Mary moved to the bank of windowed doors at ground level for the walk-out basement. She paced, waiting for Matt. A few minutes later, Matt appeared in his uniform behind Rich and Brandi, who were hanging on to each other. Mary opened the door, letting them inside.

"Thank you, Matthew," Mary said, as she hugged her son.

"I can't do this again," he replied.

"I know." She turned to Rich and Brandi, her face rigid. "Did you hear that, you two? Next time you'll rot in jail."

Rich and Brandi laughed.

"Shut up," Matt said.

They stopped laughing but had big dopey grins.

"I love you, brother," Rich said. "You're the best cop ever. You should get a medal." He started to laugh, and Brandi joined in.

"That's enough," Mary said, as she moved to the kitchen counter. "Come over here and drink some water."

"This place is a wreck," Matt said, looking around.

Mary acknowledged Matt's comment with a wag of her head and a scowl.

"We're going to bed," Rich said.

"Drink the fucking water," Matt said, pushing them toward the counter.

Rich and Brandi laughed again. "So forceful," Brandi said. "Can we borrow your handcuffs?" She winked at Rich.

"Isn't she hot?" Rich said to Mary.

Brandi wore a short skirt, tight shirt, and no shoes. Rich leaned down and kissed her openmouthed.

Mary rolled her eyes.

When they came up for air, Mary thrust the McDonald's cups of water at them.

"Drink," Mary said.

Rich and Brandi drank the water. Rich set the cup down on the counter with a long-drawn-out *aah*.

"I love water," he said. "Without water, there's like no … life."

Brandi set her cup down and turned to Rich. "He's so smart. I just love him." She touched his chest, glancing at Mary. "Your son has a hot bod." Brandi gazed at Rich, raking her teeth over her lower lip.

"Go to bed," Mary said.

"You don't have to tell *me* twice," Rich said, grinning from ear to ear.

Matt shook his head, his jaw set tight.

The teens headed off to the bedroom, fingers interlocked.

"And we'll have a conversation about this basement tomorrow," Mary called out. She sighed. "I'm sorry about that," she said, turning her attention to Matt.

"You can't keep letting him do whatever he wants," Matt said. "He's not a baby anymore."

"I know. I baby him too much. It's just … he's the youngest. He'll always be my baby."

Matt blew out a breath. "He's headed for disaster. You told me about Tara, and you were right. Now I'm telling *you* this has to stop. You have to have consequences for him."

"You're right. I'll take care of it."

"You might wanna call Dad."

Mary nodded and kissed her son on the cheek. "Thank you for everything."

"You're welcome." Matt glanced at his watch. "I have to get back to work."

18

Wes and BiggusDickus

Wes sat in his car in the school parking lot. He felt sick to his stomach. He had watched Nick's video on his phone. There were already three million views and over fifty thousand likes. Fifty thousand people had enjoyed watching Wes cry, seeing Wes fumble with his computer to turn off the gay porn, seeing his fear when Roy had questioned him. But mostly the viewers had enjoyed watching Wes cry. There were some dislikes but only a few thousand. The title was perfect click bait: "School Employee Gets Caught Watching Gay Porn and Cries."

Wes scrolled through the comments. He knew better, but he couldn't help it.

NeatoBurrito: at 1:14, face transforms to cryface

GoGo Gadget Arm: Fucking awesome

Tommy Souza: What a tool. Everyone knows theres no crying at work.

BiggusDickus: That's baseball. Bitches cry at work all the time.

Jason Coltrane: He's not a bitch, but he plays one on YouTube.

BiggusDickus: He's not? My mistake.

Fanny Fae: Am I the only one who thinks this video is mean?

Magestic Watermelon Eating Unicorn: Yes

Thanks, Fanny Fae. The published date for the video was May 2,

2015. *Five weeks ago. The day Roy chose me over Nick.*

Wes lifted himself a few inches off the seat and shoved his phone in his pocket. He shut his eyes. *Be a man. For once be a man.* He opened his eyes and climbed from his car. It was already hot and sticky. He slogged into school, his stomach tied in knots, his pits sweaty, and his head down. He ignored the whispering and the laughing. *It could be anything, right? But, if Colleen had found out, how many others? Maybe it would be forgotten in the excitement of the last day of school.*

Wes entered the technology office. Nick sat at the end of the table, tapping on his phone. Roy was in the back office, his eyes on his computer. Wes set his laptop bag on his chair and marched up to Nick.

"Take it down," Wes whispered between gritted teeth.

Nick looked up at Wes, a grin spreading across his face. "Take what down?"

"You know what."

"Wes," Roy said.

Wes turned around to see his boss.

"In my office, now."

Wes followed Roy into the office.

"Shut the door," Roy said. "Sit down."

Roy sat behind his wooden desk, Wes on the chair across from him. Roy's desk was spotless, not a speck of dust, just a single sheet of paper in front of him. He placed his elbows on the desk, his hands interlaced as if he were praying. His square jaw was rigid, his eyes narrowed.

"We're letting you go," Roy said.

Wes's mouth hung open.

"Principal Taylor got ahold of that video. I stuck my neck out for you. I told him that Nick probably put that filth on your computer." Roy shook his head. "Then he had me check the servers for times when you were here alone. Now *I* look like a jackass. I don't need to tell you what I found, do I?"

"No, sir." Wes looked down at Roy's hands. They were gnarled and thick.

"There'll be no severance. You'll need to hand over your ID badge, laptop, and parking pass. I'll walk you out and grab the parking pass." Roy pushed the single sheet of paper and a pen across the desk. "This acknowledges that you've been counseled and terminated for the consumption of pornography on school grounds. Sign at the bottom."

Wes had a lump in his throat. His eyes were wet. He signed, his signature messy. He took off his lanyard with the ID badge and set it on the desk.

Roy exhaled. "If it makes you feel any better, we're not keeping Nick either. Cocky bastard thinks we're gonna keep him because he got rid of the competition. We're moving in a guy from the high school. He'll find out in a few minutes."

Wes nodded.

Roy stood up. "Let's go," he said.

Wes was in a daze, his eyes glassy, as Roy removed the laptop and power cord from Wes's bag. He set it on the work station. Wes glanced at Nick, working on his laptop, a hint of a smirk on his face.

"Let's go," Roy said again.

He ushered Wes into the hall. They walked in silence. Wes glanced into Daisy's classroom as he walked by. She was at the whiteboard, as beautiful as ever.

In the parking lot, Wes reached into his car, removed the parking tag hanging from his mirror, and handed it to Roy.

Roy held the tag with his left hand. He held out his right, and Wes took it. Roy squeezed his hand and looked Wes in the eyes. "You're a good worker. You take care of yourself."

Roy left.

Wes climbed into his Hyundai. He shut the door and banged on the steering wheel with both hands.

"I'm gonna kill that motherfucker!"

19

Mary, the Truth Makes an Appearance

Mary filled her wine glass at the kitchen counter. The sink was filled with dirty dishes. She resisted the urge to clean them. She did have guests.

"Allison, more wine?" Mary asked.

"No, thank you," Allison replied from the kitchen table. She sat with Connor in her lap, talking to Colleen. Abby was on the table in her carrier.

Mary looked out the kitchen window. Most of the men were in the backyard, tossing a football. Wes sat by himself on the deck, nursing a bottle of water. He stared off into the woods beyond their backyard. *I'm worried about him. This Tara thing. It's been three months. He's kept it a secret, but he won't even look at Matt. That may never change.* Mary sighed and turned around. The American flag cake was half eaten, part of the stripes left but no stars. Kyle walked in haphazard circles, grabbing his crotch.

"Sweetie, if you have to pee, go to the bathroom," Allison said.

"I can pee outside, like Rocky." Kyle grinned.

"Not funny, Kyle. And what did I say about grabbing your private area in public?"

"This isn't public. It's Nana's house." Kyle fast-walked to the bathroom, his hand still gripped on his crotch.

Mary smiled, grabbed her wine glass, and sat down at the kitchen table.

Allison shook her head at Mary. "He's a handful."

"Boys always are," Mary replied.

Allison wore a sundress, her pale skin tinted with a bit of pink. Colleen sat in an oversize T-shirt and baggy shorts. Her knees had a layer of fat. Her hair and nails were done, like new rims on a jalopy.

"How did you deal with three boys?" Allison asked.

"I'm still figuring it out," Mary replied. "Lately Richard's been *more* than a handful."

"He needs discipline," Colleen said.

Mary smirked. "I distinctly remember *you* as a rebellious teen."

"I wasn't near as bad as Rich, and you guys *did* discipline me. Remember when Dad caught me sneaking beer? He didn't let me go to senior week."

"One day Abby will be sneaking alcohol and giving *you* gray hairs."

Collen mock-frowned at Mary. "Not my little angel." Colleen leaned forward and kissed the sleeping Abby lightly on the cheek.

"Has he calmed down since the night with the Ecstasy?" Allison whispered the last word.

"Underneath that teen boy bravado, I think Rich was scared by the police," Mary replied. "He's been better. Now if I could just get him to keep the basement clean."

Kyle slid in his socks on the hardwood floor toward them. "Can we go upstairs and play?" he asked, flashing a grin of tiny teeth.

"Of course," Mary answered for Allison.

"Come on," Kyle said to Connor, grabbing his hand.

Connor climbed from Allison's lap, and the boys ran up the carpeted steps.

"How's Wes doing?" Allison asked. "He seems sad."

"The breakup with Tara's been hard on him," Mary replied. "He's always been sensitive."

"You know she's still living in his apartment," Colleen said.

"*Really?*" Allison asked. "Is she paying rent?"

"That skank? I doubt it."

"That's terrible."

Mary exhaled. "I knew she was bad news the first time I laid eyes on her."

"Doesn't that make you mad?" Colleen asked Mary. "He's living here, when he could easily have his apartment. He's so afraid of conflict."

Mary sighed. "I told him that he needs to deal with her sooner rather than later. He asked me to stay out of it. At some point I may have to force the issue."

"When will that be?" Colleen asked. "When he runs out of money?"

"I don't think that's an issue yet," Mary said. "Your brother may not make a lot of money, but he doesn't spend any either. He's always been very careful with his money."

Colleen cleared her throat. "If you say so."

"What does that mean?"

Colleen shrugged, her large breasts moving up and down with her shoulders. "Nothing."

Mary narrowed her eyes. "Colleen Elizabeth, what is going on with your brother?"

"I'm surprised he hasn't told you. Especially since he's living here."

"Now you have me worried."

"He lost his job."

Mary's eyes were like saucers. "What do you mean, he lost his job?"

"He got fired."

"When?"

"Like a month ago."

"They can't do that. They renewed his contract."

"They can with cause," Colleen said.

"What cause?" Mary replied, with a furrowed brow.

"He was looking at porn on his school computer, and there's this video."

Mary gasped.

Allison had her hand over her mouth.

"What video?" Mary asked.

"It's on YouTube," Colleen said. "It shows Wes watching gay porn, and he gets in trouble with his boss, and then it shows him crying about it. It has like five million views."

"Who would film something like that?"

"This tech guy, Nick Gillespie. He worked with Wes."

"This Nick guy probably set him up for the video. It was staged, I'm sure of it."

Colleen nodded. "Probably. They fired Nick too."

"Then why fire Wesley? He's the victim."

"He was watching porn on his school computer, not just on the video."

"How do you know that?" Mary asked.

Colleen frowned. "I know everyone there."

Mary glanced over Allison's shoulder. Brandi stood near the basement door, frozen. *I wonder how long she's been there?* Colleen and Allison looked at Brandi. She stepped closer.

"Umm, where's Rich?" Brandi asked.

"The backyard," Colleen said.

The group remained quiet until Brandi went outside.

Mary shook her head. "What was Wes thinking?"

"I can tell you what he was thinking," Colleen said.

"Do you think he has an addiction to pornography?" Mary asked.

"How should I know?" Colleen replied.

"Addiction, I think, has seven possible characteristics," Allison said. "If I remember correctly from my psych classes, you just need three of them to classify the substance or activity as an addiction."

"Do you think he has any of the characteristics?" Mary asked.

"I don't know. I was a psych major, but I'm certainly no psychologist. He does have at least one of the characteristics—negative consequences."

"He's been going through a lot. I worry that ..." Mary sighed. "I don't know."

"I hate it when you do that," Colleen said. "You can't start to say something, then say you don't know. Just say it."

"Okay, fine." Mary held up her palm. "It was hard for me, raising him on my own. I worry that my sadness at the time affected him. Maybe that made him different."

The door to the deck opened, and Wes stepped inside. The women quieted. He trudged into the kitchen, his shoulders slumped. His face was covered in stubble, his eyes hollow.

"Hi, honey," Mary said.

"I think I'm gonna go to bed," Wes said.

Colleen frowned. "It's six o'clock."

"I know what time it is."

"Would you like something else to eat?" Mary asked.

Wes shook his head. His wavy hair was long enough now to partially cover his ears.

The door to the deck opened again, and the men spilled into the sunroom.

"I'm going to bed," Wes said. "Thanks for the food, Mom."

Wes started for the stairs. Rich and Brandi entered the kitchen. Rich was in front, tossing the football to himself. He saw Wes headed for the stairs.

"Where you goin', Wes?" Rich asked with a shit-eating grin.

Wes turned around, his hand on the bottom of the bannister. Rich raised his fist and jerked it up and down.

"Richard Derek," Mary said.

Wes stalked to Rich, reared back, and threw a punch that connected with Rich's cheek.

"Wesley!" Mary said.

Allison and Colleen were bug-eyed and frozen.

Rich's smile evaporated. He spiked the football on the hardwood, tackled Wes, and pummeled him. Wes covered his face as his younger brother took his shots. Brandi stood back. Colleen picked up Abby and moved a safe distance from the scene, but still close enough to observe. Matt, Greg, and Warren entered the kitchen.

"Whoa, whoa," Matt said, bursting onto the scene, but Rich continued the beating.

Matt pulled off Rich and put him in a choke hold. Wes scrambled to his feet. Matt was on his knees with his muscled arm tight around Rich's neck. Rich struggled for air.

"He can't breathe," Mary said. "Let go."

"Matt!" Allison said.

Abby started to cry.

Greg approached and touched Matt on the shoulders. "Let go, man."

Matt relented, standing up, his breath heavy.

Rich gasped for air and stood, rubbing his neck. "What the hell, man?"

Wes was in a daze, his mouth and nose bloody.

"Everybody calm down," Warren said with his flabby arms held out, like an impotent referee.

"What the hell are you two fighting about?" Matt said.

"That fucking douche punched me," Rich said.

Matt glared at Wes. "What the fuck, Wes?"

Wes hung his head.

"Yeah, Wes, what the fuck?" Rich said.

"Shut up, Rich," Matt said.

"Richard did something to provoke him," Mary said and looked at Rich. "Go to your room, now."

Rich frowned. "This faggot gets fired for jackin' off to gay porn, and I'm in trouble?"

"Go," Mary said, her face tight.

Rich went to the basement, nudging Wes with his shoulder as he moved past. Wes stumbled but regained his balance. Brandi followed Rich. Mary grabbed some tissues from the box on the counter. Abby quieted.

"What's this about gay porn and getting fired?" Matt said.

Mary handed the tissues to Wes.

"It's nothing," Mary said. "Rich was making fun of Wesley for losing his job."

Wes wiped his face and held the tissues against his nostrils to stem the tide of blood.

Matt shook his head. "So I just put my brother into a choke hold because Wes lost his job for jerkin' off at school? At *school*. That's disgusting."

"We don't know if he was masturbating," Colleen said from the edge of the kitchen. "He was just watching porn."

Matt glared at Wes. "You're a dumb-ass. You work in a school. With *kids*. What the hell is wrong with you?"

"Matthew, leave him alone," Mary said.

"Something's wrong with him."

Wes dropped his hand, removing the tissues from his face. The edges of his nostrils were dark with blood. His eyes were red rimmed. "At least I don't fuck around on my wife."

Allison stood from the table, her eyes opened wide. "What is he talking about?"

Matt froze, grinding his teeth, his eyes narrowed at Wes. "I should kick your fuckin' ass for spewing that bullshit."

"Everyone should just go home," Warren said to a deaf audience.

"Stop this, you two, now," Mary said.

"What is he talking about, Matt?" Allison said in a low tone.

"Tara," Wes said. "He was having an affair with Tara."

Matt headed toward Wes, his fists clenched. Greg stepped in front, wrapping up Matt, holding him back. "I will fuckin' kill you," Matt said, pointing at Wes over Greg's shoulder. "You fuck with my family like that."

Abby started to cry again.

Allison stalked to her husband. "You will not lay a hand on him. This is your fault, not his. That was his girlfriend, you selfish asshole."

20

Wes and the Sins of the Father

"Maybe I'm like him," Wes said.

Judy's face was expressionless, but she couldn't suppress the empathy in her blue eyes. "What makes you think that?"

Wes took a deep breath. "Because I lose my temper. With Rich, the other day—Matt, Tara, Nick, anyone who pisses me off. It's like I can't control myself."

"Anger can be a good thing, and a natural reaction to what has happened. Obviously you want to avoid violence, but feeling angry is normal and is no indication that you are like your father."

"I guess."

"What else are you feeling?"

Wes shrugged. "Depressed, ... confused, humiliated. I mean that shit's on YouTube racking up views right now. Everyone thinks I'm some kinda freak. My mom asked me if I was addicted to porn."

"How did that make you feel?"

"I don't know. I should feel more embarrassed, but I think I've hit the embarrassment limit. Now it's like everyone already thinks these things about me, so whatever." Wes pursed his lips. "Do you think I could be addicted to porn?"

Judy was stone-faced. "How much time do you spend consuming pornography?"

Wes's face felt hot. "An hour maybe."

"Every day?"

Wes nodded and hung his head.

Judy was silent.

Wes looked up. "That's bad, isn't it?"

"It's not good, and, if it's holding you back from making connections—or causing problems, as it has—it is cause for concern. Do you think you could stop for a few days?"

"I think so."

Judy sat, silent, her hands resting on her yellow notepad.

Wes shut his eyes for a moment. "I think there's a bigger problem than how much I watch."

Judy remained silent, her gaze on Wes.

"I like to see it … rough."

"Do you enjoy seeing women in pain?"

Wes paused for a moment. "I don't know if it's the pain. I don't want her to be hurt really, but it's like she knows who the man is."

Judy scribbled on her notepad. "Did your sex life with Tara mirror the pornography you view?"

"No. She liked it that way, but I had … I had trouble with it."

"What do you mean by *trouble*?"

Wes frowned. "I couldn't do it." He huffed out a breath. "I couldn't perform."

"Could you perform when it wasn't rough?"

"Yes."

They sat in silence.

"Do you think I get these sex problems from my father?" Wes asked.

"I don't think so. You've had no contact with your father."

"You said before that being a sociopath can be hereditary."

"I don't know if your father is a sociopath."

"He is a rapist."

"That doesn't mean he's a sociopath. He may simply have poor impulse control."

Wes frowned. "But he's more likely to be a sociopath than someone who doesn't go around raping women."

"Probably."

"And it's hereditary."

"There is evidence to suggest increased rates of sociopathology among the offspring of sociopaths, but they are still much more likely to have a conscience than not."

"Maybe I'm a sociopath."

"Do you feel bad if you hurt someone?"

"Yes."

"Do you feel empathy for the pain of others?"

"Yes."

"Then you're not a sociopath."

"Maybe I'm just manipulating you."

* * *

Wes approached the sprawling one-story brick building. A haze reverberated off the asphalt. Wes wore jeans, despite the triple-digit temperature. The entryway had a concrete walk, pillars on the building, and a bank of glass doors. Inside, it was chilly by comparison, the air-conditioning consuming BTUs. Tables and chairs were in the middle of the room. The perimeter was lined with metal bookshelves. One corner had a cluster of computers. The library was mostly empty. Wes walked to the front desk. A frumpy white-haired woman with glasses sat behind a computer screen. She stood with a groan.

"May I help you?" she asked.

"I'm looking for an old newspaper article," Wes said. "It would be from 1984 or maybe 1985."

"Do you know which newspaper?"

"I don't, but I think it would be a local paper, like the *Alexandria*

Gazette. It might have even been in the *Washington Post*. I think the thing I'm looking for happened in Alexandria."

"Do you have a date or names involved in the ..." The woman raised her eyebrows over her wire frames.

"It was a crime in 1985. I don't have the names. Well, I have one name, but it's the victim, and she wouldn't be in there. I don't think they put things like that in the paper."

The woman nodded. "Well, we do have a digital searchable archive now. Be thankful you don't have to use microfiche. You'd be here for weeks."

The old woman showed Wes to the computer cluster. She demonstrated how to do a general search and how to do an advanced search.

Wes sat by himself. He tried an advanced search, using 1985 for the date. He chose the sources: the *Washington Post, Washington Times*, and *Alexandria Gazette*. He used the search terms: *rape, gang rape, Alexandria Catholic High School student*, and *Mary Katherine Sullivan*, just in case he was wrong about the newspaper naming the victim. He hit the Enter key. Wes's stomach turned; his eyes widened. *Holy shit*. A dozen or so articles appeared about the same rape case. Wes clicked on the top article from the *Washington Post*.

Alexandria Catholic Grads Accused of Rape

By: Amy Watson

August 18, 1985

Joseph Esposito and Jeremy Gilbert were arrested and charged with raping a classmate at a graduation party in June. Esposito and Gilbert, both 18, were arraigned yesterday. They entered pleas of not guilty and are being held without bail.

Grand jury testimony revealed an eyewitness account of the rape. According to testimony, Esposito and Gilbert held the victim's boyfriend, 17, at gunpoint, while the victim, 17, was raped alternately by both men. The rape allegedly took place in Jeremy's bedroom, inside the Gilbert family home.

Gilbert, an All-Met and All-State linebacker for Alexandria Catholic, earned a football scholarship to attend the University of Virginia. The scholarship for the four-star recruit has been suspended, pending the outcome of this case.

Esposito had plans to join his father in the family business, Esposito and Sons Plumbing.

When asked about his son's arrest, Joe's father, Vincent Esposito, said, "That boy's been nothing but trouble. I hope they lock him up for life."

"We have a very strong case. We will be seeking the maximum penalty for this heinous crime," District Attorney Dennis Holland told court reporters.

"I would like to remind everyone that we are talking about eighteen-year-old kids, barely out of high school at a party filled with alcohol," Public Defender Randy Pace told court reporters.

Wes scrolled down the headlines. He clicked on the last relevant article.

Alexandria Catholic Grads Plead Guilty

By: Amy Watson

October 7, 1985

Joseph Esposito, 18, and Jeremy Gilbert, 18, each pled guilty to one count of aggravated assault and one count of rape. They have been sentenced to fifteen years in a state penitentiary, without the possibility of parole.

The rape occurred on June 15, 1985 during a graduation party at the family home of Gilbert. The victim's boyfriend, 17, was held at gunpoint while the victim, 17, was alternately raped by Gilbert and Esposito.

Gilbert was an All-State football player at Alexandria Catholic High School. Esposito was described as a "troublemaker" and "poor student" by staff at ACHS.

ACHS Principal Louis Walker made the following statement. "In my twenty-five years at Alexandria Catholic, I've never seen so much as a shoplifting charge for one of my students. The Alexandria Catholic community is shocked, dismayed, and deeply saddened. We are praying for the victim and her family."

District Attorney Dennis Holland described rape cases as "notoriously difficult to prosecute." He congratulated his office for "doing a tremendous job seeing that justice was served."

Wes typed *how long from conception to birth* into the Google search bar. Thirty-eight weeks was the average. He looked at his calendar on his phone. He counted thirty-eight weeks, starting with June 15. He counted three times. His heart pounded. Thirty-eight weeks from June 15 would be March 8. Wes shook his head. *It's true. One of these pieces of shit could be my father.*

Wes typed *background checks* into Google. The first site after the ads was CheckOnPeople.com. Wes clicked on the link. He was prompted to fill four empty boxes with information. He typed the first and last name, *Joe Esposito*. He skipped the city and typed *Virginia* into the state. *Why would he stay here? He may not even be in Virginia*. Twenty-eight

Joe Espositos showed up in the query. Most of them had ages. Wes did the math in his head. He should be forty-nine or fifty now. Two were in that age group, and three others had unknown ages.

Wes clicked the button that read Access Report next to the fifty-year-old. A questionnaire popped up and asked Wes if he was over eighteen and whether or not he agreed not to harass or blackmail anyone with the information or deny employment. Wes answered appropriately, and a green progress bar began, stating that information was downloading. Wes was then prompted to enter his email. He went back and forth on his email and paid ten dollars to get the full information, including the criminal record. This Joe Esposito was clean. He went through the same process for the forty-nine-year-old, this time spending $49.99 for a bundle of twenty background checks. This Esposito had a rape and aggravated assault on his criminal record from 1985 in Alexandria. *Bingo.*

Jeremy Gilbert was a little more difficult to find. Thirty-eight records were found, and eight had no age. He accessed six different records before finding the Jeremy Gilbert with a 1985 rape on his record.

21

Wes and Paternity

The GPS on Wes's phone took him to an apartment complex in Woodbridge. The buildings were three stories tall with dirty vinyl siding. The parking lot was half full with economy cars and a few work trucks. Maybe the tradesmen had called it quits for the day, on account of the heat. There were approximately twenty buildings. Wes found Building 10. He parked in a visitor's space. A single staircase ran up the middle of the building. Each floor had two units on either side. The apartment he sought was on the ground floor—1B.

Wes knocked on the door, holding a plastic bag labeled CVS. There was no answer. He knocked again, harder. He waited. Nothing. Wes double-checked the address on his phone. *Building 10, Apartment 1B.*

A man approached through the first-floor stairwell, coming from the back of the building. He carried a tool box and wore a T-shirt that read Carlisle Property Management.

"You need somethin'?" he asked in a deep voice.

Wes looked at the man, and his jaw dropped. The man was wiry, his black hair slicked back. He had a black-and-white beard that was a little bit longer than stubble.

"You need somethin'?" the man asked louder.

Wes took a breath. "I was looking for Joe Esposito."

The man narrowed his eyes. They were too small, too close together, giving him a perpetual look of distrust. "You found him. Your AC take a dump?"

"Um, no. I, uh ..."

"Come on, boy. Spit it out. I ain't got all day."

"I'm Wes Shaw."

Joe looked at him with a blank look. "That supposed to mean somethin' to me?"

Wes's heart pounded. "My mom's Mary Sullivan."

Joe clenched his jaw. "What do you want?"

Wes searched Joe's weathered face. Like Wes, Joe's nose was too big, but the beard evened it out. He had beady eyes, but they didn't look weak like Wes's; they looked hypervigilant.

"I think you might be my father."

Joe gritted his teeth. "I ain't got time for this bullshit."

Wes clenched his fists to stop his hands from shaking. "I was born on March 12, 1986. Nine months from the date of that graduation party."

Joe shook his head. "Christ, I can't get away from that fuckin' cunt."

Wes glared at Joe. "Don't call her that, you, you, fucking rapist."

Joe blew out a breath from his nose, like a bull. He stepped into Wes's personal space. He smelled like grease and sweat.

Wes stepped backward until his back was against the wall. Joe moved with him, still too close.

"That make you feel big?" Joe asked. "To call me a rapist? That supposed to shock me, boy? I've heard that a thousand *fuckin'* times, and it don't mean shit to me. What the fuck do you want? Revenge?"

Wes held up the CVS bag. "I came for the truth."

Joe stepped back. "How you gonna figure that?"

Wes removed the small box from the CVS bag. It read Home DNA Paternity Test, 99.99% Accurate!

Joe cackled. "You got some balls comin' here with this shit."

"It's just a swab to the inside of your mouth. It'll take two seconds."

"And what if I am your father? What then?" He smirked. "I hope you ain't expectin' an inheritance, because I ain't got a pot to piss in."

Wes clenched his jaw. "I don't want anything from you."

"Right, you just want the truth."

Wes nodded.

"I'll give you that swab thing, but you're gonna hear my side first."

"Your side of what?" Wes asked.

"What really happened that night."

Joe stepped toward his apartment and opened the door. He faced Wes. "You want the truth or not?"

Wes hesitated, then followed Joe into the apartment.

Inside was a wooden coffee table and a gray couch with some of the spongelike material exposed on the armrests. *Probably pulled that from the trash.* His flat-screen television sat on two flipped-over milk crates. The walls were barren, the decor jail-cell chic.

"Have a seat," Joe said, walking past the living room into the tiny kitchen.

Wes inspected the couch and sat down. He peered into the kitchen from his seat. A calendar with a naked woman was on the fridge.

"You wanna beer?" Joe called out.

"No."

"What was that?"

"I said, no," Wes said louder.

Joe returned to the living room with an open beer can. He took a few gulps and sat in the ratty recliner, kitty-cornered from Wes.

Wes glanced over at Joe, his stomach in his throat.

Joe smirked. "You look like you're about to shit a brick."

"I'm fine."

Joe laughed. "If you say so."

"Just get on with it, okay? I'm listening."

"No shootin' the shit?"

Wes went silent.

"Down to business. I like that." He chugged the rest of his beer, leaned forward, and set it on the coffee table. He sat back in the recliner with a groan.

Wes was blank-faced.

"I was eighteen, your mother seventeen," Joe said. "We went to Alexandria Catholic. I hated that school. Pompous pricks. She was at the top of the class. I was at the bottom. They only graduated me to get me outta there. There was a graduation party at Jeremy Gilbert's house. He was the big man on campus, had some football scholarship. We had a business relationship. That's why I went."

"What kind of business relationship?"

"I sold steroids to him and a couple other guys."

Wes frowned.

"Don't judge me, boy. I didn't say it was right. I'm tellin' you what happened."

Wes nodded.

"A lot a girls at the party. They all wanted big Jeremy's jock. I didn't do too bad myself." The corners of his mouth turned up. "They wanted the bad boy. These rich Catholic bitches wanted to give the ultimate FU to Mommy, Daddy, and God. I was in Jeremy's room, makin' the deal, and he told me how Mary's coming to his room to fuck, and her faggoty boyfriend wants to watch."

"That's bullshit," Wes said.

Joe glared. "You want that swab or not?"

"Who was her boyfriend?"

"This rich prick, Ben Armstrong. Fuckin' valedictorian. Piece of shit. Anyway, Mary waltzed in with this prick. I started to leave, and she looked me up and down, like I'm a fuckin' steak dinner. She said somethin' like, 'Where are you rushin' off to?' I ignored her, and she grabbed my arm. She said some shit about how I should stay. Then she took off her clothes right there. She looked damn good." Joe had a wide grin. "I looked at Jeremy to see if it's all right that I stay. It was their party, not mine. He just shrugged, so I stayed."

Wes rubbed his temples.

"I'm not gonna lie. We worked her over pretty good. I tried not to look at Ben. That queer motherfucker stood in front of the bed, jerkin' it. Jeremy yelled at Ben to get some toilet paper. Jeremy said he would kick Ben's ass if he came on the carpet. Jeremy had condoms, but Mary said she just had her period. Still the nastiest shit I've ever done. But it wasn't worth the price we paid."

Wes was white as a ghost.

"She was fine after. Everybody got off. We didn't hear shit for two months. Fuckin' cops started comin' around, askin' questions about that night. I told 'em what happened. So did Jeremy. Big fuckin' mistake. Don't ever talk to the cops without a lawyer. Next thing we know, we've been indicted."

"What did Ben say?" Wes mumbled.

"Speak up, boy."

"Ben, what did Ben say?"

Joe shook his head and stroked his beard. "This is where it gets really fucked up. That motherfucker sided with the prosecution and backed up Mary's story. He got immunity. He said Jeremy held him at gunpoint while I fucked her, then we switched. Jeremy's dad had a glass gun case with some old rifles. They said we used one of 'em. None of our fingerprints were on the guns, but the cops said we cleaned 'em. Of course they were clean. They were fuckin' antiques.

"Then Mary double-crossed Ben, saying that he brought her there because he wanted to watch her get raped. Ben had immunity, so Mary hit him with a civil suit. I bet she had some shit on Ben. His family had a lot a money at the time. I'm guessin' they settled to save the embarrassment. Jeremy and I got fifteen years hard time, and Ben paid her off."

"Do you still talk to Jeremy?"

"We had beers a few times over the years, but what the fuck are we gonna talk about? Ain't nothin' between us but shit we both wanna forget. Last I heard he was drivin' a forklift in Hampton."

“What happened to Ben?”

One side of Joe’s mouth raised in contempt. “That motherfucker’s a plastic surgeon. Tit jobs and shit.”

“Have you seen him?”

“I saw him. He didn’t see me.” Joe clenched his fists. “Let’s just say, he’s lucky he has kids.”

Wes’s face was rigid. “I think you’re lying.”

“How you figure?”

“If you were so innocent, why did you plead guilty?”

Joe exhaled. “I was a kid with a public defender. My parents were done with me, wouldn’t pay for a lawyer. The public defender told me, if I didn’t take the deal, I’d prob’ly get life. Fifteen years was a helluva lot better than life. Jeremy was in the same boat. His family wasn’t rich. He was on scholarship at Alexandria Catholic.”

“I’m supposed to believe that cliché? Poor kids get screwed over by the system?”

“I don’t give a fuck what you believe.”

22

Mary, Holding It Together

Mary sat behind her maple desk, her cell phone to her ear. Outside her fishbowl office, people busied themselves in cubicles on laptops and phones.

"I'm so sorry, Allison," Mary said into her cell.

"He didn't come home last night," Allison replied.

"He's at Colleen's."

Allison exhaled. "At least he's not with *her*. I just don't think I can do it anymore. I'm afraid we might be headed for divorce. I'm taking the kids to stay with my parents. I need some time to think."

"That's probably a good idea. It'll give Matthew a chance to see what he's missing. Your parents are in Hershey, right?"

"Yes. I'll take the kids to the park and Chocolate World. I've told them it's a vacation. I'm not sure how to tell them the truth. It breaks my heart."

"I'm so sorry, honey. These situations are always so much harder for the woman. We have to deal with the fallout with the children, and men move on so much easier than we can. Have you thought about where you'll live or work?"

"I … I haven't. I just need space to figure it out."

"These things are disastrous to finances. As you know, they don't pay police officers near enough."

"I have to go," Allison said. "I just wanted to say that I'm sorry for this mess ruining your party."

"There is absolutely nothing for you to be sorry about. Matthew's to blame. Has he apologized to you?"

"He did, but I question his sincerity."

"He stopped by yesterday," Mary said. "I'm not sure if he told you."

"He didn't."

"I've never seen him this distraught. Sometimes it takes losing someone to realize what you had. I think that's where he is now. Of course he didn't get my sympathy. He made his bed."

"I should go. Thank you for your support."

"Of course, sweetheart. Would you mind if I give you one piece of advice before you go—as someone who's been where you are?"

"Okay."

"Ed was seeing Sheryl behind my back. I'm not sure if you knew that."

"Matt told me."

"Like you, I felt angry and hurt—betrayed. It was awful. I couldn't even look at him. Ed apologized profusely. He broke it off with Sheryl immediately, and he wanted to work it out, go to counseling. I refused, and I filed for divorce." Mary exhaled. "I love Warren. He's loyal and uncomplicated, but we don't have that same connection that I had with Ed. If I could do it over, I think I should have at least tried forgiveness and counseling.

"When I started dating again, it was a disaster. When I was younger, I had my pick. As a divorced woman with kids, men weren't exactly lining up. Men my age wanted someone younger with less baggage. My kids were considered baggage. Can you believe that? It was a pride-swallowing experience. Men are wired differently, and I'm sure Warren would be just as likely as Ed to cheat, but, for obvious reasons, he doesn't have the same opportunities."

"What are you saying?" There was an edge to Allison's voice.

"Matthew made a terrible mistake, but most men are prone to this disgusting behavior, especially the good-looking ones. If he can change with counseling and love, it might be better to rebuild what you have than to start over with someone who might be much worse, especially considering all the negative ramifications for Kyle and Connor."

"I really have to go." Allison hung up.

The line went dead. Mary sighed. She tapped on the tiny screen and put the phone back to her ear. It rang.

"Mom," Matt answered. He was groggy.

"I know you worked late last night, but we need to talk," Mary said.

"Stay out of it. I'm handling it."

"By handling it, do you mean getting a divorce?"

"What? No. Nobody's talking about divorce."

"Allison is."

Matt drew in a breath. "You talked to her."

"Yes."

"She wants a divorce?" His voice was small.

"Do you want to lose your family?"

He sniffled. "No."

"Then listen to me very carefully. Allison's taking the kids to her parents'. Give Allison and the kids two weeks of space. Then call her and beg her to meet with you. Tell her that you only want fifteen minutes and that you'll drive to Hershey. Meet her someplace where you two can be alone. Maybe that lake you guys talk about."

"I really fucked this up. What am I supposed to say to her?"

"Tell her that you made the biggest mistake of your life. Tell her that you love her."

"I've already told her those things."

"Did you try to justify what you did because of what you think happened when you were deployed?"

"You think she did it too."

"Do you want your family back or not?"

"I do."

"Then be a man and let it go. Her past indiscretion, if it even was an indiscretion, does *not* give you the justification to have an affair."

"I know Allison. It won't work."

"You have to suggest counseling. And you have to have the appointment set up in advance, so she knows you're serious."

Matt groaned.

"This is about you getting better, so she can trust you again."

"If I do all this, do you think she'll take me back?"

"I don't know, but I guarantee you that she won't if you *don't* do it. I can get you the name and number of a good therapist."

"Thanks, Mom."

Mary hung up and set her phone on her desk. She hung her head and massaged her temples. *I'm holding this family together with duct tape*. Her desktop phone rang. She picked it up.

"Can I come over and talk to you?" Dan asked.

"Can we do it this afternoon?" Mary replied. "My plate is a bit full at the moment."

"It's urgent."

"Okay."

Dan waddled into Mary's office. He plopped into the chair in front of her. His chubby face was turned down.

"What can I do for you, Dan?" Mary asked.

"I know you're busy," Dan replied. "And you know how I worry. I just wanna go over this thing with Megan one more time."

"I already told you. She wasn't hitting her numbers. She was often late in the mornings, and we counseled her three times, all with signed statements. She doesn't have a leg to stand on."

"I spoke with Robert a few minutes ago. He spoke with her lawyer this morning. She's making some serious claims. She said that you set her territory goals too high. She said you changed it right after she was hired."

"Of course I did. The goals hadn't been raised in a decade. Inflation alone would account for an increase in the goals, not to mention population growth. Someone competent would have had no problems." Mary shook her head. "I feel like I'm being attacked here."

Dan frowned. "I'm not attacking you. I know you did the right thing. We just have to get our ducks in a row. Her lawyer thinks they have a strong case for wrongful termination."

"What does Robert think?"

"He thinks, if the goal was doable, we should be fine. They'd have to prove that it wasn't reasonable. The burden of proof is on them. But I'd rather not get caught up in litigation." Dan crossed his arms, resting his forearms on his gut. "Her parents came up to me after church and gave me an earful. It was extremely embarrassing."

Mary narrowed her eyes at Dan. "What did I tell you about hiring friends? Do I need to remind you that this was your hire?"

"I know."

23

Wes and Hulk Hogan

Wes puttered through the neighborhood in his Hyundai. The late afternoon sun was low in the sky. The streetlights were on, but kids were everywhere—black kids. Kids without shirts. They ran in front of his car with no regard for their safety. They crowded the street with their football game. Men sitting on porches glared at Wes as he drove by.

Wes found the house among the redbrick duplexes and parked in an empty space next to an old Harley-Davidson motorcycle. The lawns were mostly compacted dirt, dormant grass, and weeds. The trim on 1310 needed some paint. Wes removed the DNA kit from the CVS bag and shoved it in the side pocket of his cargo pants. He hurried up the concrete walk. He pressed the black button next to the doorknob and waited. He glanced over his shoulder. A handful of black men stared at him. He pressed the button again and listened. The bell didn't work. He knocked on the door and again glanced over his shoulder. The men were coming his way. He knocked once more, harder this time.

The door yanked open. A gigantic white man appeared with a horseshoe mustache and a bandanna on his head.

He glowered at Wes. "What do you want?"

"I'm looking for Jeremy Gilbert."

"I said, what the *fuck* do you want?"

"I'm Wes Shaw, Mary Sullivan's son." Wes winced.

Jeremy clenched his jaw, shaking his head. Long blond hair touched his shoulders. He looked like Hulk Hogan.

"I wanted to ask you a few questions," Wes said. "I talked to Joe yesterday."

Jeremy frowned. "Fuck it." He stepped aside.

Wes stood, frozen.

"You gonna come in or not?"

Wes stepped into the house, glancing over his shoulder as the black men walked down the street. Inside Jeremy's house was a black leather couch and a forty-eight-inch plasma hanging from the wall. Wes followed Jeremy past the living room to the "dining room" where a square wooden table sat next to the kitchen with four metal chairs. Jeremy pulled a handgun from the back of his jeans and set it on the table in front of him.

Wes stared at the gun with wide eyes, his mouth open.

"What's wrong?" Jeremy said with a chuckle.

"Can you put that away?"

"You're not one of those gun-control faggots, are you?"

"I, umm …"

"Sit the fuck down."

Wes sat down across from the man.

Jeremy grinned. "I ain't even supposed to have this. My life was taken from me, along with my first amendment rights. But I suppose you know that already."

Wes nodded.

"How am I supposed to defend myself if one of those fuckin' niggers breaks in here?"

Wes remained silent.

"They break in here, they're leavin' in a fuckin' body bag. I can tell ya that."

Wes froze.

"If you're scared, say you're scared."

"I don't understand." Wes furrowed his brow.

"I used to have a football coach who'd say that. That nigger was black as night. Hard-ass motherfucker though."

"I'm not really sure ..."

"I'm tellin' you to quit bein' a fuckin' pussy and to say what you came here to say." Jeremy leaned forward and rested his elbows on the table. He put his hands together, cracking his knuckles.

"Joe told me that my mother set up the, uh, meeting, that night."

"Is that a question?"

"Is it true?"

"Would it matter if it was?"

"Yes."

"What the fuck are you doin'?"

"I just wanna know the truth."

"Bullshit." Jeremy glared at Wes.

"I thought my father was dead. If that was a lie, what else is a lie? I'm trying to piece it together."

"Fuckin' people don't want the truth. They wanna believe what they already believe."

Wes took a deep breath, his stomach in his throat. "Did you do it?"

Jeremy smirked. "If I say no, what the fuck does that prove?"

"Why did you take the plea deal if you were innocent?"

"Fifteen years is better than life."

Wes reached into his cargo pants.

Jeremy placed his hand on his gun. "Watch those hands."

"It's just a paternity test," Wes said, slowly removing the DNA kit from his pocket and setting it on the table.

Jeremy cocked his head, like a confused dog.

"I was conceived on that night," Wes said.

Jeremy stared at Wes for a beat, then exploded with laughter.

Wes frowned. "What's so funny?"

"You look like Joe. A pussyfied version but you definitely look like him. He's your daddy, not me."

"Will you take the test anyway? It's just a mouth swab."

Jeremy smirked. "Yeah, I'll take your test, on one condition."

"What's the condition?"

"Gimme a hundred dollars. Cash."

* * *

Wes drove through the well-lit neighborhood of McMansions. The large houses sat on quarter-acre lots with diagonally striped green lawns. Luxury cars were parked in the driveways, the occasional late-model Honda for the teenager. Wes parked along the curb. He looked up at the brick-faced colonial. The front of the house and walkway were lit with landscape lights. The green grass was still wet from the underground sprinklers.

Wes checked his phone. It was 9:14. It had been a long day. His car was running on fumes, and his wallet was one hundred dollars lighter. He marched up the driveway to the brick walkway. He climbed the stoop and rang the doorbell. The door opened, and a balding man in athletic shorts and a T-shirt appeared. He narrowed his eyes at Wes.

"May I help you?" he said.

"I'm looking for Ben Armstrong," Wes said.

"I'm Dr. Armstrong. What is this about?"

"My parents are Joe Esposito and Mary Sullivan." *Probably.*

Ben's face turned white.

"Who is it?" a female called from inside the house.

"It's a patient. Give me a minute," the doctor called back.

He stepped onto the porch in bare feet, shutting the door behind him. "What do you want?" he said, his jaw clenched.

"What happened that night, with Joe and Jeremy?" Wes asked.

Dr. Armstrong shook his head. "You show up at my house unannounced and ask me to relive this?"

"I'm just trying to find the truth."

“They pled guilty. I saw them do it with my own two eyes. It was the most traumatic thing that’s ever happened to me. Now, if you’ll excuse me, I’d like for you to get off my property.” His hands were on his hips. He was soft around the middle.

“I could come back tomorrow, or I could go by your work,” Wes said.

Dr. Armstrong stepped closer to Wes. “I could have you arrested for trespassing.”

“Why did she sue you?”

“I’m done talking to you. I’m calling the police.” He turned and went back inside, slamming the door behind him.

Wes went back to his Hyundai and sped away.

24

Mary and Her Past

Mary sat in her SUV in the garage, the engine off and the garage door down. She hung her head, massaging her temples. A tapping on her window jolted her upright. It was Warren.

"Are you coming inside?" he asked through the glass.

Mary nodded, grabbed her purse, and stepped from the BMW. She slogged around the vehicle. Warren met her at the garage door.

"You okay?" he asked, his brow furrowed.

Mary sighed.

"Rough day?"

"Unfortunately it's more than that," Mary said.

They walked into the kitchen. Mary dropped her purse on the counter. She slipped off her high heels.

"Why don't you sit down?" Warren said, ushering her to the family room.

Mary sat on the couch, and Warren plopped down beside her, his breathing elevated, his belly and breasts jiggling under his golf shirt.

"You wanna tell me what's going on?" Warren asked.

Mary exhaled, her shoulders slumped. "I don't know what I'm doing."

"What do you mean?" Warren put his hand on top of hers.

Mary's eyes were glassy. "I just can't do it anymore."

"What can't you do?"

"It's too much." Mary wiped the corners of her eyes. "Working these long hours with my mother's health deteriorating."

"She seems to be doing better since her fall."

"Until the next one. I wasn't there for her then, and I'm not here for her now."

"What are you saying? You wanna quit your job?"

She sighed. "I don't know. Maybe. I just don't know how much time she has left."

"Can we afford it?"

"We'd have to tighten our belts a bit, but I think we'd be okay."

"It's up to you, cuddle cakes. I trust you."

Mary leaned over and kissed Warren on the cheek. "You're a good person."

Warren smiled wide, his bulbous nose scrunching.

"I'm taking tomorrow off and I'll think about it over the weekend," Mary said. "I don't want to make a rash decision when I'm tired and emotional. I appreciate your support, honey." She forced a smile.

"There's my girl."

Mary glanced past Warren through the sunroom windows. Wes was on the deck, sitting on a camping chair, facing the woods.

"How long has he been out there?" Mary asked.

Warren shrugged. "Don't know. He was out there when I got home. I stuck my head out and said hello, but he didn't move. I think he has earphones in."

"I'm really worried about him. I should talk to him." Mary stood.

Warren grabbed the remote from the coffee table and turned on the television.

Mary walked out to the deck, her feet protected only by panty hose. It was overcast but warm. She stepped gingerly and placed her hand on Wes's shoulder, making him jump. He turned, sat up straight, and removed his earbuds.

"Hi, honey," Mary said.

"Hi, Mom," Wes replied.

Mary sat down on the built-in bench across from Wes. "I'm worried about you."

His dark eyes were hooded, his face stubbly, his mouth turned down. He needed a haircut. "I'm okay," he said.

"You don't look okay."

"I'm trying to figure some things out."

"Tara?"

He shrugged. "There's not much to figure out *there*."

"It's been over three months. Maybe it's time to get her out of your apartment."

"I know."

"Is there something else?"

He exhaled and looked at the deck.

"Honey, I'm really worried. Please talk to me."

He looked up, his eyes red. "I know my father's alive."

Mary sucked in a breath, her mouth open. "I didn't …"

"Nana said some things, and Dad confirmed them."

Mary's eyes filled with tears. "I wanted to protect you. I didn't want anyone to think—"

"To think what, Mom? That I might be a rapist, like my father?"

Tears streamed down her face. "You could never be like him. Never."

Wes wiped his eyes. "Joe and Jeremy—"

"How did you find out their names?"

"Newspaper."

"Then you know what they did to me."

"Did they do it?"

"Wesley Steven!"

Wes hung his head.

"How could you possibly ask me that?"

He looked up. "They said—"

"You *talked* to them?"

"I, uh, … yeah."

Mary stood, her hands balled into fists. "Are you out of your mind? They're violent, awful, awful men."

"I'm just trying to find out what happened."

"You already know what happened."

Wes bit the inside of his cheek. "The details."

Mary scowled. "The details? You wanted the details of your mother's rape?"

"Mom, I, uh—"

"I'll give you details. They smelled like alcohol. They were heavy on me. It hurt. It physically hurt me. Emotionally I was broken. I still am. How's that for the damn details?"

"I'm sorry, Mom. I'm just confused. Why did you sue your boyfriend?"

She let out a quick breath and shook her head again. "You really have been digging. Why didn't you just come to me first?"

"I didn't wanna upset you."

"Too late for that." She had her hands on her hips, glaring down at Wes. "He was in on the whole thing. The gun, everything. He's sick, and he wanted to act out his sick fantasy. They're all sick, but rape is hard to prosecute. The DA said we had to give Ben immunity to get his testimony against Joe and Jeremy. The DA was the one who told me that I could still sue Ben in civil court."

"Oh, … I didn't know."

"You do now. I think it's best you go back to your apartment and handle things with Tara. You've been hiding out here long enough."

25

Wes, Play the Hand You're Dealt

Wes parked in a visitor spot near Building 10. The streetlights cast a yellow glow on the full parking lot. Wes walked across the lot in jeans and a T-shirt. He knocked on Apartment 1B.

Joe opened the door, eyeing the folded paper in Wes's hand. "You get that test back already?"

Wes nodded. "Only takes a week. I also have a few more things to ask you."

"All right then." Joe stepped aside, and Wes entered the apartment.

The television was on. Local news. An empty plate, a beer, and a pair of reading glasses were on the coffee table. Joe grabbed the remote and turned off the television.

Wes handed Joe the piece of paper.

"Make yourself at home," Joe said as he grabbed his reading glasses from the table.

"Thanks," Wes replied, sitting on the couch.

Joe sat in his old recliner, kitty-cornered from Wes. He wore a pair of long jean shorts and a stained white tank top. He slipped on his reading glasses and unfolded the paper.

Wes sat in silence as Joe read.

Joe looked up from the paper, his glasses on the end of his nose.

"It's a 99.99 percent probability of a paternal match."

Wes nodded, his face drawn.

"You must be disappointed."

"I just want the truth. I'd like to ask you a few more questions."

Joe nodded. "Go on then."

"My mother told me that Ben was in on it. That he was living out some sick fantasy. She said the DA told her that they had to give Ben immunity to get you and Jeremy. She also said the DA told her how she could still sue Ben in civil court."

Joe smirked. "You believe her?"

"I don't know." Wes cleared his throat. "Do you have anything to say about what she said?"

"The best liars know how to put enough truth in the lies. Ben *was* a sick fuck. That's true. Shit, we're all sick fucks. Ben did what he did to save his ass. That was his only crime. Jerkin' off while two guys plow your girlfriend ain't a crime. I suspect the embarrassment factor had somethin' to do with it. I'm sure she had him wrapped around her finger."

"So, you're saying that she's lying?"

"That's all I've been sayin'."

"Why? Why did she lie?"

"That's the sixty-four-thousand-dollar question. You'd have to ask her."

Wes hung his head and rubbed his eyes.

"You look like shit," Joe said.

Wes glanced up at Joe.

"You look like someone ran over your dog and fed it to you for dinner."

"I've had a ..." Wes shook his head. "Forget it."

"Finish what you were sayin'."

"I've had a shitty few months."

Joe nodded, stroking his beard. "It's a damned-if-you-do, damned-if-you-don't situation. If you believe me, then your mother's a lyin' sack a shit. If you believe her, you gotta rapist for a father."

"That's not helpful."

"I'm not gonna blow smoke up your ass. Shit is how it is. Sometimes you gotta accept shit, move on, play the hand you're dealt."

"Is that what you did?"

"No, but I wish I had. Would a made my time in prison a lot easier."

"What was it like? Prison."

"There's no peace in prison. No quiet. You're always watchin' your back, always calculatin' the situation to not get jumped or stabbed or fucked in the ass. I was a tough kid, but I was scared shitless when I went in. And I had every reason to be."

"Did you ever get jumped or stabbed?"

"A lot a shit happened to me. You can't dwell on it. Play the hand you're dealt and move forward."

"Is that what you're doing now?"

Joe grinned, his beard stretching across his face. "You're a nosy little shit."

Wes frowned.

"I'm just fuckin' with ya. You shoulda been a lawyer. Shit, I don't even know what you do."

"I work with computers."

"Makin' the big bucks."

"Not exactly."

"What do you mean, not exactly?"

"Being a tech guy doesn't pay much. It pays even less when you don't have a job."

"Economy sucks. They been talkin' about a recovery for five years, but I ain't seen shit."

"I got fired."

"Damn, boy, the hits just keep comin'."

"They sure do." Wes nodded. "And my girlfriend was sleeping with my brother."

Joe's face went taut, his eyes fiery. "That ain't right. Did you kick his ass?"

"No. He tried to come after *me*."

"That's bullshit."

"Yeah."

"You're not still with this whore, are ya?"

"No."

"You're better off. Bitches ain't worth the hassle. That's why I never got married."

Wes took a deep breath. "She's still in my apartment."

Joe let out a low whistle. "You pay for that apartment?"

"Yeah."

Joe winced. "God damn, boy, didn't anyone teach you shit about women?"

"I'm gonna ask her to leave."

"There's your problem. You don't need to *ask* her shit. It's your apartment. You pay for it. Tell her to get her ass out before you throw her out. If she says no, wait for her to leave, take all her shit, throw it outside, then change the locks. Ask your property manager to change the locks. Tell 'em you lost the keys or somethin'. They change locks all the time. They'll charge you, but it ain't much."

"But how do I get the property manager to change the locks at a certain time?"

"Does she work?"

"Yeah."

"You can schedule an appointment for a lock change. I do a couple of 'em a week."

"Thanks."

Joe nodded.

"Is that what you do? Like maintenance for the apartment complex?"

"Yeah. Before this, I bounced around. I did some plumbin', construction, landscapin'. I've been workin' at this complex for eight years. Doesn't pay shit but at least it's steady. I ain't gonna be here forever though." Joe grinned. "I got plans."

"I should get going," Wes said, standing.

"Already? You don't wanna hear about my plans?"

No, I don't. Wes was dumbfounded.

"Come on. Humor an old man. I don't get many visitors."

Wes sat down. "Five minutes."

Joe smirked. "You wanna start the timer?"

Wes scowled.

"I'm gonna start my own business."

You and every other idiot. "What kind of business?"

"You know how, when you live in an apartment, you gotta take your trash out to the Dumpster?"

"Yeah."

"Then you know what a huge pain in the ass it is. So, I got this idea to pick up the trash for people. So, I come by a couple times a week, pick up the trash, and throw it out."

"That's not a new idea. It's like valet trash. Other companies are already doing that."

"No shit. There's thousands of landscapers too. That don't stop new landscapin' companies. My company's gonna be different. I'm gonna have these bags made. They look like those bags you see from the cleaners. They're gonna be heavy duty and washable, with a handle you put on the doorknob. People put their trash bags inside and hang it from the door. I come by and haul the trash. I leave the heavy-duty bag, so they can use it again."

Wes didn't know what to say.

"You don't think it's a good idea?" Joe asked.

"I'm sure it is."

"It's gonna be a cash cow. I just need more start-up money. I figure I need about sixty thousand to make the bags, do my marketin', get a truck, and some savin's to tide me over while I'm gettin' started."

"I should get going." Wes stood up.

Joe stood from the recliner. "I got almost forty thousand saved. That's why this place is such a shithole."

Wes moved toward the door. Joe was right behind him. Wes opened the door and stepped outside.

“Maybe you can help me with my website?” Joe asked.

Wes turned around. “I don’t do that type of work.”

“No?” Joe paused for a moment. “Well, thanks for stoppin’ by.”

Wes nodded.

“Lemme know if you got any more questions … or if you just wanna stop by.”

26

Wes and Ho-Be-Gone

Wes parked in the back of the lot, next to the Dumpsters. He crept past the playground, behind a couple apartment buildings. His sneakers were wet from the dew on the grass. A row of cypresses ran along the edge of the property. He hid behind the trees, fifty yards from his apartment building. Tara's white Volkswagen was parked in front. He waited, periodically sticking his head out to check if she was still there. *I hope to God that she's going to work today.*

He surfed the internet on his phone to pass the time. He heard men talking and laughing. He peered out from behind an evergreen. Two muscled black men—one bald, the other with cornrows—stood in the parking lot. *Shooting the shit, as Joe the rapist would say. Those two guys are always out there. Jesus, don't they have jobs?* Wes wondered what it would be like to walk around without fear, to stand in the middle of the parking lot, knowing nobody would say shit.

The bald one looked at Wes. "Hey, you," he called out in a deep baritone.

Wes whipped his head back behind the tree. His heart pounded. He stood frozen, like a rabbit in the wild, hoping that the predator couldn't see him.

"Hey, what are you doin'?" The man's voice was closer. "I said, what are you doin'?"

Wes stepped out from behind the tree. The men stood in front of him. "Sorry, I, uh, I was just waiting for someone."

The man with cornrows was a little leaner. He was tall and well-defined with a muscular upper body and thin legs, like a comic superhero. The bald man was beefier with legs like tree trunks and arms like anacondas. They were both scowling.

"Doesn't look like you're waitin'," the bald man said. "Looks like you're spyin'."

"I wasn't spying," Wes said, his palms up in surrender.

"Who you waitin' for?" the man in cornrows asked.

"My girlfriend … actually ex-girlfriend," Wes said.

"You're a stalker then," the bald man said.

They moved closer; Wes stepped back.

"Where you goin'?" the man with cornrows asked.

Wes stopped. The men were in his personal space.

"I'm not stalking her," Wes said. "She won't leave my apartment."

The bald man smirked. "What do you mean, she won't leave?"

"We broke up over three months ago. I told her that she could have a week to find a place, but she said she'd leave when she wanted to."

"And you pay for the apartment?"

"Yes. I pay for everything."

The man with cornrows laughed. "Damn, she's playin' you."

Wes frowned.

"What's your name?" the bald man asked.

"Wes Shaw."

The man reached in the pocket of his cargo shorts and removed his cell phone. He tapped on the screen and put the phone to his ear.

"Hey, Chuck," the man said. "I got this guy creepin' around. Says he lives here. Says his name's Wes Shaw." The bald man glared at Wes. "He's checkin'. You better not be lyin'." The three of them stood in silence. "He got anyone else on the lease?" The man listened. "Really?" There was a pause. "Thanks, Chuck." The man shoved his phone back in his pocket. "Lemme see your license."

Wes pulled his wallet from the back pocket of his jeans and handed his license to the bald man. The man inspected it, looking at the picture, then looking at Wes. He handed it back with a nod.

"You're gonna lock her ass out, huh?" the bald man said.

Wes raised his eyebrows. "How'd you know that?"

"Chuck told me that you have an appointment to change the locks. That's some underhanded shit. Why don't you just kick her ass out?"

"You don't understand. She won't go for it."

"She stronger than you?" the man in cornrows asked.

Wes shook his head. "She'd probably have her brother beat me up or some other guy she's sleeping with."

"Damn, you're dealin' with a straight-up ho."

"Yeah."

"Hold on a second," the bald man said. "You live in that building right there?" He pointed to Wes's apartment.

"Yeah."

"I remember you. You haven't been around for a while. You drive a Hyundai, right?"

"Yeah, good memory."

"I'm a salesman at the Hyundai dealership in Woodbridge. I can't help but notice 'em. I'm Derrick, by the way." The bald man extended his hand to Wes. They shook hands. "If you ever wanna upgrade, let me know. I'll hook you up."

"Thanks," Wes replied.

"This is Luther." Derrick nodded to the man with cornrows.

"What's up," Luther said.

"Nice to meet you," Wes replied.

Luther laughed. "*Nice to meet you,*" he mimicked Wes's formal tone. "I like white people. Y'all are so damn polite."

"Thanks?"

"So, what's the plan here, Wes?" Derrick asked with a smirk.

"I was gonna wait for her to leave, then I was gonna put all her stuff outside, and change the locks.

Luther cackled. "She's gonna be mad as hell."

Derrick laughed. "You got that right."

"Should I do something different?"

"Naw," Derrick said, "this situation's like a Band-Aid. You gotta rip it off."

"What'd she do anyway?" Luther asked. "She steppin' out on ya?"

"She was sleeping with my brother."

Luther winced. Derrick shook his head.

"That's dirty," Luther said.

"And she's been stayin' in your place for three months?" Derrick asked.

"Three and a half," Wes replied.

Wes glanced past the men to see Tara hurrying into the parking lot in a short skirt and a tight shirt. Wes hustled behind the tree.

"That's her," Wes said.

"Damn, that's your girl?" Luther asked. "She's fine. I see how she got you all twisted."

Wes peered through the tree. Her chest was huge. *I can't believe she did it. They look stupid. I wonder how she paid her boss back.*

"She's got that crazy look to her," Derrick said.

"Must be," Luther said. "She got Wes hidin' behind a tree and shit."

Tara zipped from the parking lot in her Volkswagen. Wes stepped out from behind the tree.

"I hate to tell you this," Derrick said, "but I think your brother might be livin' there."

"Oh, that's right," Luther said. "Some big-ass corn-fed white boy."

Wes raised his eyebrows. "My brother broke it off. At least I think he did."

"Does he drive a souped-up Honda?" Derrick asked.

"Vin Diesel wannabe motherfucker," Luther said.

"He drives a pickup truck," Wes said.

"Must not be him," Derrick replied.

"Then you're payin' for some other dude to hit that." Luther shook his head. "Damn, she's doin' you dirty."

Wes nodded and hung his head.

"Don't sweat that shit," Luther said.

Wes looked up. A black Honda with chrome wheels and a coffee-can-size exhaust pipe was parked in a visitor's spot near his apartment.

"That's his car?" Wes pointed.

Derrick and Luther turned.

"That's it," Derrick said.

"I don't know if he works," Luther added.

"I guess I could just stop paying. Then they'd get evicted."

Derrick shook his head. "That'll take at least three months, and you'll lose your security deposit."

"And your credit'll be *fuuucked*," Luther added, dragging out the "uh" in "fuck."

"You gotta get him outta there," Derrick said.

Wes's armpits started to sweat. He wiped his brow. "I can't."

"Naw, fuck that," Luther said. "That motherfucker's gotta go."

"You gotta do it, Wes," Derrick added.

"I'm just supposed to go up there and tell this guy to leave?" Wes asked. "What happens when he says no? Because I guarantee you, he's not gonna listen to me. He'll probably beat me up, thinking I'm a burglar."

Derrick checked the time on his phone. "What time you headed to work?" he asked Luther.

"I got the late shift tonight."

"You wanna give him a hand?"

Luther nodded.

"We'll go up there with you to make sure he doesn't try anything," Derrick said.

"Wow, thanks, guys. I don't know what to say."

"You gotta talk to him. We're not gonna do that for you," Derrick said.

"Let's do this," Luther said.

Wes was wobbly as he climbed the steps to his third-floor apartment. Derrick and Luther were behind him. Wes stood in front of the door.

"Should I knock or just walk in?"

"It's your house," Luther said.

"It's your call," Derrick said.

Wes knocked. Luther frowned. Wes knocked again. They waited. Wes looked at the men and shrugged. Luther stepped up to the door and banged on it, hard enough to shake the door frame. He stepped back with a small grin.

The door flew open, and the Vin Diesel wannabe stood with a scowl. Like Luther said, he was a big corn-fed white boy. He wore basketball shorts and a T-shirt with the sleeves cutoff. He glowered at Wes.

"Why are you bangin' on my door?" he said.

"No, he didn't," Luther said.

"This is, umm, my apartment," Wes said.

The man crossed his meaty arms. His bald head was shiny. "It's my girlfriend's."

"Tell him," Luther said.

"My name is Wes Shaw, and I'm the only one on the lease. She hasn't paid a dime to be here. I pay all the bills."

He glared at Wes. "Bullshit." He glanced up at Derrick and Luther. "Who are these guys? Can't handle your own shit?"

"Watch your mouth," Luther said.

The man narrowed his eyes. "I'm gonna call her." He tried to slam the door, but Derrick stepped forward and inserted his boot.

Derrick and Luther pushed Wes forward, and the three men stood just inside the apartment.

"Don't move," the man said and walked into the kitchen. He returned with his phone, alternately eyeing the screen and the men. He put the cell to his ear.

"I couldn't text you," he said. "It's an emergency. There's a …" The man pulled the phone from his ear and said to Wes, "What's your name again?"

"Wes Shaw."

"There's a Wes Shaw here, and he says this is his apartment." He nodded, listening. His eyes dropped to the floor. "I don't think I can do that." He took a few steps back, listening. "He has backup." He tried to say the last part low enough that his "guests" couldn't hear. He hung up.

"She's comin' back," he said. "She'll be here in like fifteen minutes."

"Hey, Wes, mind if we watch some TV?" Luther asked.

"Go ahead," Wes replied.

"Hold on," the man said, his palms in the air.

"You pay for this TV?" Luther asked, sauntering over to the couch.

The man was unresponsive.

"I thought so," Derrick said, brushing past the man on his way to the couch.

"How 'bout the couch?" Luther asked.

The man remained unresponsive.

"I bought that at Value City," Wes said.

Luther smiled and plopped down on the couch. "Love me some Value City. Got my bedroom set there."

Derrick sat down on the opposite end of the couch. He gave Wes a nod.

Luther turned on *SportsCenter*. The theme song was on. Da da da. Da da da.

"You should start packin'," Luther called out from the couch with a wide smile. "You ain't gotta go home, but you gotta get the fuck outta here."

The man scowled and shook his head. He turned and went into the bedroom, shutting the door behind him. Wes sat on the couch between Derrick and Luther.

"You're doin' good," Derrick said.

"We'll see when she gets here," Wes replied.

"It's your house. After what she did, no way in hell should she still be here."

Wes sat on the couch upright, his body tense. Luther and Derrick leaned back, laughing and commenting on the highlights, as if they were at a friendly get-together.

The door opened and slammed. Tara stood in her short skirt with tan legs and her top stretching across her new breasts. Her mouth hung open, staring at Wes and his new friends on the couch.

"What the fuck are you doing here, Wes?" Tara said. "And who are these people in my house?" She gestured to the couch.

Wes stood, moving closer to Tara. "I need my apartment back."

She let out a quick breath. "I don't give a fuck. You can't just barge in here unannounced. You don't live here anymore. You left, remember?"

"I pay all the bills. You're not even on the lease, remember?"

"Fine, whatever. I can leave at the end of the summer. I'll have a place then."

"Do you have an exact date?"

She lifted one shoulder. "September sometime. I'll let you know. Now get out of my house and take your thugs with you."

Luther and Derrick stood, moving behind Wes.

"Who you callin' a thug?" Luther asked.

"We were invited here by the legal tenant," Derrick said.

The Vin Diesel wannabe emerged from the bedroom.

"You and your boyfriend are livin' here illegally," Derrick continued. "That makes you two the thugs."

Tara pursed her lip gloss-covered lips and turned to Wes. "Just give us until September."

"I can't," Wes said. "My mom wants me to move out."

She made a clicking sound with her tongue off the roof of her mouth. "Just move in with your sister for a few months."

"I can't do that. You guys have to leave today."

"Today!" Tara said. "Fuck you. I'm not going anywhere. I'll leave in September."

"We'll go in September," the Vin Diesel wannabe echoed.

"You know where the door is," Tara said.

"I'm not leaving," Wes said.

"Get the fuck out, douchebag." Vin Diesel pointed at the door.

Wes stepped back; Derrick and Luther stepped forward. "You need to stay out of it," Derrick said to Vin Diesel. "This man's been payin' your rent, and this is how you talk to him in his own house?"

Vin Diesel stepped back and unpuffed his chest.

"Better step off," Luther said.

"I'm calling the police," Tara said.

Luther laughed. "What the fuck are they gonna do 'cept kick your vagrant asses out on the street?"

"He's got a point," Wes said.

"Come on, Wes. Just let me stay until September." Tara's tone was sweet. "Aaron's just a friend. He doesn't live here."

"That's some bullshit," Luther said.

"Shut up," Tara said to Luther. "Why are you even here?"

"Because I was invited. Why are *you* even here?" Luther said, in perfect mimicry of Tara.

She frowned.

"I would like for you both to leave now," Wes said.

The group went quiet.

"You heard the man," Derrick said, breaking the silence.

"Better get packin'," Luther said with a grin.

"I don't have anywhere to go," Tara said.

"Not my problem," Wes replied.

"When did you turn into such an asshole?"

Wes remained steadfast, not reacting to her taunts.

Tara's eyes welled with tears.

Luther shook his head. "You ain't gonna turn this around."

"Would you *shut up*," Tara said to Luther, tears spilling down her face.

"I guess I could—" Wes said.

"No, Wes," Derrick said, shaking his head. Then he glared at Tara. "You got one hour."

"Let's go, babe," Aaron aka Vin Diesel said. "This apartment sucks anyway."

Tara wiped her face and cackled. "He can't even get it up," she said, motioning to Wes.

Wes ducked his head, his face hot.

They started packing their things. Wes and his new friends supervised.

"Do you have to watch me the whole time?" Tara said to Wes.

"Yes," Wes said.

"Ten minutes left. You better hurry," Derrick announced.

Tara started to cry. "I can't get all my stuff in only an hour."

Wes didn't respond.

Tara and Aaron departed with twelve garbage bags full of clothes and nine cardboard boxes of miscellaneous items. One of the bags Tara carried split on the stairs. She sat on the steps and cried while Aaron picked up her scattered clothes. Aaron and Tara bickered as they packed up their cars.

"We're out, Wes," Derrick said.

"Thanks, guys. I really appreciate it," Wes replied. "There's no way I could've done that without you."

Luther smiled and smacked Wes on the shoulder. "Wes, my man, it's been real."

Derrick handed Wes his business card. "When you wanna trade up, let me know."

Wes took the card and shook Derrick's hand. Then Luther and Derrick headed down the stairs.

"That was some funny shit," Luther said to Derrick, "when her clothes fell outta that trash bag. Drawers and shit all over the place, she's cryin', Vin Diesel's pickin' up her drawers. Damn that was funny. We should start a business. We could call it Ho-Be-Gone."

27

Mary, Down but Not Out

Mary sat in her home office, hunched over her cherry desk. She leafed through bills with a scowl. She took a deep breath, began writing checks and adding stamps to return envelopes. Mary set the bills in her outbox.

She stared out the window into the trees. *Wesley might be a problem. It's been a month since he went back to his apartment, and he's still a zombie when I call. "Yes. No. I don't know." It's like talking to a brick wall. I wonder if he's depressed about his biological father. He has to understand why I lied.* Mary sighed. *It might have been better to let him stay, to keep an eye on him. He's been acting erratic. I think it's more than just his father. I need to figure out what's going on with him. Matthew's another problem, not entirely unrelated.* Mary frowned at the thought. *I should give him a call and see how counseling went today.*

Mary picked up her cell phone and tapped *Matthew*.

"Hey, Mom," Matt answered.

"Hi, honey," Mary said. "I was just calling to see how you were doing."

"You wanna know about the counseling session."

"Only if you want to talk about it."

"It was fine. I'm still sleeping on the couch, but I think we're making progress."

"That's great to hear, honey," Mary replied.

"Even if we get past it, I don't know if we'll ever really be past it."

"These things take time. You just have to love her the best you can and be patient."

"Can I call you tomorrow? I need to get ready for work."

"Of course, honey. Be safe tonight."

Mary ended the call and set her phone on the desk. She trudged up the carpeted steps to Nana's room.

"Mom," Mary said. She tapped on the door and entered. Nana was slumped to the right, her glass of orange juice toppled over. Her tray of food was barely touched. Mary sucked in a breath and put her hand over her chest.

"Mom!"

Nana mumbled, her speech incoherent.

Mary rushed to her side. "Mom, what happened?"

More mumbling.

Mary rushed downstairs and grabbed her cell phone from her desk.

"Nine-one-one, what is your emergency?"

"It's my mother. I think she's had a stroke."

* * *

Mary and Warren stood in a corner of the waiting room with an Asian doctor. The tiny man had a young face with symmetrical features. Mary couldn't help but think that he and his wife must have adorable little children. Warren, by comparison, looked like he could eat the doctor as a light snack.

"Your mother's stable," the doctor said.

Mary breathed a sigh of relief. "Thank God."

"But there were a few complications," the doctor added.

"What does that mean?" Mary asked.

"Your mother suffered an ischemic stroke," the doctor said. "It's caused by blockages or narrowing of the arteries that provide blood to the brain. We treated her with medication to relieve the blockage. However, during the time that her brain received inadequate blood, some damage occurred."

"What kind of damage?"

"The stroke damaged the left side of her brain, which affects the right side of her body. She has some paralysis on the right side of her face and body. She has some difficulty speaking, and she has some memory loss."

"Is it permanent?" Warren asked.

"Time will tell," the doctor said. "Half of stroke sufferers still have symptoms six months after the stroke. Given her age, I expect that she will have some difficulties, but I also expect her to improve with rehabilitation."

Mary's eyes were red and glassy. "What does this mean for her … life span?"

The doctor offered a small smile. "There's no reason why she can't live for many more years. She'll need increased care, but, like I said, I expect her to improve. I'd like to schedule her right away for rehabilitation with the occupational therapist, physiotherapist, and the speech therapist."

28

Wes and Attachments

"Is she okay?" Judy asked.

"She's sort of brain-damaged," Wes replied, from his usual chair opposite his therapist. "The right side of her body's paralyzed. The doctor said she can improve a lot with the rehab, but she probably won't be the same. She is like eighty."

"How does that make you feel?"

Wes shrugged. "Can I be really honest?"

"Therapy doesn't work very well if you're not."

"I don't feel anything. I'm not sure I even care."

Judy scribbled on her notepad. "Why do you think that is?"

"Because she's always been kind of mean to me."

Judy remained silent.

"She's never been the regular nice grandmother, but she's nicer to my siblings. Matt used to make fun of me, saying that Nana hates me. It was one of those jokes that we both knew held a kernel of truth."

"How old were you when this happened?"

"I don't remember a time when she wasn't mean to me, but my first memory of it was when I was six or seven. My mom used to bathe us kids together when we were little. I remember we were at Nana's house, and she had this huge Jacuzzi tub. I wanted to play in the bath with Colleen and Matt. Nana screamed at me and slapped me across the face. So I took a shower in the guest bathroom."

"Why do you think she did that?"

Wes exhaled. "Knowing what I know now, she probably didn't want the seed of a rapist near the good kids ... especially naked."

"How does that make you feel?"

Wes frowned. "I'm not stupid. I know if you do things like this to kids, it can really mess them up later in life. I think I'm messed up. I just don't know how to fix it."

"That's why you're here."

Wes nodded. "Can we change the subject?"

"Sure."

"I got a job," Wes said with a smirk.

"Congratulations." Judy smiled, creases emerging around her mouth.

"It's at Best Buy, part of the Geek Squad. I don't know why they have to call it that. It's kind of humiliating. Actually I do know why they call it that. It's marketing. It's a stupid job, for half of what I was making at school. It is enough to pay my bills though, especially with Tara gone."

"How has it been without Tara?"

"It hasn't been too bad. At first it was rough, but, after I got away from her, I realized I didn't miss being treated like crap. I spend a lot less money too. It's been good to be back in my apartment. I love my mother, but I couldn't stay there anymore."

Judy scribbled in her notepad. "Because she asked you to leave?"

"She just said that it would be best if I dealt with Tara and went back to my apartment. And she was right. If I would have asked her to stay longer, she would have said yes."

"Then why did you leave?"

"She was upset with me because I was questioning what happened with Joe."

Judy nodded.

"I think she was right to be upset with me. I was questioning her word on what must have been the most traumatic experience of her life."

"Do you think she's telling the truth?"

Wes took a deep breath. "I do. It's just ..." Wes shook his head. "I don't know. I'm having trouble figuring out what's true and what's a lie. I mean, I thought my biological father was dead until a couple months ago. It seems like Joe's telling the truth, but it also seems like my mother's telling the truth. Someone's lying, and it's a really big lie." Wes paused. "How do you know if someone's lying?"

"I read an article recently that said that the traditional tells that the police look for to identify suspects are inconclusive. Nervousness or avoiding eye contact. Those behaviors were thought to show deception, but research has shown that to be untrue."

"What if Joe's a sociopath? Wouldn't he be able to lie really well?"

"It doesn't work that way. If he's a cunning, smart sociopath, he'll probably be adept at lying, but, if he's a bumbling low-IQ sociopath, his lies will likely be more transparent."

Wes nodded. "Last time I saw him, I tried to figure out if he fit the profile you gave me."

"There's really not a set profile. Sociopaths are very different from each other."

"But you said that they can have trouble forming attachments, and they often have immature hobbies and addictions."

Judy nodded. "And they often prey on the sympathies of others. But they are notoriously difficult to spot."

"I don't think Joe has any immature hobbies, but I think he does have trouble forming attachments. He's never been married. I think no kids, besides me, but I don't think I count as an attachment. I'm not sure he even has any friends. He has had a beer every time I've seen him. Maybe he's an alcoholic."

Judy let Wes talk without interruption.

"As far as preying on my sympathy, he did give me a sob story about the cops railroading him because he didn't have any money for a decent lawyer." Wes blew out a breath and frowned. "What do you think?"

"His history, and what you've told me, gives me reason to pause. If you continue to have contact with Joe, I would recommend that you proceed with caution. Sociopaths spend their lives figuring out how to blend in and how to mimic the emotions of others."

29

Mary and Hindsight's Twenty-Twenty

The right side of Nana's face was lazy, and her right shoulder was weak, but she had regained movement. She was feeding herself with her left hand. Mary tried to feed her, but Nana wasn't having it. *She still has her fighting spirit.* Nana's movements were slow, robotic, and deliberate. Mary sat in the chair next to her bed. Sharks were attacking cages filled with divers on the television. Mary had a Nicholas Sparks novel open in her lap. She was stuck on the same page. Mary kept losing her train of thought as she alternately read and watched Nana eat.

Nana shoved a large piece of dry turkey into her mouth. Mary tried to cut her food for her, but Nana had slapped her hand and said, "Not baby, not baby." After a couple weeks of regular therapy, her speech had improved. The occupational therapist had remarked about her "indomitable spirit." Swallowing was a struggle at first, but she was back on solid foods.

She stopped chewing. She tried to swallow over and over. She gasped for air, her eyes wide. She gasped again. Her skin turned pale.

Mary froze, slack-jawed.

She awoke from her stupor and ran from the room, down the stairs to her office. Mary surveyed her desk. Her phone was upstairs.

She ran back to Nana's room and snatched her phone from the bedside table.

Nana was turning blue.

Mary fumbled with her phone, her fingers betraying her. She tapped 9-1-1.

"Nine-one-one, what is your emergency?"

"My mother's choking," Mary said.

"What is your location?" the operator asked.

"I'm at 9700 Cardinal Rose Court in Fairfax Station."

"I'm dispatching an ambulance. Is your mother breathing at all?"

"I don't think so."

"Is she still conscious?"

"Yes."

"You need to perform the Heimlich maneuver."

"I don't know how."

"Sit her up, if she's not already standing. Wrap your arms around her from behind. Make a fist with your dominant hand, and cover the fist with your other hand. Place your fist just above her belly button and just under her rib cage. Give her a succession of rapid forceful thrusts, inward then upward, like the letter *J*."

"Okay, I'll try. I'm putting the phone on Speaker."

Mary placed the tray of food on the dresser. She sat Nana upright and climbed into the bed behind her. Mary reached around her mother's waist and put her fist above her mother's belly button. She placed her left hand on top and pulled inward, then upward. Nothing happened. She did it again, harder. She thrust her fist into Nana again and again in rapid succession.

"Nothing's happening!" Mary called out.

"Keep trying," the lady on the phone replied.

Mary continued to work on Nana. "It's not working. Somebody help us!"

"An ambulance is already en route. They should be there in less than five minutes."

* * *

Warren drove Mary home from the hospital. The late afternoon sun glared through the windshield, partially blocked by the car's sun visors. Her cheeks were blotchy, her eyes puffy. She leaned her head on the window in a stupor. Warren hit a pothole, and her head bounced off the glass. She sat upright.

"It's my fault," she mumbled.

Warren put his right hand on top of hers, his left still on the steering wheel. "It's *not* your fault. It was an accident."

"I ran downstairs to get my cell phone." Mary shook her head. "It was in the room on the bedside table. It was like I had lost my mind. I wasted all that time. That was the difference between her living and her dying." Mary hung her head, a couple tears slipping down her cheeks.

"It's stress. Stress makes people forget simple things. It could have happened to anybody." Warren glanced at Mary, then back to the road.

Mary stared at Warren. "But it didn't to anybody. It happened to me." She gazed out the window. "I tried to cut her food, but she wouldn't have it."

"I know you did."

"I should have just let her be angry with me."

"Come on, cuddle cakes. Hindsight's always twenty-twenty."

Mary sighed, turning from the window back to Warren. "I should have known how to perform the Heimlich maneuver."

"You did the best you could. I don't want you blaming yourself, okay? You took excellent care of your mother. You quit your job for her. I didn't see Grace lifting a finger."

30

Wes and It Seems Fishy

Wes sat in the parking lot of Joe's apartment complex. His car idled with the air conditioner on. His cell phone was pressed to his ear.

"You don't think it seems a little fishy?" Wes asked.

"Do you have any idea what you're saying?" Colleen replied.

"I'm just saying, how does she not know her phone's in the room? It was right next to her."

"So you think Mom killed Nana?"

"I didn't say that. I just said it seems fishy."

Colleen blew out a quick breath over the phone. "Either she's telling the truth or she killed Nana. You do understand that, don't you? You do realize that you're suggesting that Mom's a murderer?"

"I'm not saying that. I just don't think she's always as perfect as everyone thinks."

"Nobody's perfect. Jesus. But she's not a freaking murderer. What is wrong with you?"

"You don't understand what I'm trying to say."

"I understand perfectly well."

"Maybe part of her didn't wanna help Nana. Maybe it was more than just her making a mistake."

Colleen didn't respond.

"Colleen?"

"Keep this shit to yourself at the funeral," she said and hung up.

Wes frowned and shoved his phone in his pocket. He cut the engine and stepped from his Hyundai. It was a cloudless day. Wes was the only person outside, despite the break in the heat. As he walked across the asphalt, he was simultaneously warmed by the sun and cooled by the breeze. He knocked on the door of the ground floor apartment.

Joe answered a few seconds later with a big grin. "Come in," he said.

Wes sat on the couch, Joe in his usual recliner. Pro football was on the television. Joe pressed Mute, silencing the crowd and the announcers. A vinyl bag lay on the coffee table. It was black with white lettering that read Esposito Trash. Joe was in long jean shorts and a gray T-shirt that also read Esposito Trash.

"This becomin' a regular thing?" Joe asked.

"I wanted to ask you a few more questions."

"Whaddaya think about my new shirt?" Joe adjusted his shirt so the lettering was straight.

Wes was expressionless. "Looks good."

Joe smiled. "And check out the bag." He motioned to the sample on the coffee table.

Wes nodded.

"Pick it up. Check out the handle for the doorknob."

Wes picked up the vinyl bag for a couple seconds and set it back down.

"I packed it with as much weight as I could, and it held just fine."

"Are you making a fortune yet?" Wes asked with a small smirk.

"It ain't about makin' a fortune. It's about makin' somethin' for myself. I still need about twenty K before I buy the bags in bulk and get a truck."

Wes nodded again and leaned back.

"I could use some help," Joe said.

Wes didn't reply.

"You wanna get involved?" Joe asked.

"I'm good."

Joe frowned. "You ain't got a job."

"I do now."

"Good for you." Joe cracked his neck back and forth. "What kinda job you get?"

"Same stuff I was doing before. Computer stuff."

Joe nodded, his eyes narrowed. "If you ever want a real opportunity, you let me know."

Wes nodded.

"Let's have it then, Mr. Down-to-Business."

Wes cleared his throat. "My grandmother died."

Joe was blank-faced.

"My mom's mom. She choked to death. My mom was there, and she ran down the stairs to get her phone to call for help, but her phone was in my grandmother's room all along. My mom ran back upstairs and called 9-1-1. They told her how to do the Heimlich maneuver, but it was too late."

"*Hmmph*."

"What's that mean?"

"Nothin'."

"She feels terrible about wasting time looking for her phone. She thinks it was her fault."

Joe stroked his black-and-white beard. "Lemme get this straight. She's with her mother, and the old bag starts to choke."

Wes nodded.

"Instead of pickin' up the phone that's right next to her, she runs out the room, thinkin' her phone is someplace else. Then she realizes it's in the room that she just came from?"

"Yeah, that's what happened."

Joe smirked. "You believe that pile a dog shit?"

"She feels awful. I mean, I can see how it could happen. Stress can make you do weird things."

"Really?"

"Yeah, I think so."

"You got it all figured out then."

"You don't believe it?"

Joe let out a breath. "Of course I don't believe it."

"I thought you might have some insight."

"Bullshit. You have your doubts, but everybody you talk to thinks you're an asshole for even thinkin' the unthinkable. Right?"

Wes shrugged and hung his head.

"You come here because you know I'll give it to you straight. Right?"

Wes looked up. "It doesn't make sense. I mean my mother took care of Nana for all these years. She just quit her job to take care of her. Why would she do all that if she was gonna let Nana die on purpose?"

The corners of Joe's mouth turned up. "Did she have a good job?"

"She did. She was pretty high up in this charity for children's heart disease."

Joe chuckled.

"What?"

"The bitch without a heart, helpin' kids with heart problems. I'm not buyin' it. You really wanna know the truth? I'd start by findin' out if she really did quit."

Wes nodded. "I have one more question."

Joe held out his palms. "I'm an open book."

"Do you have any hobbies?"

31

Wes, the Racist

Wes approached the concrete office building. The beltway reflected off the tinted glass as he entered the marble lobby. His stomach churned as he approached the front desk. Greg recognized Wes from afar and stood behind his desk, his uniform pressed and his arms crossed.

"Hey, Greg," Wes said.

"What are you doing here?" Greg asked. "You know Mary doesn't work here anymore."

"I know. I wanted to talk to Dan Nelson."

"About what?"

"He told me, if I ever needed a job, they always need tech guys."

"I can't let you up there."

"I'll just call him then." Wes pulled his phone from his pocket. He tapped on his phone until he found a phone number for We Heart Children. Wes dialed and put the phone to his ear, striding a few feet away from Greg.

Greg stood staring.

"We Heart Children, how may I direct your call?" a female asked.

"Dan Nelson, please."

"Hold, please."

The phone rang.

"Dan Nelson's office," a female answered.

"May I speak to Dan Nelson please?"

"May I ask who's calling and what this is regarding?"

"This is Wes Shaw. I met Dan at a family picnic a few years ago. He'll know who I am."

"Hold please."

Wes looked up at Greg. "I'm on hold."

Greg sat again behind the marble desk, which was more like a built-in access barrier.

"I'm sorry, but he's unavailable," the female said.

Wes turned away from Greg to make the phone call more private. "Is there a time when he will be available?"

"I really don't know."

"May I make an appointment to talk to him?"

"What is the appointment regarding?"

"Employment."

"I'm sorry. We're not hiring right now."

"Can I—"

She hung up.

Wes put his phone in the front pocket of his jeans.

"I made an appointment," Wes called out to Greg. "See ya later."

Wes turned his car around, so he had a good view of the expensive cars in the rock-star parking spots. He cracked his windows, letting the fresh air in. Thankfully it was in the seventies. He waited for hours, surfing the Internet, glancing up often to make sure he didn't miss Dan.

Wes tried not to think about how bad he had to pee. The pressure was unbearable. He glanced around. No people outside. No trees either, at least none of any size for concealment. Nothing but a concrete and asphalt jungle.

Wes stepped from his Hyundai. He moved to the back of the car. His car was between him and the office building. Behind him was a chain link fence. Beyond that, beltway traffic roared. He kneeled on one knee, positioning his body so he faced downgrade. He unzipped his fly and pulled his penis through the hole in his boxer shorts. Wes felt immediate relief as urine snaked along the concrete curb.

He shoved his penis back in his pants and stood, surveying the scene. Dan waddled toward a Range Rover. Wes zipped up and ran across the parking lot. Dan was backing out.

Wes yelled, "Mr. Nelson, hold on."

Wes ran in front of the silver SUV, waving his hands back and forth. Dan put the truck in Drive and looked forward. He slammed on the brakes. Wes was in front of his vehicle. Dan put the SUV in Park and powered down his window. Wes jogged over to the driver's side window.

"I'm sorry, Mr. Nelson," Wes said.

"Wes Shaw?" Dan asked.

"Yes, we met at the company picnic a couple years ago."

"We're not hiring."

"I know. I just need to ask you a couple questions."

"If this has to do with your mother, my lawyers advised me—"

"Lawyers?"

"I can't talk about it."

"She didn't quit?"

Dan frowned. "All I can say is that she worked here."

Wes stepped back from the car in a daze. Dan drove away.

"Wes," a man with a familiar deep voice said.

Wes snapped from his daze, his head turning instinctively toward his name. Greg stood in the parking lot, a minicooler in hand.

"What are you still doing here?" Greg asked as he approached.

Wes shrugged. "I needed to talk to Dan."

Greg glared. "You can't be harassing people here. Next time I'll call the cops."

"Do you know why my mother doesn't work here anymore?"

"She quit to take care of her mom. You know that."

“Anybody here tell you differently?”

“No, but I don’t work for the charity. I work for the realty company that owns this building. I know names from checking badges, but they don’t talk to me.”

“You don’t like me, do you?” Wes asked.

Greg shook his head with a smirk. “You really wanna do this?”

Wes nodded. “I do.”

“Look, man, I get that you have issues and that’s why I don’t say anything to you, but I’m not gonna pretend to be okay with your racist bullshit. And I definitely don’t want Abby around it.”

Wes frowned.

Greg pointed his finger for emphasis. “If you say one racist thing in front of my daughter, that’ll be the last time you see her.”

“I did say that stupid comment about her getting picked on because she’s half white and half black, but I didn’t mean anything by it. I was genuinely concerned—”

“I really don’t wanna hear your excuses.”

“So, I make one comment, and I’m a racist?”

Greg shook his head. “I know a lot more than you think.”

Wes held out his palms. “What does that mean?”

“I was warned by a very good source.”

“What are you talking about?”

“I’m not gonna get into it with you,” Greg said. “Look, I know who you are. Maybe it’s best you stay away from me, and I’ll stay away from you.” Greg turned and marched toward his car.

32

Mary and the Doll Fight

The guests were dressed in black. Mary pulled back the foil on the catered food. Warren hovered behind, playing the supportive spouse.

"Can you go tell Richard and Brandi that the food's ready?" Mary asked Warren.

"Are they downstairs?" Warren asked.

Mary nodded.

Mary moved from the kitchen to the sunroom, her heels tapping the hardwood. Matt and Allison sat next to each other, but a gap separated them.

"Food's ready, you two," Mary said.

"Thanks, Mom," Matt said, standing. "The service was really nice."

Allison stood. "I'm so sorry for your loss," she said.

"Thank you, honey," Mary replied.

"I should get the boys," Matt said.

"Let them play. You two should eat in peace."

Allison nodded and offered a small smile.

Mary walked into the family room. Cousins Jill and Wayne sat on the couch, watching a talk show on the television. They were in their fifties and looked every bit their age, complete with wrinkles and the paunches associated with first-world living. Colleen chose the opposite end of the couch with Abby in her arms. Greg sat in the recliner with his black suit jacket open and his hands folded in his lap.

"Food's ready, everyone," Mary announced.

Greg popped up, glanced at the others still seated and blushed.

Jill and Wayne stood from the cushy couch with groans. "We need to be going soon," Wayne said. "We have an early flight."

"Hopefully you can eat something before you go," Mary said. "My mom would have really appreciated you two traveling to be here."

Wayne huffed. "It is quite the trip. I remember when you didn't have to show up an hour before your flight leaves."

"And the traffic here is outrageous," Jill added. "I don't know how you stand it."

Mary pursed her lips. "Well, we don't have much choice, do we?"

"You could always move, like I did. I'm so much happier in Florida—"

"We should probably eat," Wayne said, putting a hand on his sister's forearm.

The cousins ambled to the kitchen.

"You two doing okay?" Mary asked Greg and Colleen.

"We should be asking you that," Greg said. "How are you doing?"

Mary shrugged and took a deep breath. "I'm hanging in there."

Greg hugged Mary. They disengaged, and Mary looked at Colleen and Abby on the couch.

"I appreciate you and Greg being here—and Abby of course," Mary said.

Colleen smiled. "I love you, Mom."

Mary bent down for a moment to kiss her daughter on the cheek and the sleeping Abby on the forehead. "Don't wait too long to eat. It's getting cold."

"We won't," Colleen replied.

"Have you seen Grace?" Mary asked.

"I think she's out front, smoking," Greg said.

"Can you let her know that the food's ready?"

"Sure."

Mary walked outside on the deck. Wes leaned on the railing, staring into the woods.

"The food's ready, honey," Mary said to his back.

Wes turned around. He was clean shaven, his suit a bit too big, no doubt purchased many years ago when the baggy look was in.

"Thanks, Mom," he said.

"You okay?" Mary asked.

Wes nodded.

Mary approached and hugged her son. "I love you."

"Me too."

Mary returned to the kitchen. Warren had a beer in hand, his jacket undone, his face beet red.

"What's wrong?" Mary asked.

"I walked in on Rich and Brandi … you know."

"I know, what?"

"They were having sex."

Mary sighed. "Where are they now?"

"They left."

"That's great, just great. He's really trying my patience."

"We probably won't see him for the rest of the day."

Mary frowned. "Obviously."

Greg walked into the kitchen and picked up two plates. "I'll get Colleen's plate too," he said.

Mary forced a smile in his direction.

Wes entered the kitchen, but stayed at the edge, waiting for Greg to finish with the food. The smell of cigarettes wafted into the kitchen with Grace. She wore a black dress that was too short and too tight for the occasion.

"Can I talk to you for a minute?" Grace asked Mary. "In private."

"Can it wait?" Mary replied.

"No."

"Fine."

Grace followed Mary outside on the deck.

Mary turned to face her sister. "What is it, Grace?"

"What's the status on the will?" Grace asked. "I'm not trying to be crass, but my finances are, … well, you know me, I won't bore you with the details."

Mary's mouth quivered, and she broke eye contact for a split second.

Grace put her hands on her hips. "The will's already been read."

"I'm sorry, Grace."

Grace narrowed her eyes. "What are you sorry for?"

"I'm sorry it didn't work out for you."

"So, I got nothing?" Grace gritted her teeth.

"I tried to tell Mom to include you—"

"You think she should've included me?"

"It was mom's choice, not mine."

"You didn't answer my question."

"Yes, I think she should've included you."

Grace crossed her arms, glaring down at Mary. "We can fix it right now. You can write me a check for half the money."

"Well, first of all, there are tax implications."

"Whatever. Pay the taxes, and give me half of what's left."

"So you can blow the money, like you've always done?"

"Fuck you, Mary." Grace dropped her arms, her hands balled into fists.

"You think that kind of talk will help your cause?"

"I got nothing to lose." Grace moved into Mary's personal space.

"I'm done talking," Mary said, attempting to brush past her sister.

Grace grabbed Mary by the shoulders. "You're not going anywhere."

Mary's face was taut. "You're hurting me."

"I don't give a fuck." Grace was spitting as she talked. "You're gonna give me my half."

"Maybe if you get your life together."

Grace shook Mary. "My life is none of your *fucking* business."

Mary's eyes filled with tears. "Let me go."

"I want my money." Grace squeezed tighter, her long nails digging into Mary's upper arms.

"Ow, you're hurting me." Tears spilled from Mary's eyes. "Let go."

Grace continued to squeeze, one side of her mouth raised in contempt.

"Help, help," Mary called out.

The door from the house opened. Matt, Greg, and Warren stepped onto the deck. Colleen, Allison, and Wes watched through the sunroom.

"What are you doing?" Matt said.

"Let go of her," Greg said.

Grace let go, and Mary scurried toward her protectors.

"Your mother stole my money," Grace said.

Mary's face was tear-streaked. She shook her head. "I didn't do anything. It was Mom's decision."

"Oh, bullshit."

"It's not my fault," Mary said.

"You should leave," Matt said.

"Matt's right," Warren said. "You should leave."

Mary rubbed her upper arms.

"Not until I get my money," Grace said, her hands on her hips.

Matt clenched his jaw. "Don't make me call the police, Grace. You'll go to jail for assault."

Grace glowered at Mary. "I hope you and Mom rot in hell."

Grace stomped down the deck steps. She disappeared around the side of the house, presumably headed for her car in front.

"What is going on?" Matt asked when Grace was out of earshot.

Colleen appeared on the deck, holding Abby. Allison and Wes remained in the sunroom.

Mary shook her head and wiped her eyes with the side of her index finger. "It's just Grace. You know how she is."

"Why is she upset about money?" Matt asked.

"It has to be the will," Colleen interjected.

Mary sniffled. "Nana didn't leave her what she wanted. I knew this would happen. I pleaded with Nana to change her mind, but she thought Grace would waste the money."

Grace's Ford Mustang roared to life in the distance.

Warren hugged Mary. She kept her arms in, allowing Warren to envelop her up in a bear hug.

There was an audible screech of tires as Grace drove away.

"Back inside everyone," Matt said.

The door to the house shut, leaving only Mary and Warren outside on the deck.

"You okay?" Warren asked, letting go of Mary.

Mary sniffed. "I think so. My face must be a mess."

"You look beautiful as always."

"That was really embarrassing. I don't want to go back inside."

"I think people are gonna leave soon anyway. And nobody faults you for Grace's craziness. Everyone knows what she's like."

Mary sighed. "Thank you, honey."

Warren smiled. "Come on, cuddle cakes."

They entered their house.

"I'm going upstairs to fix my face," Mary said.

She climbed the staircase and heard her grandsons playing upstairs.

"Bam," Kyle said. "He just punched your doll."

Mary rushed to the doll room.

"Don't do that," Connor said.

"Bam, punched you again," Kyle said.

"Stop it," Connor replied.

Mary stood in the doorway, her stomach in her throat. Kyle and Connor had on matching dark suits, no jackets, their shirttails out. "Kyle and Connor, what on *earth* are you doing in here?"

The floor was covered with dolls; the shelves were not. Kyle held an antique life-size boy doll, its arms out in a boxing stance. Connor was protecting another life-size boy doll.

Connor put his head down and retreated to the corner.

"Just playing," Kyle said.

Mary had her hands on her hips, looking down on the boys. "What did I tell you about playing in here?"

"You said we can't play in here because the door's locked," Kyle said. "The door was open."

Mary grabbed Connor and Kyle by the arms and dragged them from the room.

Connor started to cry.

"Nana," Kyle said, "you're hurting me."

Mary stopped just before the stairs and let go of the boys. Kyle and Connor ran down the stairs away from their nana.

33

Wes and Emotional Blackmail

Wes sat down in his usual chair.

Judy grabbed a book from her desktop. "I have something for you." She handed it to Wes. "The book we talked about."

She sat down across from him and crossed her legs. She wore a skirt suit and heels.

Wes scanned the cover. "Your colleague?"

"We were classmates in the same PhD program at Stony Brook."

"Thank you," Wes said, holding up the book for a second. "When do you need it back?"

"You keep it."

"Thanks."

They sat quietly for a moment.

"My grandmother's funeral was a disaster," Wes said. "Not the funeral part exactly but the thing after, like the get-together."

Judy nodded. She brushed her auburn bangs away from her eyebrows.

"My aunt Grace tried to beat up my mother because Grace didn't get anything from my grandmother in her will."

"How did you feel about that?"

"Part of me thought it was funny."

Judy scribbled in her notepad. "And why would that be funny?"

Wes shrugged. "I don't know. It just confirms what I've been thinking."

Judy and Wes exchanged glances.

"Are you going to tell me what you've been thinking?" Judy asked.

"I wanted to see if you would ask."

Judy nodded.

"Just that my mother's not as perfect as everyone thinks she is," Wes said.

"Nobody's perfect."

"I know that, but there are some things. At the reception or whatever, she got mad at my nephews."

"What did they do to upset her?"

"I didn't get the details. I've been keeping my distance from Matt and his family, and they left right after that. I think the boys made a mess or something."

Judy nodded.

"Connor, my younger nephew, always seems scared of my mother. He's different. He has darker hair and eyes like me. Of course everyone favors Kyle, because he's more athletic, more blond, less introverted. Seeing Connor brings back a lot of my childhood memories."

Judy waited for Wes to elaborate.

"I remembered something that my mother did when I was young." Wes adjusted himself in the chair and swallowed. "When I was bad, she used to tell me that she was going to kill herself, and it would be all my fault because I was bad."

"How old were you?"

"I don't know. I was young but old enough to go to school. Maybe five or six."

"Do you remember how you felt when she said that to you?"

Wes hung his head for a moment, his eyes watering. He snatched a tissue from the box on the coffee table and blotted his eyes before they overflowed. "Scared. … I was scared."

"At that age, you're totally dependent on your parents. The idea that your mother would be leaving you would be terrifying to a five-year-old. That must have been very hard on you."

Wes's eyes were glassy. He wiped them with his tissue again. "Am I supposed to hate my mother? I mean, is she a bad person?"

"People often do terrible things that they wish they could take back. We all have times of weakness—"

"Is that what you think? It was just a time of weakness to tell a child some bullshit like that?"

"I'm in no way excusing her behavior. I'm suggesting that people may act poorly. We should judge them on their entire person, not only on their bad behavior."

Wes frowned. "If someone does something terrible to me, I'm supposed to forget it because they aren't *all* bad?"

"If someone does something so egregious that you simply cannot forgive, you may have to cut that person from your life."

"So I'm supposed to tell my mother to go *F* herself and have no contact with her?"

"I can't make that decision for you, but, in your mother's case, you may want to try talking to her."

"How do I know if I should continue in the relationship?"

"That is your decision."

Wes held out his palms. "I'm asking for help. I know you have some advice."

"If a relationship is a net positive in your life, by all means, you should continue it, and you also need to do your part to be a positive influence in the other person's life. But, if that relationship is a net negative, you might want to reconsider continuing with the relationship."

34

Wes and Sugar's Addictive

Wes sat down on his couch, his phone in hand. The television was off. He tapped *Colleen* on his cell.

"Hi, Wes," Colleen said.

"Do you have a few minutes to talk?" Wes asked.

"Yes. Abby's asleep, and Greg's at the gym."

"How's school going?"

"I miss Abby terribly, but it's nice to be back at work."

"You must be tired."

"I am, but I'm used to functioning on no sleep."

"If you ever wanna go out with Greg, I could babysit sometime."

Colleen laughed. "Do you even know how to take care of a baby?"

"Well, no, but you could show me. How hard can it be?"

Colleen laughed again. "You can take care of her while I'm here to supervise. If you can do that, I'll *consider* leaving her with you."

"Okay. I liked holding her that time."

Colleen sighed.

"I'm sorry I haven't been over since then."

"I'm not begging you anymore."

"I know."

"What did you really want to talk to me about? I know when you're buttering me up."

"Mom—I think something's not right with her."

"Give it a rest. I know she's not perfect, but she's a pretty damn good mother. We're *all* lucky to have her."

"When I was a kid, she told me that she was going to kill herself, and it was my fault."

"I don't remember that."

"Of course you don't. You were like one."

"How do you know you're remembering correctly? I don't hardly remember anything before the age of like seven."

"It happened numerous times. I'm sure of it."

"Why didn't you ever say anything before?"

"I just remembered it."

Colleen let out a breath. "Come on, Wes. You have to understand that you might not be remembering what really happened. Memories are unreliable, especially from early childhood."

"But it's true. I remember it like it was yesterday."

"Just like that, out of the blue?"

"Yes. I'm positive."

"Okay, fine. Let's say it might be true. Why did she say that to you? What was the context?"

"I don't know. Maybe I made a mess, or I upset her in some way. I really don't remember what I did. Maybe she was upset about something else and took it out on me."

"That's a lot of maybes. What are you going to do? Hate Mom for something she did like twenty-five years ago? Maybe she was having a rough time. She had three little kids. Dad was always in the field."

"Would you ever say something like that to Abby?"

Colleen sighed. "I would hope not, but at times I feel very frustrated. I can see how a parent might say something like that—"

"And you think that's okay?"

"I'm not saying it's okay. I'm just saying that being a parent is really hard. If you ever have kids, you'll understand."

"It's not just me that she did things to. She used to feed you tons of junk food. That's why you were overweight."

"So, now Mom made me fat? You're unbelievable. I used to sneak cookies and ice cream and every other dessert we had. Mom didn't force me to eat like that. That's my problem, and it's something I still struggle with. I can't believe you'd bring it up."

"I'm sorry. It's just … sugar's addictive, and when she gave you all that crap—"

"They didn't know about food like they do now."

"All that sugar, it made you—"

"That's enough, Wes. I'm hanging up."

35

Mary aka Cuddle Cakes

"I feel bad that I yelled," Mary said into her phone. She wore a silk nightgown with a plunging neckline. She sat up on the king-size bed, her lower body under the covers.

"It's not a big deal, Mom," Matt said. "They were being brats. They deserved worse."

"I just love my little guys. It breaks my heart that I hurt their feelings."

"Seriously, Mom, it's not an issue. They've forgotten all about it."

"And Allison. Is she upset with me?"

"Of course not. She understands better than me how frustrating they can be."

"I let Grace upset me, and I—"

"Mom, let it go. You have nothing to explain and nothing to apologize for."

"Thank you, honey."

"I gotta go. I love you, Mom."

"I love you too."

Mary ended the call and placed her cell on the bedside table.

Warren flipped his book facedown in his lap—some hardback biography of an ex-president. He wore light-blue pajama pants and a matching button-down pajama shirt.

"I told you that you were making something out of nothing," Warren said.

Mary sighed. "I still feel bad."

"It's been a difficult time. You should cut yourself some slack."

"I suppose so. I'm just tired."

"If you need some help with things, I can help."

Mary chuckled. "You want to start doing the laundry?"

Warren smiled, showing his tiny teeth. "I was thinking I could handle the bills."

"I've been taking care of our bills since we've been married."

"I know. But I also know how much money stresses you. I manage money for a living, cuddle cakes. Let me help."

"You already manage our investment accounts. You don't pay bills for a living."

Warren placed the book on his bedside table and turned to Mary. His shirt crept up and exposed the bottom of his gut. "I got a call at work about a past due bill."

Mary put her hand to her chest. "For what? Our bills are up-to-date. I'm certain of it."

"It was from Discover. I took care of it. My finances have to be impeccable. My job's on the line. I think it would be good for both of us if I got involved."

"I really wish you hadn't paid that. It could be a scam."

"I don't think it was a scam."

Mary hung her head. "When my mom died, I did let things slide for a few weeks, but I'm on it now." She looked at Warren. "I'm really sorry if I made a mistake."

"Cuddle cakes, please don't worry about it. Let me help."

"Things were a little tight with me not working on top of my mother's medical bills, but we're okay now, especially with the inheritance."

"I still think—"

"You can get that boat you've always wanted. Wouldn't it be nice to take everyone out on the Chesapeake?"

"We can't park it here, and those slips are expensive."

"We can afford a slip."

Warren shrugged. "I'm not sure I wanna deal with all the upkeep."

"A new car then. I just want you to be happy."

"I am happy. I have you. I'm more concerned about *your* happiness. And I think you'd be happier if I took over the bills."

Mary frowned and crawled closer to Warren. She put her head on his chest, her arm on his keg-size belly. She moved her hand beneath his gut, inside his pajama bottoms. She grabbed his flaccid penis, covering it entirely with her hand. Mary squeezed.

Warren gasped.

"Maybe we can leave it as it is for now," Mary said.

His penis filled with blood. Mary crawled under the covers. She unsnapped the hole in the crotch of Warren's pajamas and pulled out his penis. It wasn't hard enough for vaginal sex. Mary grabbed his semierection, holding it upright. She kissed the circumcised tip, then covered it with her mouth.

Warren groaned as she moved down the shaft, completely covering him.

Mary sat up with a grin, one strap of her nightgown sliding down her upper arm. "I think I can handle … *things*, … don't you?" She raised her eyebrows when she said "things."

Warren nodded, his face flushed, his belly moving up and down with his labored breathing.

"It's settled then. I'll let you know if it becomes too much. And don't you worry. You'll never receive another one of those calls again, okay?"

Warren nodded.

Mary grabbed his penis and squeezed. "Okay?"

"Okay."

36

Wes and the Sweet One

Wes walked toward the couch. Joe smacked him on the back, causing Wes to flinch.

"Two weekends in a row," Joe said.

"I went to her work," Wes said as he sat on the couch.

Joe sat in his recliner. "Oh, yeah? How'd that go?"

"Her boss said that his lawyers advised him not to say anything."

Joe grinned and stroked his beard. "I knew it."

"It doesn't mean she did anything wrong."

Joe chuckled. "Come on. Use your head."

Wes rubbed his temples. He looked at Joe. "Everywhere I look, I get more questions. I need answers."

"You really wanna know somebody? You gotta go to the beginning."

"What does that even mean?"

"I know where she lived in high school."

"So do I."

"Then we go there and knock on doors, ask the neighbors. Some old bag might remember her."

"That was like thirty years ago."

"You got a better idea?"

* * *

Wes drove through downtown Alexandria, past the trendy bistros and the stores selling boutique clothing and designer jewelry.

"This place got all hoity-toity," Joe said from the passenger seat. "Wasn't like this when I was a kid."

Wes didn't say anything.

"I used to live a couple miles from here. Not as nice as your mom's place, but it was nice."

"Do they still live there?" Wes asked. "Your family?"

"Don't know. I haven't talked to anyone in my family since 1985."

They were quiet for a few minutes.

Joe cleared his throat. "My dad was a plumber. Your grandfather. He was a *fuckin'* asshole. Wanna know what the name of his business was?"

Wes nodded. He already knew the name.

"Esposito and *Sons* Plumbing. When I got arrested, that piece of shit was in the paper sayin' he hoped I got life. Then he changed the company name to Esposito and *Son*. I don't know if my younger brother ever went into the business. If my pops were smart, he would've changed the Esposito part too. He was a stubborn old bastard."

Wes glanced at Joe, staring out the passenger window, then back to the road.

Wes parallel parked his Hyundai in one of the few empty spaces on the tree-lined street, kitty-cornered from Nana's old house. Wes stepped from his car and stared at the brick home. No vinyl siding and none of that brick-facing crap. Her old house was built to last.

Joe slammed the passenger door. "I bet these are worth a fuckin' fortune now."

"I guess we should start with her old house," Wes said, turning to Joe.

Joe wore stained jean shorts and a Carlisle Property Management T-shirt.

"Let's go," Joe said as he walked toward the house.

They opened the wrought iron gate and walked up the brick walkway to the front door. An Audi sat in the driveway. A light breeze rustled the leaves on the trees. Wes rang the doorbell.

A man in shorts and a Georgetown Law T-shirt opened the door. "There's no soliciting," he said.

"We're not selling anything," Wes said. "My grandparents used to live here, and I was wondering if you knew anything about their daughter, Mary Sullivan, my mother?"

"When did they live here?"

"My grandfather died in the early '90s, but my grandmother lived here until, I think, 2003."

"I bought in 2012. Sorry."

"Do you know where the previous owners went?"

"Florida maybe. I'm not sure."

"Okay, thanks."

Wes and Joe tried both next-door neighbors, but they were relatively new to the neighborhood. They walked across the street. An Alexandria police car with flashing lights pulled into the neighborhood and parked at an angle in front of Wes and Joe. Joe put his hands up. Wes stood there, frozen.

A burly officer stepped from the cruiser. He lifted his chin in their direction as he marched closer. "What are you two doin' here?"

"My mom used to live here," Wes said. "I just wanted to talk to a neighbor who might remember her."

Joe still had his arms up.

The cop has his hand on the butt of his Glock. "There's no solicitin' here."

"We're not selling any—"

"I don't give a shit what you're doin'. You need to get movin'."

Joe lowered his hands.

"But we weren't—" Wes said.

"Thank you, officer. We're leavin'," Joe interrupted. He grabbed

Wes by the elbow and led him to the Hyundai. As they walked to the car, the officer followed them with his glare. An old lady in the house across from Nana's parted the curtains and peered out the window.

"What the hell, Joe?" Wes said, sitting in the driver's seat of the Hyundai. "We can be here. He can't do shit."

"Think so, huh? Cop was about to arrest us."

"How do you know that?"

"He had his hand on his gun. He was lookin' for trouble."

"Whatever." Wes started the engine. "We're not gonna find anything here anyway."

"Old lady in that white house with the columns was looking out the window." Joe pointed to the house.

"I saw her. So what? She's nosy."

Wes pulled out of the neighborhood, making sure to fully stop at the stop sign while the cop looked on.

Joe said, "Jesus Christ, boy. You're the dumbest smart kid I ever met."

Wes gripped the steering wheel, his knuckles white.

Joe continued. "If she's old and nosy and lives right across the street—"

"We can't go back there."

"What happened to 'We can be here. He can't do shit'?" Joe mimicked Wes's voice, a higher version of his own.

"You're the expert on the police, not me."

"Turn right … up here," Joe said, pointing.

Wes turned. "For what?"

"You should ask before you do it." Joe grinned.

Wes frowned.

"Relax. We'll circle back, and you can park a block over. Then just go to that old bag's house. If she doesn't know anything, hightail it back to the car."

Wes found a space a block over and parked. He stepped from the car, his door still open. Joe was in the passenger seat, making no attempt at an exit.

"You coming?" Wes asked.

"It's better you do this alone," Joe said. "You don't need me scarin' the old lady. Leave me the keys so I can listen to the radio."

Wes looked at his keys for a moment and shoved them in his pocket. "I'm gonna keep them on me."

"Suit yourself."

Wes hurried down the sidewalk. He turned up the walkway to the white brick house with black shutters. Wes rang the doorbell. The old lady opened the door. She wore an off-kilter curly haired wig and a light-blue housecoat.

"Yes," she said, her voice high with a raspy undertone.

"Hi. I'm sorry to bother you. My name is Wes Shaw. My mother is Mary Sullivan."

The woman stared blankly, standing in her doorway.

"She used to live across the street." Wes pointed to the redbrick house.

She continued to stare at Wes.

"Do you remember Elizabeth Sullivan, my grandmother?"

She remained quiet.

"Ma'am, did you hear me?" Wes asked loudly.

She blinked. "I remember the Sullivans."

"You do?"

"Oh, yes."

"Is there anything you can tell me about them—or Mary in particular?"

"We weren't very friendly, I'm sad to say."

"Why not?"

"They didn't associate with Jews." She said this in a whisper, as if it were a secret.

Wes frowned. "Are you sure about that?"

"Oh, yes."

"Do you remember anything about Mary? She was the oldest girl."

"I remember her." The woman scowled, her eyes narrowed.

"Do you remember anything about her?"

"Oh, yes." The old lady quieted, in a daze.

Wes exhaled. "Could you tell me what you remember?"

"I'm afraid it's not something I should repeat."

"Please, I'm trying to find out something very important."

"I don't see how it's important."

"Let me be the judge of that."

"I'm not going to use any naughty words."

"That's fine."

"You'll just have to use your imagination."

"Okay."

"Jacob used to play poker on Saturday nights. Sometimes he would stay out until midnight—"

"Who's Jacob?"

"My husband of course," she answered as if it were a ridiculous question. "God rest his soul." She stared at the sun.

"Ma'am?"

She looked at Wes. "My Jacob was a terrible poker player, but he liked being one of the boys. They just played for pennies."

"What does that have to do with Mary Sullivan?"

The old lady frowned. "I'm getting there. All good things to those who wait."

Wes took a deep breath and forced a polite smile.

"I always looked out the window when I heard a car on Saturday night, thinking it might be Jacob. I worried when he was out so late. We didn't get too much traffic back here in those days. I heard a car one Saturday in the summer. I remember it was such a hot summer. It was a lot like this past summer, … so hot." She pursed her lips.

"So, you heard a car?"

"Oh, yes. I saw a red sports car pull into the Sullivans' driveway. It was a convertible. They were in the car for a long time. I wondered when they would go inside. I looked outside every few minutes. I thought he was going to kiss her."

"Who was in the car?"

"I told you. It was Mary and some boy."

You didn't tell me. "Okay, please continue."

"That's when it happened."

"That's when what happened?"

"The thing."

"Ma'am, please, I have no idea what you're talking about."

The old lady blushed. "Her head was in his lap." She crossed her arms. "That's all I'm going to say."

"Are you sure it wasn't the other daughter, Grace?"

"Oh, I'm sure. Grace was the sweet one. She used to wave to me when I was in the front garden. Mary never waved."

37

Mary and the American Dream

Mary sauntered across the marble floor, shopping bags in both hands. She passed Zales and ivivva athletica on her right, Call It Spring and New York & Company on her left. There were other well-dressed patrons, but her personal space was in no danger of being violated. Prices at the Tysons Corner Center mall were high enough to keep out the riffraff.

Her eyes were drawn to the bright yellow floor and walls of the Lego store where a life-size lion had been built from thousands of tiny bricks. Inside the store, she browsed the building sets, stacked along the wall. There was a race car team complete with a tractor trailer to haul the stock car. There were houses, castles, and towns. There were themes styled after pirates, Star Wars, and Minecraft. She found the perfect one.

Mary set down her bags, reached into her purse, and grabbed her cell. She dialed her daughter-in-law.

"Hi, Mary," Allison said.

"Hello, Allison. I'm sorry to bother you. I'm at the Lego store in Tysons, and I wanted to get something for the boys."

"That's really nice of you, but it's not necessary. They have so many toys."

"Don't be silly. It's my job as Nana. I'm supposed to spoil them.

I found this Lego building set with a police station and police cars. Anyway, I think the boys would just love it, but I wanted to get your opinion first. I was going to buy two, so they didn't fight."

"Mary, it's nice of you, but really, it's not necess—"

"Oh, it's no trouble. I'll go ahead and pick them up. Would it be okay if I brought them over on my way home?"

"We're here, so that would be fine."

"Thanks, honey. See you soon." Mary hung up and placed her phone back in her purse.

Mary spent over three hundred dollars on Legos. She consolidated her bags and left the store. She rode the escalator to the second floor. Mary gazed upward, through the glass ceiling. The sky was bright blue with scattered clouds.

On the second floor, she breezed into Janie and Jack and picked up a few outfits for Abby. Afterward she just had to stop at Banana Republic—her *discount* clothing store. She left Banana with another bag. She passed the Microsoft Store on the way to Victoria's Secret, where the smiley young woman at the register was happy to hold her bags while she shopped. Mary picked out a few bras and some underwear with plenty of lace. She found a pearl thong. There wasn't much to it—a little white lace around the hips and a string of pearls that went up the ass crack and the vaginal nether regions. Mary added it to her stack of unmentionables. *Warren will love them.*

She paid and exited the store, her arms taut from the weight of the Legos. *I should have bought those last.* She turned her attention to the shiny burgundy automobile in the Tesla store. Mary sashayed into the dealership. The recessed lighting overhead was perfectly spaced, like an airport runway. The walls had flat screens with images of the cars performing in their natural habitat.

"Good afternoon. Welcome to Tesla. I'm Kurt," the salesman said.

Mary smiled. "Nice to meet you, Kurt."

He was a handsome thirtysomething with a manicured beard and tight pants.

"Is there anything I can help you with?" Kurt asked.

"I'm just looking."

"Can I take your bags while you look?"

"That would be great," she said, handing them to Kurt. "They're heavy."

"I'll put them at the desk."

Mary looked inside the burgundy sedan—tan leather interior, a large screen in the center of the dashboard. The hood was open. Mary looked inside—no motor. Kurt returned, hands free.

"We call it the frunk," Kurt said with a grin.

Mary giggled. "It is a beautiful car. These are electric cars, right?"

"Yes, ma'am."

Mary cocked her head with a mock frown. "Hopefully, I don't look *that* old."

"I'd say mid- to late-twenties."

Mary smiled. "You must sell a lot of cars. Please, call me Mary."

He grinned, his teeth perfect. "So, Mary, what are you driving now?"

"A BMW X5 but my husband drives a 7 series. This would be for him."

"What year is it?"

"I think it's a 2012."

"Are you looking to trade it in?"

"I don't know. I may give it to one of my children."

"Wow, I'd love to be in your family."

"I'm very lucky."

"I think your husband's very lucky."

Mary flipped back her hair with a grin. "May I take a brochure and quote to my husband?"

"Of course."

Kurt escorted Mary to the desk at the rear of the store. She sat down across from him. He went through the options. Mary wanted them all. He printed a quote that topped one hundred grand. Mary took the quote and a brochure.

"They really are beautiful cars," Mary said. "It would be nice not to have to go to the gas station."

"And great for the environment. We're very proud of our commitment to the planet. Electric cars are the future."

38

Mary and Pearl Thongs and Electric Cars

Mary drove through a neighborhood of quarter-acre lots and brick-faced McMansions. Most of the lawns were green, despite the September drought. No doubt the result of underground sprinkler systems. Mary parked in the Shaws' driveway, behind Allison's SUV.

She grabbed two large shopping bags from the backseat of her BMW and stepped to the front door. She rang the doorbell. Allison answered in workout gear and no makeup. She was still beautiful but a little pale without the enhancing effect of petroleum-based products.

"Hi, Allison," Mary said with a smile.

Allison smiled, her eyes still. "Hello, Mary," she said as she stepped aside. "Come in."

Mary stepped inside the foyer.

"May I take those?" Allison asked.

"Oh, sure," she said, handing the bags to Allison.

"The boys are in the family room."

Mary followed Allison through the foyer, past the kitchen, and into the family room. The room was framed by a sectional couch facing a wall-mounted sixty-inch flat screen. The boys were on the floor, alternately watching a cartoon on the television and ramming toy trucks together.

"Nana's here," Allison said.

Rocky, the black lab, lifted his head from his dog bed and greeted Mary with a half-hearted bark.

Kyle turned around. "Nana!" He ran to Mary and hugged her around the waist.

Mary bent over and wrapped her arms around his back. "You're getting so tall," Mary said.

Connor was still glued to the colorful characters on the flat screen.

Kyle and Mary disengaged. Kyle's eyes went wide at the sight of the Lego store bags in Allison's grasp.

"Is that for me?" Kyle asked.

"One's for you, and one's for your brother," Mary said, grinning.

"Connor, Nana brought you a present," Allison said.

Connor glanced at his mom, then back to the screen.

"Connor, come give Nana a hug," Allison said.

He didn't speak or move.

Allison frowned. "He's so moody sometimes."

"It's okay," Mary replied.

"Can I have Connor's Legos?" Kyle asked.

"No," Allison said. "And how do you know Nana brought you Legos?"

Kyle smirked. "It says Lego store on the bag. I can read, you know."

"You can?" Mary asked.

"It's easy," Kyle said.

"I've been reading to them at night," Allison said. "His little brain is like a sponge."

"Can I have my present now?" Kyle asked Allison.

"What do you say to Nana?" Allison asked.

"Thank you, Nana," Kyle said, as if it was a recording.

"You're welcome, sweetheart," Mary said.

Kyle grabbed the bag from Allison and scurried to the floor near Connor. Allison set the other bag on the couch next to a folded comforter and pillow.

How long does she plan to hold a grudge?

"Connor," Allison said, "your present from Nana is on the couch when you want it." She turned to Mary. "Thank you. That was really thoughtful."

"It was my pleasure," Mary said. "So, how have you been?"

Allison forced a smile. "Oh, busy. You know how it is with the little guys. How about you?" She winced slightly.

Mary sighed. "It's only been a week since the funeral, and it still feels surreal, like she'll be there when I get home."

"I'm really sorry, Mary."

Mary moved closer to Allison. She reached out and squeezed Allison's hand. Allison edged back, mere inches.

Mary glanced at the boys. "Enjoy this time. It goes by so fast."

Allison nodded.

Mary let go and stepped back.

An uncomfortable silence evolved. Mary looked at the kitchen and the teapot on the stove. *I just spent a fortune on Legos. Not to mention that monthly check to Chase Bank. Aren't you going to offer me something to drink?*

"Thank you for stopping by," Allison said. "I should get dinner started."

"Is there anything I can help you with?"

"No, of course not. I'm sure you have your own dinner to prepare."

Mary nodded, her eyes still. "I'm sure I do. Well, I'll leave you to it."

Mary left with another thank-you from Allison and drove the short distance home. She set down her bags in the kitchen, next to the stairs. She carried the brochure and the tiny pearl thong into the family room. Warren had his feet up in the recliner, the remote resting on his gut. Golf was on the television.

"Hi, honey," Mary said.

"Hey, cuddle cakes." Warren's eyes were glued to the flat screen. "How was Tysons?"

"I have something for you." Mary strutted in front of the man chipping from the rough. She had the brochure and the thong behind her back.

Warren craned his neck to see the television.

Mary frowned. "I guess you don't want your present."

Warren smiled. "I'm sorry. I'm paying attention now."

"You sure?"

"I'm sure."

"Pick a hand."

Warren pointed to her left hand. Mary transferred the thong to her left hand and revealed the prize.

Warren's eyes bulged. "What is that?"

Mary tossed the thong in his lap.

Warren held up the underwear with a grin. "I'm not sure I can fit into them."

Mary giggled.

"You gonna model these tonight?" Warren asked.

"If you're a good boy." Mary raked her teeth over her bottom lip.

Warren stared at her like a predator about to strike.

"What do you have in the other hand?" he asked.

Mary moved closer, revealing the brochure. She bent over, kissed Warren on the lips, and handed him the glossy advertisement.

"You want a Tesla?"

"It's not for me, silly. It's for you."

"My car's fine."

"This is electric. It's much better for the environment."

He glanced through the brochure. "It is a nice car."

"They have a dealership in Tysons. I saw the car, and I thought of you. You don't have to get it. I was just thinking you might like it."

"That's really sweet of you, cuddle cakes. Maybe we can go by there next weekend and look."

"Have you given any more thought to the beach house?"

Warren exhaled. "I know we can afford it with the inheritance, but

I wanted to invest more of the money. We really need to think about our retirement. I see it every day, people underestimating how much they need to put away for retirement."

"Real estate *is* an investment. Arguably much safer than the stock market. We can rent it when we're not using it, and, when we're ready to get out of the DC rat race, we have a place to retire."

Warren frowned. "It's almost five million dollars."

"And the prices keep going up. If we don't buy now, we'll pay more later."

"I don't know, Mary. We need to be very careful with this money. You never know what kind of medical bills we might have in the future."

"The Realtor said we could finance it and make more from rent than our mortgage. Then we wouldn't be spending anything, and we wouldn't have to worry about paying a higher price later."

"I'd have to look at the numbers."

"I don't think it'll be on the market much longer."

"There'll be other beach houses for sale."

"Think about walking out our back door right to the beach. Not to mention the pool. And I love the off-season."

"Can we at least give it some time? I feel like we have this money burning a hole in our pocket."

"I'd like to take you down there next weekend to see the place and to talk to the Realtor. We don't have to do anything, but, if we really want to retire in Duck, we should at least look at the numbers."

"I'm not getting out of this, am I?"

Mary had her hands on her hips. "Absolutely not."

39

Wes and the Actress

"What do you want?" Grace stood in the doorway of her condominium.

"I wanted to talk to you about my mother," Wes said.

"I have to go to work." She wore black pants and a white button-down shirt.

"Can I come back tomorrow?"

"Don't bother. You're not gonna convince me of some bullshit manipulation your mom told you." She shut the door in his face.

Through the door, Wes said, "I'm not here to defend her. I'm here for the truth."

Grace opened the door. "You got ten minutes. I really do have to go to work."

"Okay."

Grace led Wes to the living room. The condominium had wall-to-wall white carpeting and modern furniture—lots of glass and lots of black. Wes sat on one end of the couch, Grace on the other.

Wes said, "I think my mother's done some things … maybe some really bad things."

Grace blew out a quick breath. "No shit, Sherlock."

"What happened with Nana's will?"

"She manipulated our mother."

"Why?"

"What do you mean, why?" She frowned. "To keep all the money for herself."

"How could she do that? Nana was always strong-willed."

"Hell if I know. She wasn't exactly all there at the end. Your mother had access."

"Do you have any proof?"

"I know how she operates. She might seem as wholesome as apple pie, but she's rotten to the core."

"How does she operate?"

"She acts nice to your face. She tells you what you wanna hear. But, behind the scenes, she's plotting to screw you over."

"Can you give me a specific example?"

Grace pursed her lips. "When I was a kid, I had this piggy bank. I put my money in there from birthdays and chores and whatnot. There was a plug on the bottom, where you could get the money. I was like thirteen, and I wanted to buy some clothes that my mother wouldn't buy for me. My best friend and I were going to the mall. Her mom was gonna drop us off. So, I had plans to update my wardrobe from Catholic schoolgirl to something more grown-up. Anyway, I emptied my piggy bank, and there were no twenties. The change and the ones and fives were still there, but the twenties were all gone. I had at least ten of them."

"Mary took the money?"

"Of course she did. Who else?"

"Did you ever have friends in your room?"

"They wouldn't steal from me. Your mother, that's a different story." Grace shook her head. "The stealing isn't even the worst part."

Wes raised his eyebrows.

"The way she bold-faced lied to our parents, she should have been a fucking actress. She's the best liar I've ever known, and my ex-husbands were pretty damn good liars."

"But it could have been a friend?"

Grace shook her head. "Still drinking the Kool-Aid."

"I'm just saying, it's not real proof."

"You don't believe me, fine. Go talk to Doris. She'll give you an earful."

"I thought she went crazy."

40

Wes and a Wolf in Sheep's Clothing

Wes glanced up at the mammoth brick building with an ambulance parked in front. The clouds in the sky were dark and heavy. He thought of one word to describe the place—death.

Inside was a reception desk, a waiting area, and a security guard next to a set of double doors. On the wall was a picture of a cell phone with a red *X* through it. The guard eyed Wes as he approached the front desk. The receptionist was reading. Wes tapped on the wooden partition. She continued to read, finishing her sentence, then turned the book over to hold her place. The cover had a bare-chested man with long hair flowing in the wind.

"Can I help you?" she said, with no enthusiasm.

"I'm here to visit Doris Parsons," Wes replied.

"I need to make a copy of your photo ID, and you'll have to fill out this form." She set a clipboard with a questionnaire and a pen attached on the partition.

Wes opened his wallet and handed the middle-aged woman his license. He smiled at her.

She stared back, her expression emotionless. "Once I have your information, I'll call to ask if she'll see you."

The waiting area was a cluster of plastic chairs with metal frames.

Wes sat down and filled out the paperwork. He turned in the questionnaire, retrieved his license, and returned to the rigid seat.

Wes waited patiently, fighting the urge to break the no-cell-phone rule. A dark-skinned man in light-green scrubs emerged from the double doors.

"Wes Shaw," he called out.

Wes approached the man and showed his ID again. The man gave him a visitor tag, which Wes attached to his polo shirt. The orderly led Wes down a corridor lined with hand railings. They passed a few residents—old women shuffling along, two by two.

"She's in the rec room," the orderly said.

"Does she get many visitors?" Wes asked.

"Not sure. I've only been here a few months."

"Since you've been here?"

"Not on my shift."

The rec room consisted of plastic-covered furniture arranged around a big-screen television plus a card table and chairs. Dr. Phil was on the screen, his head big and shiny. A handful of residents watched the talk show. Doris sat alone at the card table, staring at Wes and the orderly as they approached.

"Mrs. Parsons," the orderly said. "Wes Shaw is here to see you."

"I've been waiting for you," Doris said, her eyes narrowed at Wes.

Her hair was gray and stringy, her face wrinkled and slack.

"Hi, Aunt Doris," Wes said, sitting down across from her. "Do you remember me?"

The orderly walked away.

"You're the dark one." Her teeth were red from the generously applied lipstick.

"I do have darker hair and skin than my brothers and sister."

"Dark on the inside too."

Wes's stomach churned. "I wanted to talk to you about my mother."

"They come to you in sheep's clothing, but inwardly they are ferocious wolves."

"Are you talking about me or my mother?"

"Apple doesn't fall very far."

Wes frowned. "What have I ever done to you?"

"You were there. *You* let it happen."

"Let what happen?"

"You let her take everything from me."

"I have no idea what you're talking about."

"My David was a good man." She shut her eyes for a moment. "He was a good man."

"What did she take from you?"

She glared. "Don't get smart with me. I know what you are."

Wes took a deep breath. "Aunt Doris, please tell me. I forgot."

"I remember. Oh, I *remember*. 'Help us get into the house,' she said. 'I'll take care of you,' she said. 'I found Jesus,' she said. She said 'I think of you as my mother, not Liz.'" Doris narrowed her eyes. "She tricked me because she knew I always wanted children. Then she threw me out like trash."

"My mother said it was your decision to leave." *She also said that you were insane and that you were institutionalized.*

"It was. I was like a prisoner. But she wouldn't return my money. It was everything David left me."

"Why didn't you ask Nana to help you get the money back?"

"My little sister?" Doris shook her head. "She always did believe her daughter's lies. She'll take everything Liz has too. You'll see."

"Nana died last week."

Doris stared at the card table.

"I'm sorry," Wes said.

Doris looked up, the right side of her sagging mouth raised in contempt. "What are you sorry for?"

Wes showed his palms. "Nothing. I'm just offering my condolences."

"I know what you are." She pointed a shaky finger at Wes. "Devil, … devil."

Wes stood and backed away. The orderly approached.

"Is everything okay? Mrs. Parsons?"

She glowered at Wes. "I know what you are."

"I think this visit is over," the orderly said to Wes.

41

Mary and When It Rains, It Pours

The doorbell rang, breaking the monotony of the rain. Mary glanced at the clock on her laptop, which read 7:51 p.m. *Who on earth?* She stood from her desk and stepped out of her office. Warren was in the family room, watching Fox News. He hadn't moved a muscle in the recliner. *Don't get up. I'll get it.*

Mary padded across the hardwood in her socks. Wes stood on the covered stoop, his hands in the pockets of his rain jacket. Mary opened one of the double doors.

"You could have just come in," Mary said.

"I don't live here anymore," Wes said. "I didn't wanna intrude."

"Nonsense, honey. Come in." Mary stepped aside, motioning him inside.

Wes stood, frozen on the stoop. "Can we talk out here?"

"I suppose." Mary stepped onto the Welcome mat, shutting the door behind her. "Is everything okay? You're scaring me."

"No." Wes shook his head. "I'm confused, and I want you to be really honest with me."

The air smelled clean. Rain blew under the small roof that covered the stoop. Mary was protected, close to the house, but Wes's back was probably getting wet.

"I'm always honest with you," Mary said.

"Grace said that you manipulated Nana into giving you all her money."

Mary put her hand on her chest, her eyes wide. "Why on earth would you take my sister's word on anything?"

"I'm not. That's why I'm asking you."

Mary's face was flushed, her fists clenched. "What are you asking me? If I coerced my mother for … money?" She said "money" as if it were a dirty word.

"So you didn't do it?"

"Of course not. Jeez Louise. I can't believe you'd even *think* such a thing."

"I went to see Aunt Doris."

Thunder cracked in the distance, followed by a jagged streak of lightning.

Mary frowned. "I can only imagine what *that* crazy woman said about me."

"She said she helped you get into this house, then she wanted to leave, but you wouldn't give her money back."

Mary shook her head. "I can't believe I'm having this conversation with you. She did give us money to help with the down payment, but it wasn't because we needed it."

"Then why?"

"Because she wanted to move in, and she wanted to contribute. We said no, but she was adamant. Warren and I let her, because it was a tiny sum of money, a few thousand dollars maybe."

Wes hung his head, staring at Mary's socks. "She said that her husband left her a lot of money."

Mary blew out a breath. "That deadbeat didn't even leave enough for his own funeral."

Wes was quiet, the rain pelting the back of his jacket.

"Honey, you have to be really careful with some of my relatives."

Wes looked up, his eyes red. "When I was a little kid, you told me that you were gonna kill yourself."

Mary huffed. "I really have no idea what you're talking—"

"You said it was my fault." His voice caught on "fault."

"Honey, I—"

"You said it was my fault you were gonna kill yourself." Tears slipped down his face.

Mary held out her palms. "Honey, I have no idea why you would think that. I would *never* say something so awful to you. I love you so much." Mary took a step toward her son, reaching.

Wes stepped backward into the rain.

Mary stopped, as if the rain line were a force field.

"Please, come inside," she said. "You're getting soaked."

Wes backed up again, stumbling on the step. He regained his footing at the bottom of the stoop, turned, and ran toward his car.

"Wesley, … Wesley!" Mary called out.

But he was gone.

42

Wes and the Email Bomb

Raindrops pelted the bedroom window. Wes rolled onto his back. He stared at the shadows on the ceiling—long slits created by the streetlights filtering through the blinds. He closed his eyes. He saw his mother admonishing him, pleading with him, reaching for him. There was thunder in the distance. He opened his eyes and sat up with a groan.

Wes put on his sweats and staggered to the bathroom. He peed, washed his hands, and padded to the "family" room. He sat on the couch, leaned forward, and picked up his laptop from the coffee table.

He logged into his Gmail account and clicked Compose. He left the To and Subject lines empty.

Matt, Colleen, and Rich,

I'm sending you guys this email because I wanted to talk to you about something that I've been struggling with. I thought that maybe you might be having a similar issue or had one in the past. I'm hoping we can be a support to each other. I know we haven't always seen eye to eye, but you guys are my brothers and sister.

I'm concerned that our mother is not truthful and that she may not be the person we think she is. I'm very conflicted about this statement, and I recognize that I may be wrong. I'm hoping that you three will have additional information that may clarify the situation.

I spoke with Dan Nelson, Mom's boss when she worked at the charity. I asked him about Mom. He said his lawyers told him not to talk about it. I don't think she quit. I think she was fired, and they must have had good cause.

I spoke with Aunt Grace. She said that Mom coerced Nana into leaving her entire estate to Mom. Grace also said that Mom stole from her when they were kids, then lied about it with the skill of an award-winning actress.

I also went to see Great-Aunt Doris. She lives in a state retirement facility. It is not a very nice place. Doris said she gave Mom the money Great-Uncle David left her, so Warren and Mom could get into their house. The agreement was that Mom and Warren would take care of Doris. She said she was a prisoner, and she wanted to leave, but Mom wouldn't return her money.

I recently remembered an incident from my childhood. When I was five or six, Mom used to tell me that she was going to commit suicide, and it was my fault.

I think the circumstances surrounding Nana's death are suspect. I'm not saying that Mom killed her, but maybe, in the back of her mind, she knew that there would be a big payday if Nana died, and Mom wouldn't have to worry about Nana's medical bills eating into the money. By Mom's own admission, it took her too long to call for help, and she was unable to perform the Heimlich.

The big shock is that I found out that my biological father is still alive. According to the newspapers from 1985, Mom was raped. I am the product of that rape. I've met my father, and he claims the sex was consensual. His name is Joe, not Tony as Mom has been saying my entire life. To be honest, I'm not sure who to believe. I do know that Mom lied about my father's death. If she lied about that, who's to say she wouldn't lie about the rape? Maybe Nana found a pregnancy test in the trash. She would have been pissed that Mom was pregnant outside of wedlock. Maybe Nana threatened to cut her out of the will, and that's when Mom came up with the rape story. Abortion would have been out of the question for a strict Catholic.

I don't think she's a truthful person. Maybe you've seen it too. Please let me know what you think.

Your brother,
Wes

Wes inserted the email addresses of his siblings: MattShaw@FairfaxPD.gov, Colleen.Jensen@FCPS.edu, and BigDickInYoFace33@gmail.com. In the subject line, he typed *Conflicted, Please Help*. Wes hovered the cursor over the Send button. His stomach turned. He clicked it. *Boom.*

He glanced at the time on his laptop, *2:11 a.m.* He closed the screen and went back to bed.

Wes awoke to the sound of his phone ringing. He reached over to his bedside table, grabbed his cell, and turned off the alarm. It was 8:00 a.m. There was a text message from Matt.

> **Matt**: You ever contact me at work with this shit again I'll kick your fucking ass. Stay the fuck away from my family. You have serious issues.

Wes's heart pounded, his stomach in his throat. He tapped his Gmail. Rich had responded with a single word: *faggot*.

Wes's cell phone chimed.

"Hey, Dad," Wes said.

"Good morning, Wes," Ed replied. "I got a call from your sister, and she sent me that email you wrote."

"What did she do that for?"

"Don't be upset with your sister. She's worried about you."

Wes blew out a breath.

"I thought we agreed that you weren't gonna mention what happened in the past with the, uh, attack," Ed said.

"I didn't agree to anything."

"Well, I really wish you didn't involve your siblings. This is the type of thing that drives wedges between family members."

"So, we're supposed to live a lie?"

"Nobody's askin' you to live a lie. I thought you understood why she lied."

"Maybe, but I keep finding more lies. Why did she take Doris's money or what about Grace? There's something not right here."

"I know this thing with your father is hard to take, but you're lettin' your emotions run wild, and I think that might be cloudin' your judgment."

"Do you think Doris and Grace are telling the truth?"

"I don't know. Your mother's extended family, ... well, let's just say they have their problems."

"Warren has a good job, and Mom had a decent job, but I still don't see how they could get into a house worth over a million dollars. I mean, you see how much money she spends."

"I know. She cleaned me out when we got divorced."

"What do you mean, she cleaned you out?"

"Well, maybe 'cleaned me out' is too strong. I gave her everything, but I had a stock account that I was gonna keep. That was the agreement, but she liquidated it and took the money. These things happen when emotions are high, and emotions are definitely high during a divorce."

"Don't make excuses for her. She stole your money."

"Not exactly. Her name was on the account. So, technically she didn't steal anything."

"That doesn't matter, and you know it."

"It was a long time ago. I would appreciate it if you would cut her a break, and let this stuff go. It's bad for family relations. There's a reason why I put on a happy face and come to your mother's get-togethers. I do it for the good of everyone. That's what I'm askin' you to do."

Wes scowled.

"Do you understand what I'm tellin' you?" Ed asked.

"Yeah, I get it."

43

Mary Coming Clean

Mary leaned closer to the screen and read the forwarded email from Colleen. *Damn him.* She clicked Reply.

> Unfortunately Wes is going through a personal crisis. I'm not angry with him, but I am concerned. I'm concerned that some of the crazy people in my family may have influenced him.
>
> I would like to get you kids together so we can talk about it and clear the air. It's not something we should discuss over email or the phone. I was thinking tomorrow at 6:00 p.m. because Matt is off. Feel free to bring Greg. And please don't mention any of this to Wes. He needs some time to cool off.
>
> Love you,
> Mom

Mary clicked Send. She sent a similar message via text to Matt and Rich.

* * *

The smell of grilled salmon and garlic mashed potatoes hung in the air. Mary tossed the baby kale and chard salad. A cake sat on the counter—freshly iced. Warren entered the kitchen from the garage. He smiled wide, his eyes mere slits.

"Smells great, cuddle cakes." Warren looked at Mary. "You look beautiful."

"I bet you tell all the girls that," Mary replied.

Mary wore a dark blue dress that hung just beneath her knees and a maroon cardigan. Her blond hair was in an updo, her makeup flawless.

Warren set his keys on the counter and sauntered to his woman. He pulled her close and kissed her openmouthed, his gut mashing against her.

Mary stepped back, her face hot. "What was that all about?"

Warren hiked his slacks over his belly. "It's about how much I love you."

Mary touched his forearm. "I love you too."

"So, what's the special occasion?"

"I just thought it would be nice."

Soft music was on the sound system as Mary and Warren ate. The conversation was sparse. After the main course, Mary served cake.

Warren took his final bite of buttercream layer cake. He patted his belly with a grin. "I am *stuffed*," he said. "Great dinner."

"Thanks, honey." Mary was expressionless.

"You okay? You've been quiet."

Mary hung her head.

"What is it?"

She shrugged and glanced up at Warren with glassy eyes.

"Cuddle cakes?" Warren stood and moved from the chair across the table to the one next to her. "Look at me." He put his hand under her chin and tilted her face upward. "What is it?"

She rubbed her eyes with the side of her index finger. "I have something really difficult to tell you."

Warren nodded, putting his hand on top of hers. "You can tell me anything."

"Do you remember when I told you about what Ed did to me?"

Warren nodded, his jaw clenched.

Mary took a deep breath, her eyes red. "Do you remember when you asked me if anyone else ever hurt me like that?"

"I don't remember what I said. I just remember that I wanted to kill the bastard." Warren scowled. "I still do."

Mary looked down. "It happened before."

"When? Who?"

Mary looked up, tears blazing trails through her foundation. "At a high school graduation party. Joe Esposito and Jeremy Gilbert."

Warren held out his palms. "I don't understand. You were raped by two men?"

Mary nodded. "One of them is Wesley's dad. Probably Joe." She sniffled. "Wesley looks just like him."

"I thought Tony was Wes's dad?"

Mary shook her head. "There's no Tony." Mary put her head in her hands and sobbed.

"That's how you got pregnant with Wes?"

She nodded, her head still in her hands.

Warren sniffed.

Mary looked up, her face blotchy and wet. "I'm so sorry I lied. I … I didn't want anyone to think badly of Wesley."

Warren wiped his eyes and took Mary's hands in his. "I'm so sorry that you had to go through that. Do you wanna talk about it?"

Mary shook her head. "No. But we need to talk about it because Wesley found out."

"How did that happen?"

"Some old newspaper articles."

"What did they say?"

Mary pursed her lips. "That I was gang-raped by the two men, and my boyfriend was held at gunpoint."

"My God."

Mary shut her eyes for a moment, squeezing out a couple tears.

"That wasn't the truth."

Warren raised his eyebrows, a few tears running down his face.

"The rape was by the two men, but my boyfriend set it up. He led me there. It was his sick fantasy to watch me be attacked." Mary hung her head.

"Jesus Christ. Mary, I'm so sorry." Warren leaned forward and wrapped his arms around her in a bear hug.

44

Mary and the Spam Busters

They sat in the family room, the television black. Mary and Warren were on one end of the couch, Greg and Colleen holding Abby on the other end. Matt was in the recliner, Allison next to him in a chair from the living room. Rich stood with his hands in his jacket pockets, itching to leave.

"Thank you for coming, everyone," Mary said. "Wesley's going through some things so his behavior's been a bit erratic."

Matt frowned. "That's an understatement."

"I know Wesley sent you an email that discussed me."

"He has issues," Matt said.

Mary nodded. "It's not his fault. I'm asking you to have some compassion for him. Like I said, he's going through some things."

"Everybody has problems."

Mary took a deep breath. "Most of the email Wesley sent you is untrue, but one thing *is* true. It's something that I never intended to tell anyone, not even Warren." She glanced at Warren, and he gave her hand a squeeze. "It started with Nana telling Wesley some things about his biological father. This led him to seek out more information from Grace and Doris. We all know that Grace and Doris are not the most stable people. They said some completely untrue things about me to Wesley. I think they did this because they're angry that Nana didn't leave them anything in her will. Money can make people do things they wouldn't normally do."

"Why would Doris think she would get anything?" Colleen asked. "She's older than Nana was."

Mary shrugged. "I don't know. She's always wanted something for nothing. She never had kids, never had a job. I think she feels entitled."

Colleen nodded.

"I tried to convince your Nana that she should include Grace in the will, but Nana was adamant that she didn't want Grace to receive anything. Nana said that an inheritance is meant to strengthen a family, to be handed down to help the younger generations. Nana felt, because Grace didn't have children and she's never been particularly responsible with money, that the money would be wasted by her. Nana wanted me to have it, because ultimately she wanted all of you to have it."

Rich's eyes widened. "So, we're getting money?"

"Eventually yes."

Rich frowned. "So, we're not getting anything."

Mary scowled at Rich. "This isn't about what you're going to get. Warren and I are investing the money, and, when we die, our assets will go to all of you. Hopefully you will take that wealth and build more for your children. That's what Nana wanted. It's not so you can have a shopping spree."

"Mom's right," Matt said, glaring at Rich, then softening his gaze at Allison. "As parents, we can't be selfish anymore. For us, Kyle and Connor come first. And I'm sure Greg and Colleen feel the same way about Abby."

Greg nodded to Matt.

"I think it's incredibly generous of Mom and Warren," Colleen said. "Thank you."

"You're welcome," Warren said.

"Of course, honey," Mary said.

Colleen smiled at her mother and kissed the top of Abby's head.

"This brings me to the hard part." Mary wiped the corner of her eyes with her index fingers.

Warren grabbed a couple tissues from the box on the end table and handed them to Mary. She took them and offered her husband a small smile.

Mary took a deep breath. "Wesley was telling the truth about the rape. I was seventeen, and Wesley is the product of that incident. I've been lying about what happened because I didn't want anyone to think that something was wrong with Wesley ..." She wiped her eyes with the tissues. "And I didn't want to relive it. I know my honesty is under scrutiny now. If anyone wants proof, I can send you the newspaper articles. Matt could probably pull the court documents from Alexandria."

Colleen's eyes were glassy. "I'm so sorry, Mom." She handed Abby to Greg and walked over to Mary. She bent over and hugged her mother. After a moment, she sat down. Mary was now sandwiched on the couch between Colleen and Warren. "I understand why you wouldn't want to tell the truth. I think I would have done the same thing. Nobody here is questioning your honesty."

Matt shook his head, his eyes bloodshot. "That explains why Wes is such a freak."

"That's what I was thinking," Rich said.

Allison remained expressionless.

Mary sniffled, her face blotchy. "This is what I don't want. Wesley is still your brother, and we have to be understanding of what he's going through."

Matt frowned. "Mom, he's in contact with your rapist. I won't have Allison or my kids anywhere near him."

"Matt has a good point," Colleen said. "I don't want anything to do with him either, not unless he gets some help and comes to his senses."

"I already unfriended him and marked his email as spam. Spam busters, bitch." Rich grinned.

"I blocked him too," Matt said.

Mary exhaled. "Wesley needs some time to figure things out. It's probably best to give him some space and to let *me* help him right now."

"I don't think you should go near him either," Matt said to Mary.

"He's my son. I won't give up on him."

45

Wes and Control

Wes lay lengthwise on the couch, his head propped up. He was reading the book Judy gave him. When his cell phone rang, he sat up, put the book on the coffee table, and picked up his phone. It was a 703 number, no name identified.

"Hello?" Wes said.

"Wes, it's Allison. Are you at home?"

"Yeah."

"I need to talk to you. May I come over?"

"Right now?"

"Yes."

"Sure, but I don't think Matt would be too happy about it."

"That's why we'll keep this between us."

"Do you even know where I live?"

"You live in the Woods of Fairfax, right?"

"Yeah."

"I don't know the address exactly."

"It's Building 1210, Apartment 3B. Make sure to park in one of the visitor's spaces. They'll tow your car if you don't."

"I'll see you in fifteen minutes."

* * *

There was a knock at the door. Wes opened it a few seconds later. Allison stood in yoga pants and a fleece jacket with her blond hair in a ponytail.

"Come in," Wes said, stepping aside.

"Thanks," she replied.

"Would you like something to drink?"

"No thanks."

"Would you like to sit down?"

"Sure."

"The couch is probably the best place," Wes said, gesturing to his brown sofa.

Allison sat down on the end. She was on the edge, as if she were afraid to lean back. Wes sat on the other end, as far away as possible.

"This is, um, sort of strange," Wes said. "How did you even get my number?"

"Matt's phone." She smirked. "He lets me have access to his phone now. He's trying to regain my trust."

Wes nodded. "I never had a chance to tell you that I appreciate how you stuck up for me that day. So, thanks."

"That situation with Tara was wrong on so many levels."

"Yeah."

"You're probably wondering why I'm here."

"Yeah."

"Matt showed me the email you sent. There was a family meeting about it."

Wes frowned. "I know everybody hates me, but I don't think I did anything wrong."

"I don't think you did either. I've noticed some things about Mary too."

Wes sat up straighter.

"I've stopped letting her babysit the boys because Connor's deathly afraid of her, and Kyle comes back high on sugar."

"Did she do something to Connor?"

"I don't know. I've asked Connor, but he doesn't say anything one way or another. But I know my child. Something's not right."

"Did you talk to Matt about it?"

"I've tried. You know how he is, always the loyal son."

Wes nodded.

"And I think she's part of the reason my marriage is a mess. I mean, looking back on it, I know Matt's probably not the right guy for me, but I love my boys." She took a deep breath. "The cheating and the lies, it's been … it's been difficult. Obviously you understand that."

"Is that why you stayed? For the boys?"

"That's a big part of it." Allison pursed her lips. "The other part has to do with Mary. I don't know if you know this, but Matt's convinced that I had an affair while he was deployed. I have no idea where I would have found the time. Kyle was a handful then. But Matt was convinced and said that he knew for sure from a reliable source."

Wes had a déjà vu moment. He thought of Greg and the source that proved Wes was a racist. "Who was the source?"

"He wouldn't tell me. He just said that the person wouldn't lie and that they saw me out with some guy in a bar. That never happened. I rarely went anywhere when Matt was in Afghanistan, except to the grocery store."

"You think Mary told him that?"

"Maybe not exactly that. I think she might have told him something else, but he can't say exactly, because then I would know it was her. I think Matt was just guessing with the bar part, thinking I would admit it." Allison blew out a breath. "He's a cop. He wants the confession."

"You think Mary led him to believe you were having an affair?"

"Yes. I just can't figure out why. But I think this is the reason he had the affair with Tara. To get back at me."

"You should read this book." Wes picked up the book from the coffee table and flashed the cover toward Allison. "*The Sociopath Next Door*."

"You think Mary's a sociopath?"

Wes shrugged. "I don't know. I'm not an expert. I haven't even finished the book yet. I do know that sociopaths are pretty common, and sometimes they do things that don't make any sense, but they do them just to mess with people. I can mail it to you when I'm done."

"I'll pick up my own copy but thank you."

"Have you told Matt that you think it was her?"

Allison sighed. "No, but I know how it would go. He won't betray her."

"Do you have any evidence? Maybe if you had evidence, Matt would admit it."

"I don't have any concrete evidence, but there is the money she gives us."

Wes's eyes widened.

"I'm guessing you don't know about this?"

"I don't."

"She gives Matt and I money every month to help us with our mortgage. We couldn't live in a house around here otherwise. I didn't want to take the money, but Matt insisted. He said he wanted to be close to Mary so the kids could see her. Of course she doesn't see them any more than when we lived in Woodbridge."

"The money's for control?"

"I think so. She doesn't come out and say it, but it's like we have to be on her side now. If the checks stop coming, we'll lose our home."

"What about Greg and Colleen?"

"They have the same deal. But I don't think Colleen thinks of it as Mary having control over her. I think it's hard for her to see her mother as anything less than perfect."

"Have you ever talked to her about all this?"

"I've tried some mild criticisms, but Colleen is always quick to defend Mary, so I haven't said anything more."

"Do you think she made up the affair because, if you two are divided, Matt would be easier to manipulate?"

Allison shrugged. "I don't know. I guess it's possible."

"What are you gonna do?"

"It's not about me anymore. I'm doing what's best for my boys. I'm really dreading Kyle's birthday party this weekend, that's for sure. Apart from these special occasions, I'm keeping my kids away from her."

"Then why tell me this?"

"I don't know. I just feel bad. I feel like you're telling the truth, and you're getting burned for it. It's not fair. I just thought, if you knew you weren't the only one, maybe it would be of some comfort to you."

"It is. Thank you."

"Can we keep this between us? We're all supposed to stay away from you. Matt thinks I'm at yoga."

46

Wes, Mom's Calling

Wes drove into the shopping center parking lot. He parked near the Giant Food grocery store. He walked from the shopping center lot to Ox Road. A handful of luxury cars zipped along the four-lane highway. Wes waited for a break in traffic and jogged across the highway. He hiked along the shoulder to Roseland Estates.

Wes crept through the woods near Mary's mansion, leaves crackling and twigs snapping beneath his feet. The green leaves on the trees were just starting to turn, some tinged with red and orange. Wes sprinted from the woods across the asphalt driveway to the garage. He peered in the windows. Mary's SUV was there, but Warren's car and Rich's truck were gone. *Warren's at work. Rich is at school. She's here.* He ran back to the woods and sat behind a tree. *This is stupid. She may not even go anywhere. I could be here all day for nothing.*

Wes waited for almost two hours. The garage door startled him. He peered out from behind the tree. Mary wore running gear and earbuds connected to her phone inside her arm band. She shut the garage with a press of the keypad. She bent over and touched her toes. She stood and rotated her torso. Wes watched her jog up the driveway and down Cardinal Rose Court to the main road of Roseland Estates.

With Mary safely in the distance, Wes sprinted to the garage. He typed the code into the keypad. The garage door opened. He entered the garage and smacked the button on the wall to close the garage door. The door to the house was unlocked as usual. He entered the kitchen. It was spotless. He glanced down at his shoes and slipped off his sneakers, holding them in his hands.

Wes snuck into Mary's home office. He set his shoes upside down on the Oriental rug. He opened her laptop and sat down. He checked the time on his phone while the laptop powered on—*10:16. How long does she run? Fifteen minutes? Thirty minutes? I have no idea. I need to be gone by 10:30 to be safe.*

The laptop wasn't password protected. He opened Google Chrome and clicked Gmail. Her email loaded and opened. She hadn't logged out since the last time she had visited. Wes scanned her emails. Facebook notifications, sales from various clothing stores, a few emails from Warren, Matt, and Colleen. He saw his email forwarded to Mary from Colleen, with a subject that read, *Wes is losing his mind.*

Wes spent the next fifteen minutes scanning her email history. It was more of the same. The clock on the screen read *10:31. Shit, I need to get out of here.* He clicked on the Trash icon. At the top of the folder it stated *Messages that have been in Trash more than 30 days will be automatically deleted.* He scanned her trash folder. It was mostly advertisements for clothing and household goods. One from three weeks ago stuck out. It was from Megan Myers, and the subject was *How's Unemployment?* Wes opened the email.

Mary,

I just wanted to let you know that I'm so glad that I accepted Dan's apology and returned to work. The new HR manager is a wonderful woman who's very happy with my work, so happy in fact that I was promoted today.

I used to come home from work and cry because I couldn't

meet your impossible goals. I used to think that something was wrong with me. But there isn't anything wrong with me. There's something wrong with you.

I think you're jealous because you're on the wrong side of forty. I know women like you. Petty, vindictive, hateful, deceitful, and manipulative. There's a special place in hell for you and them.

Wes grabbed a pen from the desk and scribbled Megan's email address on his hand. He closed out of Gmail and shut down the laptop. The garage door opened. *Shit.* Wes stood and grabbed his shoes. He glanced at the front door, frozen, unsure if he could make it in time. She was in the kitchen. *Too late.* Wes looked around the room frantically. No closet. He contorted himself under the desk and pulled the chair in as best he could. He still held his shoes.

Mary's sneakers squeaked as she walked on the hardwood. There was a rumble of ice from the icemaker, followed by the barely audible stream of water washing over the ice wedges. She was walking again, her steps moving closer. *If she sits at the desk, I'm dead.* She sounded much closer. *She's in the office.* She stopped.

"Hello," she called out.

Wes held his breath.

Her steps moved closer. Her sneakers were right in front of him. She pulled out the chair, jumped back and screamed, her hand on her chest. "Oh, my God!"

Wes crawled out from under the desk and ran for the front door.

"Wesley, what are you doing?" she called out. "Wesley, come back here."

Wes ran out the front door, leaving it open behind him. He sprinted down the street, high on adrenaline, his stocking feet slapping the asphalt. He stopped for a second and slipped on his shoes. He continued running until he reached a stretch of woods near the Roseland Estates entrance. He hid behind a tree, his breath labored. He heard a car engine approaching. He peered around the tree. It was Mary, scanning the neighborhood in her SUV. He snapped his head back behind the tree and squatted down. His cell phone rang; his heart raced. He reached into his pocket and silenced the ringer. He pulled out his phone and cringed. It read *Mom Calling*.

Shortly thereafter a voice mail appeared. He called his voice mail and listened to the message.

"Honey, it's your mother. What's going on? I'm not mad at you. I understand how difficult this is for you. Call me back. I love you."

Wes waited for fifteen minutes, Mary no longer in sight. He hiked back to his car and drove to his apartment. At home, Wes typed an email on his laptop.

> Megan Myers,
>
> You don't know me. My name is Wes Shaw. I'm Mary Shaw's son. Please keep reading. I'm not on her side. I can't say how I got your email, but I heard that you had some difficulties with her. I've also had some problems with her, specifically figuring out what is true and what is a lie. This has been difficult on me, as I imagine it must have been on you. I was wondering if you would be willing to share any evidence you may have that my mother is untruthful?
>
> Thank you for your time,
> Wes Shaw

Wes clicked Send. He refreshed his email every few minutes over the next couple hours. Finally a response came.

> Wes (if that's your real name),
>
> If you are who you say you are, my condolences for having such

a f-ing bitch for a mother. The only thing I'll say to you is you should check her education. It's the reason she was fired, but it wasn't the worst thing she did. If this is Mary posing as Wes, go to hell.

47

Mary and the Confrontation

The family sat around the dining room table, eating cake.

Greg swallowed. "Great cake, Mom."

"This *is* really good," Matt said with his mouth full.

"Thanks, you two," Mary replied with a smile.

"You always did make outstanding cake," Ed said.

Warren glared at Ed.

Colleen devoured her cake. She fed bits to Abby, who sat in her lap.

"Since we have everyone here, I wanted to say a few things," Mary said, glancing around the table. She frowned. "Where did Richard and Brandi run off to?"

"They went downstairs," Greg said.

"Matthew, honey, could you please ask them to come upstairs and join us?"

"Sure," Matt replied, headed for the basement.

Kyle slid from his seat. "Can we go play with my presents?" Kyle asked Allison.

Allison narrowed her eyes at Kyle. "Did you thank Nana for the presents and the cake?"

Kyle looked at Mary blank-faced. "Thank you, Nana."

"Oh, you're welcome, honey," Mary replied.

"Only in the playroom," Allison said. "Okay?"

Kyle nodded to Allison and said to Connor, "Come on."

Connor wiggled out of Allison's lap. The boys scooped up as many action figures as they could carry and marched upstairs to the playroom.

Matt returned to the dining room followed by two sullen teens. Rich and Brandi slumped into bordering seats.

"We have to get going soon," Rich said to Mary.

"Why don't you try thinking about someone other than yourself for once?" Matt said.

"Matthew." Mary shook her head.

"I didn't even know about this party until yesterday," Rich said with a painted-on scowl. "Nobody ever considers *my* plans."

"That's enough, Rich," Ed said.

"Just a couple more minutes with the old people," Mary said with a smile. "I wanted to make a quick toast." Mary held up a glass, and everyone but the teens did the same.

"I don't have anything to drink," Rich said.

Ed glowered at Rich, shaking his head.

Mary continued. "I just wanted to thank everyone for being here for Kyle's birthday and for sticking together as a family. Nana's passing has been especially trying for me. It's only been tolerable because I have all of you. So, thank you, and I love you."

"Hear, hear," Greg said.

"We love you too," Colleen said.

Everyone touched glasses, except for Rich and Brandi.

"Love you too, Mom," Matt said.

The front door opened and shut. Everyone rubbernecked toward the sound. Wes appeared in the dining room, his hair disheveled, his eyes bloodshot.

"She's a liar and a thief," Wes said, pointing at Mary.

"Wesley," Mary said, her face taut. "This is neither the time nor the place."

Matt stood up, moving into Wes's personal space. "You need to go the hell home. This is my son's birthday party." Matt grabbed Wes's wrist and forced his arm behind his back.

Abby started to cry.

"If you don't let me go, I'll send your boss the photos I have of you at the park."

Matt let go and stepped back.

"You remember the place, don't you? Right off Telegraph?"

Matt blanched.

"Sit down," Wes said.

Matt returned to his seat. Allison didn't look at her husband.

Colleen rocked Abby. She quieted.

"You need to go home," Ed said. "Your mother's right. This is neither the time nor the place."

"You gonna beat me up if I don't leave?" Wes asked.

"I'm asking you to do what's right."

"I should do what's right, huh? Was it right to beat me senseless but never lay a hand on Matt or Colleen or Rich?" Wes's eyes were glassy.

"I made some mistakes, son—"

"I'm not your son. That was the reason, right? You beat me because I'm not your son." Tears slipped down Wes's cheeks. "I loved you like my father, even though you never felt the same way."

"That's not true—"

"Bullshit. But this isn't about you, this is about *Mary*. Anyone wanna know why she's not working at the children's charity anymore?"

"I do," Brandi said.

"Wesley, everyone knows I'm not working there anymore. It's no secret," Mary said. "I quit to take care of Nana."

Wes shook his head. "She got fired because she never even graduated from college, much less received the MBA she claimed on her résumé."

Mary wore a poker face.

"That's not true," Colleen said, still rocking Abby.

"Oh, yeah. I checked the alumni for UVA undergrads and for

George Mason's MBA program, and she is *not* on the alumni list."

"Wesley, this is insane," Mary said, as if she were making a professional diagnosis. "You're letting unstable people influence you."

"Oh, really? You're gonna tell me that you really did graduate from those schools like you said?"

"I started at UVA, but your dad and I were moving around so much that I had to finish with a correspondence course at Maryland. And I did graduate from George Mason's MBA program. They don't list online graduates as their alumni."

Ed stared at his plate of half-eaten cake.

"You're a dumb-ass," Rich said.

"Richard, no," Mary said.

"What? He can come in here saying this crap, and I can't say anything to him?"

"What about Connor?" Wes asked.

"Don't talk about my kids," Matt said.

"Someone should stand up for him. That poor kid can't stand Mary. Don't you ever wonder why?"

"Shut up," Matt said.

"I'll say whatever I want."

"We don't wanna hear any more," Greg said.

"Don't wanna hear about what?" Wes asked. "How Mary's giving you and Matt money to make your mortgage payments?"

"I knew it," Matt said. "He's mad because he wants money."

"You're wrong. Her money comes with strings. She does it for control. I'd rather live in my shitty apartment that I pay for myself."

"Because you're a child," Matt said. "No kids, no wife. Shit, you don't even have a girlfriend."

"You took care of the girlfriend for me, didn't you?"

Matt opened his mouth, then shut it. Allison glared at her husband.

"There's nothing wrong with Mom helping us out," Colleen said, giving Abby a bottle. "If you ever got your act together, she would help you too."

"Don't you ever wonder where the money comes from?" Wes asked. "Warren doesn't make *that* much money, and she doesn't even work anymore. You see how she spends money. How do you think they even got into this house?"

"Our finances are none of your business," Warren said.

"Doris would disagree. She'd like the money back that you stole."

Warren clenched his fists and narrowed his eyes. "I've never stolen a dime in my entire life. Doris gave us that money, and Mary gave it back when Doris moved out."

"I'm sure that's what Mary told you, but it doesn't explain why Doris lives in a shithole."

"We didn't even want to take it," Mary said, her face blank. "And we gave it back to her when she left."

Warren nodded along with Mary's statement.

Wes crossed his arms, glaring at his mother at the other end of the table. "What about the money you stole from Ed?"

Ed's face snapped upward. He glared at Wes. "That was in confidence."

"I'm sorry, *Dad*. But she did steal your money."

Ed ground his teeth.

"Mom, is that true?" Colleen asked.

Mary was in a daze.

"Divorces are messy," Ed said to Colleen.

"Is it true?" Colleen said, turning to her father.

"Well, … technically no."

"That's bullshit, and you know it," Wes interjected.

Ed was blank-faced.

Colleen turned to her mother. "Why would you do that to Dad?"

Mary opened her mouth, but nothing came out.

"It was payback," Warren said.

Mary scowled at Warren, shaking her head. "No," she said under her breath.

"What was payback?" Colleen asked.

"Nothing," Warren said, crossing his arms over his gut.

"You can't say 'nothing' now," Colleen said. "You brought it up."

"This conversation is over," Mary said. "Wesley, you've done enough damage. You need to leave, or I *will* call the police."

"The lies finally caught up to you," Wes said.

"You don't know what you're talking about," Warren said.

"Enlighten me then, *Warren*."

"I'm leaving," Mary said, standing up. "I'd like everyone to go home."

Nobody moved.

"It's private," Warren said. "Some of us have enough class not to air dirty laundry."

"It's time for everyone to go," Mary said, her face taut and her pupils dilated.

"Not until Warren tells the truth," Colleen said, glaring at Warren. "He said that Mom took Dad's money for payback. Payback for what? You can't just make something up because you're jealous."

Warren stood up, his fists clenched. "Jealous? Of what?"

"It's not hard to figure out," Wes said to Warren. "Look at Ed, and look at you."

"Wesley, that is shallow and rude," Mary said.

"I'm just stating the obvious." Wes glared at Mary. "Everyone knows that you and Ed are still attracted to each other."

Mary put her hand to her chest, her face hot. She looked at Warren. "That is *not* true."

"You do flirt with Dad," Rich said with a smirk.

"Richard, go to your room," Mary said.

"Fine with me." Richard and Brandi left.

"It makes sense that you'd be jealous," Wes said. "Your wife wants to have sex with her ex-husband."

"Fuck you, Wes," Warren replied. "You have no idea what you're talking about."

"Enlighten us then."

"This is over," Mary said. She tugged on Warren's arm, but he wouldn't budge.

Wes said, "Liars run from the truth—"

Warren pounded his fists on the table, rattling the china. "Ed raped her!"

Abby started to cry, now unwilling to take the bottle from Colleen.

Ed stood, looking at Warren, his eyes wide. "What?"

"Don't you fucking deny it." Warren pointed a fat finger at Ed.

"This is insane," Mary said. "We all need to calm down."

"Did you tell him that I raped you?" Ed asked Mary.

"It's all a misunderstanding." Mary's face was blotchy.

"Dad would never do that," Colleen said, rocking Abby.

Abby quieted.

"I agree," Wes said.

"What are they talking about?" Matt asked Mary.

Mary's face contorted, and her eyes were glassy. Tears streamed down her cheeks. "I was raped. You all know about it. Why are you torturing me? What did I do to deserve this?"

"But Warren said how you said Dad raped you," Colleen said, as if she were breaking bad news to a friend.

"I never said that." Mary sobbed.

Warren walked from the room and stomped up the steps. Ed marched out the front door.

"I never said that," Mary repeated. "It's a misunderstanding."

Colleen set Abby in the carrier. Matt, Greg, and Colleen moved closer to Mary. Allison stayed seated. Colleen hugged her mother. Matt and Greg stood in front of them.

"You're gonna believe this bullshit?" Wes asked.

"Happy now?" Matt said to Wes. "You're a real piece of shit, you know that?"

"She's lying. It's so obvious."

"Just go," Colleen said.

Wes threw his hands into the air and walked away.

Mary's sobbing subsided, and she wriggled from Colleen's grasp. A trail of mascara marked the path of Mary's tears. She began to clear the table.

"Mom," Colleen said. "Just leave it. We'll take care of it."

Mary stacked plates, not making eye contact with anyone. "I never would have thought my own family would make me relive the most traumatic experience of my life."

"Nobody wants you to relive anything," Colleen said. "Wes is the one acting crazy."

Mary slammed a handful of forks on the plate stack. She sniffled. "I don't appreciate being called a liar in my own home."

"We don't think you're a liar," Matt said. "I know liars. I see them every day. We all know you're an honest person. We love you, Mom."

Mary wiped her eyes. "I love you too." She looked at her children. "I don't know what I'd do without my kids." She forced a small smile. Mary kissed her son on the cheek, then Colleen, and Greg. "I'm not feeling well. I should go to bed."

"Do you need anything?" Colleen asked.

Mary shook her head. "I just need some rest."

Mary trudged past Allison, the only one still seated. In her wake were hushed conversations about cleaning up and going home. Mary went upstairs and shut her bedroom door behind her. Warren was in bed already, his nose in his book. He ignored Mary's arrival. Mary marched to her closet and took off her wedged heels.

"Boys, it's time to go home," Allison said from the hallway.

"Coming," Kyle said.

The pitter-patter of little feet ran down the hall, then the stairs.

Mary turned to Warren, still pretending to read. She stood by his bedside.

"Why did you do that?" Mary asked, her voice stern but hushed.

He slapped his book facedown on the bed. "Why did you lie?"

Mary crossed her arms. "I can't believe you think I would lie about something like that. Do you think I'm some kind of monster?"

"You said you never said that."

Mary blew out a breath. "Jesus Christ, Warren. I'm not going to tell my children that their father raped me. You see what it's done to Wesley."

Warren hung his head. "I'm sorry. I didn't think of it like that."

"No, you didn't. And look at the mess you created."

Warren rubbed his temples. He looked at Mary. "I'm really sorry. How bad is it?"

Mary shrugged. "I don't know. I had to do a lot of damage control."

48

Wes and Redemption

Wes parked in a visitor spot. He cut his headlights and took a deep breath. He was still shaky from the confrontation. He exited his car and walked across the parking lot, his hands in his jacket pockets. The streetlamps cast cold light in fluorescent circles. Wes stepped up to Apartment 1B and knocked.

Joe answered the door in sweats with reading glasses on the end of his nose. "More questions?"

"No." Wes shook his head. "There's something I wanna tell you."

Joe narrowed his dark eyes. "All right." He stepped aside.

Wes entered the apartment. There was a book on the coffee table—*Starting a Business for Dummies.*

Joe set his glasses on the table and plopped down in his recliner. Wes stood in a daze.

"You wanna sit down, or is this somethin' you say standin' up?" Joe asked.

Wes blinked. "I'll sit. Sorry." He sat on the couch opposite his father.

Joe smirked. "You find somethin' on your big quest for truth?"

Wes nodded, staring at Joe. "I believe you."

Joe was expressionless.

"I know you didn't do it."

Joe shook his head. "You can't never know such a thing. There'll always be that doubt. That's why—"

"She did it before."

Joe's mouth was open, his eyes still.

"She told her current husband that my stepfather raped her. She's sick. What she did to you was"—Wes shook his head—"really fucked up. I just wanted you to know that I believe you. I know it probably doesn't mean much—"

"It means everything." His eyes were glassy. "Nobody ever believed—" Joe cleared his throat. He stood. "Excuse me." He walked past Wes toward the bathroom.

49

Wes and the Email Dud

Wes sat on his couch, typing on his laptop.

Colleen, Matt, and Rich,

I know you guys are pissed at me. In Matt's case, I don't care anymore. I thought maybe we could salvage the relationship. We are brothers. I've finally come to terms that we can't. Matt, if you're reading this, we're finished. I'm sure you're fine with that. What happened with Tara was wrong. What you did was wrong. It's not how you treat a brother. I'm sad that I won't see Connor and Kyle, but I can't control that. The only reason I'm including you in this email is because I don't want your children to be hurt further by Mary. Please read the following.

Sociopaths make up about 4% of the population, so, for example, if you know two hundred people, you probably know eight sociopaths. Sociopaths do commit heinous crimes, with about 50% of the violent criminals in prison being sociopathic, but, by and large, most do not. Sociopaths simply do not have a conscience. They don't feel bad if they hurt others as normal people would. They are not driven by love, friendship, or loyalty. They are not even necessarily driven toward material things or money, although that can be an end to their game. They are driven to win, to control, to manipulate, to cause problems, and to watch the carnage. There is no treatment, no cure. They will never stop. They will never change.

How do you spot a sociopath?

They look just like you and me, so don't expect them to look creepy. They are adept at blending in, like a chameleon. Most of them do a good job of hiding their lack of conscience by acting normal. In fact, many of them are experts in acting. They've been faking it their whole lives. They are especially adept at manipulation. There are many traits, but, like normal people, their sociopathology manifests itself differently. One trait is most common above all others: the pity party. Perversely, sociopaths don't typically prey on our fears. They prey on our sympathies. They love to play the victim. They do this because, when we pity, we lower our defenses to their manipulations.

Other possible traits (they won't have the same ones, and remember that they will hide them as best they can.)

1. They seek out the vulnerable to manipulate.

2. They get those around them to keep secrets.

3. They are like vampires, and the truth is like the sun. They will slander and assassinate the character of anyone who sees them for who they are, tries to tell the truth, or calls them out on lies.

4. They will exhaust and drain you emotionally.

5. They will charm those in power and hurt the weak. **(Mary always said how much her boss liked her. She probably charmed the shit out of him, until he finally found out the truth.)**

6. They love to throw pity parties. They will exaggerate illnesses, money woes, how badly they've been treated. They need you to feel sorry for them. **(I saw a pretty big pity party on Saturday.)**

7. They are often unreliable.

8. They make suicide threats that are rarely carried out. **(Mary did this to me when I was a child.)**

9. They mirror your values. Do you feel like an outsider? Sociopaths will tell you that they're an outsider too. Are you a teacher? They'll tell you a story of how a teacher helped them and how they hope their kid becomes a teacher. They'll mirror your interests and desires so you feel allied with them for the sole purpose of manipulating you.

10. They use flattery, flattery, and more flattery. This is their most effective way to manipulate, and they're masters at it. Don't let your ego blind you.

11. They often have addictions: drugs, alcohol, food, sex, **shopping**, etc.

12. They lie and exaggerate. They lie big and small to cover something up or to change perceptions. Anything to make themselves look good.

13. They offer lots of promises but no positive action.

14. They're not great at holding a job. **(Mary was fired.)**

15. If caught in a lie, they'll play the victim or get very angry and blame others. **(This is exactly what she did on Saturday.)**

16. They use projection. If they're spreading lies about you, they'll accuse you of spreading lies.

17. They're immature. They're superficial. They're very concerned about their physical appearance and projecting a certain image. They love expensive cars and toys. They often have immature hobbies. **(Like collecting antique dolls.)**

18. They may have a criminal record.

19. They may fake empathy for children, old people, and animals.

20. They often leave a trail of broken marriages and relationships in their wake. They have strained relationships with family members. **(Grace, Doris, me.)**

21. They divide and conquer. Sociopaths often manipulate and pit people against each other. They exploit weaknesses in family and work relationships. **(Matt, you might want to ask Allison about this one.)**

Evidence our mother is a sociopath:

1. She lied about graduating from college and grad school to get her job. She was fired for this lie.

2. She's had two marriages.

3. She told Warren that she was raped by Ed. (Pity party.)

4. She told the police that my father and another man raped her. Two men went to prison for fifteen years for a crime I believe they didn't commit. I think Nana found out Mary was pregnant. Maybe Nana threatened to cut Mary out of the will. So, she made up the rape claim, threw one helluva pity party, and got paid in the process with a civil suit. And, most important, she stayed in Nana's will.

5. She stole from Doris, then slandered her by telling everyone that Doris was crazy.

6. She coerced and stole from Nana. I believe Grace was supposed to receive half the estate, but Mary made sure that didn't happen.

7. She stole Ed's money when they got divorced.

8. Lies, lies, and more lies. (I could go on forever here.)

9. Told me as a child that she was going to kill herself and it was my fault.

10. Lied to everyone for decades, saying that my biological father's dead. He's very much alive, and his name's not Tony. It's Joe.

11. She's a shopaholic.

12. I know she did something to Connor. That poor kid is terrified of her. (Seriously, Matt, get Connor into some counseling.)

What do you do if you encounter a sociopath?
Martha Stout, PhD, recommends the following:

1. Do not play their game. They love it, and they are better at it than you. It's what they do.

2. Question authority.

3. Question your tendency to pity. Suspect those who crave pity.

4. Do not forgive the unforgivable.

5. Never agree out of pity to conceal a sociopath's true nature.

6. Beware of grand flattery.

7. The best protection is avoidance. Preferably no contact whatsoever. If that's impossible, come as close as possible to total avoidance.

Conclusion
I refuse to be manipulated any longer, even if I'm an outcast. I refuse to be near someone of her character. I'm sure she's already started the pity party and the lie campaign against mean Wesley. Meanwhile everyone pities her. Yay, more pity parties!

She's so subtle. She's much better at manipulation than anyone thinks. If you're thinking there's no way she could manipulate you, she's probably already done it. The only way to free yourself is to stop any contact with her.

I'm not telling you to do anything. I am only providing the truth as best I can surmise. The research above comes from the book

The Sociopath Next Door by Martha Stout and various articles about sociopathology. Mary is a textbook sociopath in my opinion. SHE WILL NEVER CHANGE. SHE WILL NEVER STOP LYING AND MANIPULATING. THERE IS NO CURE FOR WHAT SHE IS.

Sincerely,
Wes

He hovered the cursor over Send and clicked.

50

Mary and Santa's Coming to Town

Mary marched into her bedroom in high heels and a tight black dress. Her blond hair was in an updo. She looked like a million bucks, without the hard work. Warren was in the sitting area, putting on his shiny shoes.

"I hope you're happy," Mary said, scowling. "Ed and Sheryl aren't coming."

Warren glanced up, then went back to tying his shoe. "Fine with me."

"He said he's not comfortable. Congratulations, you've managed the impossible—making Ed uncomfortable."

Warren closed his eyes for a moment.

"I ordered enough food for nine adults," Mary said.

"So, we'll have leftovers." Warren sat up and then stood. He wore a dark suit.

"At one hundred dollars a plate?"

Warren shrugged.

Mary shook her head. "I still can't believe you said what you said."

Warren held out his palms. "It's been three months. How many times do I have to tell you that I'm sorry?"

"When I no longer have to deal with the consequences of your big mouth. What I say to you stays between us. If I can't trust you to keep a secret—"

"I'm sorry, okay? I promise you that it'll never happen again. Can we just try to enjoy the party? It's Christmas Eve."

Mary scowled.

"Please." His voice was small.

"Fine."

"I love you, cuddle cakes."

She smirked. "I love you too. I'm going to check on the caterers."

Mary stepped down the spiral staircase. The Christmas tree was fifteen feet tall, brightly lit, and real. "Santa Claus Is Comin' to Town" played through the speakers of the whole-house audio system. The caterers talked quietly.

Mary entered the kitchen with a smile. "Is there anything I can do to help?"

The woman shook her head. "That's very kind of you, Mrs. Shaw, but that's what we're here for."

She and her adult son were each dressed in black pants, a white button-down, and a bow tie. Her son adjusted the heat on the warming trays. He looked up at Mary with a grin. "We should be ready in about twenty minutes."

"It smells wonderful," Mary replied. "And I really appreciate your willingness to work on Christmas Eve. I know you must have your own family to visit."

The woman waved her hand across her face. "We do everything on Christmas Day." She smiled. "It gave me a good excuse to make my husband do the wrapping."

"This is nice. I'm used to running around like a crazy woman before a party."

"Would you like a drink?" the woman asked. "We have most liquors and beer and sodas of course."

"I would love a gin and tonic."

The woman looked over the liquor she had set up on the counter.

"Ryan, could you go to the van and get the gin?"

Ryan nodded and hurried outside through the garage.

"Oh, that's not necessary," Mary said. "I can just have a beer."

"Nonsense, we should have brought it in. He'll just be a minute. Why don't you have a seat and relax? We'll take care of everything."

"Thanks, Ronda. You're very kind. I'll be in the living room."

Mary marched to the living room. The hardwood was covered by a handcrafted rug that cost as much as an economy car. She sat on the white couch and gazed at the Christmas tree in the corner. Heaps of presents were under and around the tree.

Ryan marched across the hardwood to the living room with a gin and tonic in hand. "Here's your drink, Mrs. Shaw."

"Thank you, Ryan," Mary replied, taking the glass. "It's nice that you work with your mother." She took a sip.

"I just help out when she needs it. I'm a senior at George Mason."

"It's a good school. I earned my MBA at George Mason."

"Do you drive the Tesla?"

"My husband. It's his Christmas present."

"Wow, that's some present. It's so cool. I wanna get one someday. I'm studying environmental science. I'm really into the environment."

Mary smiled. "We definitely need smart young men who care about the environment. If we don't take care of the planet, where do we expect to live?"

"That's what I always tell people. It's like people just don't get it."

Mary nodded and took another sip of her gin.

"Well, I should get back." He smiled and returned to the kitchen.

The doorbell rang; the door opened. Crying overpowered the Christmas music. Greg held the door open for Colleen as she shuffled inside with Abby on her hip and the diaper bag slung over her shoulder. Greg was right behind her with a shopping bag full of presents.

Mary stood from the couch, her drink in hand. "Merry Christmas."

Greg forced a smile. "Merry Christmas, Mom."

"Hi, Mom," Colleen said, frowning.

"Someone's a little cranky," Mary said in baby talk.

"Cranky's an understatement. I should feed her. I'm going to the guest bedroom. Is that okay?"

"Of course."

Colleen trudged upstairs with Abby and the diaper bag. The crying was mostly silenced with the shutting of the bedroom door.

"Wow, look at all the presents," Greg said. "Should I put these under the tree?" He held up his bag of gifts.

"Please do," Mary replied.

"I see someone's been busy," he said as he arranged the presents.

Mary smiled. "I know. I'm a spoiler."

He faced Mary, the gifts neatly placed. "It's nice."

"Will you be seeing your parents tomorrow?"

"Yep, tomorrow. The whole crew'll be there. It gets a little crazy, but it should be fun."

"Your family is so sweet. I really enjoyed them at your wedding."

"Thanks. They really liked you too."

The front door opened, and Matt and Kyle entered, followed by Allison and Connor.

"Merry Christmas," Matt said, walking toward the Christmas tree.

"Merry Christmas, honey," Mary said as he approached.

"Look at that tree." Matt hugged his mother.

"Look at all the presents," Kyle said, his eyes bulging.

"Hi, Mary," Allison said, Connor hiding behind her.

"Hi, Allison. Don't you look beautiful?"

"You guys are almost twins," Greg said, looking from one tight black dress to another tight black dress.

"I'm not the stunner that Allison is. I'm getting old," Mary said.

Greg mock-frowned. "You look great."

"Are the presents for me?" Kyle asked.

Matt laughed. "Not all of them."

"But some of them?"

"Would you like to open one before dinner?" Mary asked.

“Yes!” Kyle threw his fist into the air like a superhero.

“What about you, Connor? Would you like to open a present before dinner?”

Connor shook his head, still hiding behind Allison.

“If you change your mind, let me know.” Mary turned to Kyle. “Why don’t you find one with a tag that reads *Kyle*?”

Kyle rummaged through the presents.

“Take one from the top,” Allison said.

Kyle picked out a rectangular box about half his size. “It says Kyle. I can read.”

Allison walked over and double-checked.

“See? It says Kyle.” He pointed to his name.

“Very good, sweetie.”

“Can I open this one?”

“Of course,” Mary said.

Warren plodded down the spiral staircase, his jacket buttoned over his gut.

Kyle ripped into the wrapping paper, revealing a remote-controlled car. “It’s a police car!”

“Look at that,” Warren said, as he sidled up to the group.

“It’s remote-controlled,” Matt said. “Do you want Daddy to help you with the batteries?”

“I think that one has the batteries in the box,” Mary said.

Matt looked over the plastic-windowed box. “Yep, they’re right here. We’re gonna take this in the TV room. Come on, buddy.”

“Come on, Connor,” Kyle said.

The three Shaw boys went to the TV room. They ignored Warren.

“I gotta check this thing out,” Greg said, following the boys.

“Why don’t you go tell Richard that it’s time to eat?” Mary said to Warren.

Warren went to the basement without a reply.

Allison picked up the wrapping paper.

“You can leave it,” Mary said. “I need to bring out the trash bags before the gift exchange."

"I hate to do that," Allison said. "Everything looks so perfect."

The boys moved from the TV room to the large expanse of hardwood in the foyer. Kyle grinned as the siren blared and the police car zipped across the hardwood, banging into furniture legs and wall corners.

"This is awesome," Kyle said.

Matt stood, beaming at his son, his hands on his hips, like he was superdad.

"Be careful please," Allison said to Kyle.

"I am being careful," Kyle replied, as the car smashed into the leg of an antique dry sink.

"It's time to eat," Mary said as she approached the boys. "Greg, can you tell Colleen that it's time to eat?"

"Sure." Greg climbed the stairs in search of Colleen and Abby.

"Maybe Kyle can take his car on the driveway after dinner," Mary said to Matt, hoping to stop the damage.

Kyle frowned. "It's cold out there."

"Nana's right," Matt said. "It's time to eat." Matt snatched the controller and turned off the car.

Kyle crossed his arms. "Aw, Dad."

"After dinner, there'll be plenty of toys," Matt said. "You want me to call Santa and tell him not to come tonight?"

"No."

Mary and her family made their way to the kitchen. The caterers stood behind the stainless steel warming trays. They took drink orders and served the food, buffet-style. It was surf and turf with steamed vegetables, mashed potatoes, and salad. A variety of cheesecakes and pies were offered for dessert. The family sat around the dining room table, eating and drinking, the conversation subdued.

Colleen held Abby and tried to eat. Kyle slumped in his chair with his arms crossed. Rich sat at the far end of the table in jeans and a hooded sweatshirt—the hood up. Connor sat in Allison's lap. Matt,

Warren, and Greg ate like men.

"This is really good," Greg said.

"Great food, Ronda," Warren called out to the kitchen.

"Thank you," Ronda called back.

"Eat your food," Allison said to Kyle.

"My teeth hurt," Kyle replied, his brow furrowed.

"He needs to go to the dentist," Allison said. "I couldn't get him in until after the holidays."

"You should have told me," Mary said. "I'm sure my dentist would have taken him right away, especially if he's in pain."

"I don't think he's in that much pain. He's not hungry because he got into the Christmas candy at home, which he *wasn't* supposed to do." Allison frowned at Kyle.

"I like candy," Kyle said.

Allison shook her head. "I know you do. That's the problem."

Rich stood from the table and headed toward the basement.

Matt glared at his brother.

"Richard, where are you going?" Mary asked.

"I'm done. *Jesus*," he replied. "Why can't you stay out of my business?" Rich slammed the door to the basement.

"What's his problem?" Matt asked.

"Brandi broke up with him," Warren said.

"That's too bad," Allison said.

"More like good riddance," Matt said. "That girl was nothing but trouble."

Allison narrowed her eyes at her husband. "You would know," she said under her breath.

"The first broken heart is always the hardest," Mary said. "It is probably for the best."

"Fat, … fat," Abby said.

"No, *bad*," Colleen said, her face crimson.

"Abby's talking," Mary said, beaming. "I've never heard her talk. Is that her first word? What is she saying?"

"Sounds like *fat*," Matt said between bites.

"Fat, fat, fat." Abby grinned.

Matt laughed. "She is saying fat."

Allison glared at her husband.

"What?"

Colleen shook her head, her eyes glassy. "She must have picked it up on TV, because Greg and I don't use *that* word." Colleen wiped her eyes with her cloth napkin.

"Don't worry about it, honey," Mary said.

"It's no big deal," Greg said.

"Kids just say things. I had a coworker, and her son's first word was *S-H-I-T*, although it came out more like 'sit.' But he only said it when he was pointing at you-know-what."

"I'm still eating, Mom," Matt said.

Mary mock-frowned at her son. "If you think this is bad, how do you deal with crime scenes?"

Matt smirked. "I'm not eating my dinner over a dead body."

"Now that's too much for me," Greg said with a chuckle.

Colleen managed a giggle.

51

Wes and a Merry Christmas Eve

Wes knocked on Apartment 1B, holding a bottle of white wine. Joe answered the door with a wide grin.

"Merry Christmas, Wes. Or is it Merry Christmas Eve?"

"Merry Christmas, … Joe."

"Come in." Joe motioned with his hand.

Wes stepped into the apartment. Joe wore a sweater and khakis that were mostly free of grease stains. A tiny artificial Christmas tree sat on the coffee table. It was decorated with tinsel and a star, no lights.

"This is for you," Wes said, holding out the wine.

Joe smiled. "Thanks. It'll go good with dinner. I'm just finishin' up."

Wes followed Joe into the kitchen. It smelled like garlic. A card table with two folding chairs were set up there. Wes sat down at the table.

Joe opened the oven and shut it. He turned to Wes. "I think it's about done. I made lasagna and garlic bread. I should have asked you if you like lasagna. Hopefully you do."

"I do like it. Not sure if the wine will go. I think it's supposed to be red wine."

"That don't matter. The wine's perfect. You want somethin' to drink? You wanna open it now?"

"I'll wait for dinner."

"Take off your jacket. Relax."

Wes removed his wool jacket and hung it on the back of his chair.

Joe put on an oven mitt and removed the garlic bread and lasagna. "Looks ready."

Wes and Joe chatted over dinner. They broached safe topics, like the weather, cars, Italian food, computers, and sports.

"There's still more lasagna and bread," Joe said.

"I'm full," Wes said. "It was really good though."

Joe stood from the table. "Want me to take your plate?"

"Thanks."

Joe set the plates in the sink. He opened a drawer and removed a wrapped box the size of a man's fist. He turned around and sat back down across from Wes.

"I got this for you," Joe said, handing the gift across the table.

"Thanks. You really didn't have to."

"It's no big deal."

Wes unwrapped the gift and opened the box inside. It was a thick silver watch.

"A man oughtta have a nice watch," Joe said.

Wes put it on his wrist. "It fits perfectly. Thanks, Joe. I hope it didn't cost too much."

Joe cackled. "It ain't that nice."

Wes grabbed his jacket hanging on his chair and removed an envelope from the inside pocket. He rehung the jacket and handed the envelope to Joe.

"This is for you," Wes said.

Joe grinned, taking the envelope from Wes. He opened it and removed a check in the amount of $20,000. He looked at Wes with his eyebrows arched. "What's this?"

"I want in. I liquidated my retirement account from school."

Joe smiled wide, his beard stretching across his face. "You sure about this?"

Wes smiled. “I’m positive.”

“We’re gonna do great. You won’t regret this, son.” Joe blinked. “Sorry, *Wes*.”

“It’s okay. I am your son.”

52

Mary, She's Good

The caterers were gone. The living room was covered in wrapping paper and plastic crap. Kyle was on the floor, going from toy to toy, none of them holding his attention for very long. Allison shoved paper into garbage bags. Connor played with his action figures at her feet.

Matt and Greg fiddled with their Apple watches on the couch. Abby was asleep in her mother's arms. Colleen wore her new diamond earrings. Allison left hers in the box.

"There is one more surprise," Mary said, standing from a chair next to Warren.

Everyone looked at Mary. Warren smiled and removed two envelopes from his inside jacket pocket and handed them to his wife.

"You might wanna sit for this," Warren said to Allison.

Allison cinched the trash bag and sat in a chair, far away from Matt.

"There's one for the Shaws," Mary said, handing an envelope to Matt. "And another for the Jensens." She handed an envelope to Greg. "Open them."

Matt and Greg opened the envelopes. Inside was a white and silver Christmas card that said something sappy about how love and family make Christmas worth celebrating. A handwritten note had been added to the cards.

Matt's note started with *Matt, Allison, Kyle, and Connor*. Everything else was identical to the card Greg and Colleen read.

> Warren and I would like to invite you to an all-expenses paid vacation for two weeks in Duck, North Carolina. We are the proud new owners of a beach house in the Outer Banks. It even has a pool!
>
> This house will eventually be passed down to you and your children. In the meantime, I look forward to many wonderful summers with my family.
>
> All Our Love,
> Mom and Warren
>
> PS: A few minutes ago, I emailed you a link to the house.

"Wow, congratulations," Greg said.

Mary smiled.

"You guys really bought a beach house?" Colleen asked.

Mary nodded. "We did."

"Good for you, Mom."

"Good for us," Mary said. "There are enough rooms for everyone to have their own space."

Matt was on his phone, looking at the link Mary sent. "This place is really nice."

"Let me see," Colleen said.

Matt handed his phone to his sister.

Greg tapped on his cell.

"It looks like it's right on the beach," Colleen said, one hand on the phone, the other still cradling Abby.

"It is," Mary replied.

"I can't wait for summer. Abby will *love* playing in the sand."

"We'll have to watch Kyle around the ocean," Matt said. "That boy has no fear."

"I'll teach all the kids to swim in the pool," Mary said.

"This is very generous," Allison said.

"It's gonna be a great summer," Matt said.

* * *

Warren stood next to the bed, buttoning his pajama top. "Great party, cuddle cakes."

Mary slid her panty hose down her legs and stepped out of them. "Thanks, honey. It *was* nice, wasn't it?"

Warren nodded. "I am a little worried about Rich. He thinks you said something to Brandi."

"I know. That girl's bad news. She filled his head with God-knows-what. It'll blow over." Mary took off her earrings. "I think they're excited about the beach house, don't you?" She placed the diamond studs in her jewelry box.

"They're ecstatic. And they should be. It's a beautiful place. You do remember that we're planning to keep it rented for most of the summer? It would be nice to be cash positive the first year, especially since we're still carrying the mortgage here."

"I know. I just want four weeks."

"I thought we agreed on three."

"Well, we don't know if everyone can come down at the same time."

Warren exhaled. "I suppose one more week won't make much difference but no more."

She sidled up to her husband with bare feet and bare legs. She kissed him openmouthed and stepped back. "Merry Christmas. I love you."

"I love you too."

Mary turned around. "Can you unzip me?"

Warren slid the zipper down from her neck to the top of her ass.

Mary wore a black thong. He slid his hand inside her dress, grabbing a cheek.

She giggled and wiggled from his grasp. "You're bad."

"Maybe you can give Santa his cookies and milk now."

Mary stepped out of her dress. She stood in a black lace bra and thong. "Let me wash my face, and I'll give you the best cookies and milk you've ever had."

Warren grinned. "What about Mrs. Claus?"

"That old biddy? You'll be divorced by New Year."

Warren laughed.

Mary rocked her hips back and forth as she sauntered to the bathroom. She shut the double doors and locked them.

She washed her face in her sink and removed her makeup with a towel. She looked in the vanity mirror. She had crow's-feet spreading from her eyes, deep wrinkles on her forehead, and her mouth was starting to look like an asshole. She frowned. Then she smiled, her eyes dancing and bright. She smirked. She giggled, putting her hand over her chest. Her giggle subsided. She pulled the skin on her face back with her hands, eliminating the wrinkles. *It might be time for a face-lift. I don't think Botox is enough anymore.*

She threw her head back and laughed. Just as quickly as she started, she stopped, her face still. She stared at her reflection, her lips quivering. Her eyes watered; her vison blurred. She blinked and tears slid down her cheeks. Then she smiled.

53

Wes and Rich Pricks

Wes locked his apartment door and bounded down the steps, his keys in hand. Derrick and Luther were shooting the shit in the parking lot. It was sunny and humid—already. Luther had tight cornrows and jean shorts that hung to midcalf. Derrick's bald head was shiny with sweat.

"Good mornin', Wes," Derrick said.

"Hey, Derrick, Luther," Wes replied. "How you guys doing?"

"Not bad," Luther said. "You know how we do."

"How's that new Hyundai workin' out for your dad?" Derrick asked.

"He loves it," Wes said. "He loved the price even more."

"I told you that I'd hook 'im up."

"I appreciate it."

"We're goin' to a go-go club on Friday. You wanna come along?" Luther asked. "Some fine females."

"Thanks for the offer and I hate to perpetuate the stereotype, but I don't dance so well."

"I'd like to see Wes up in the club." Luther gyrated to an imaginary beat, his hitchhiker thumb out, then the imaginary sprinkler, followed by running in place.

Wes and Derrick laughed.

Luther stopped. "What? Too much?" Luther stepped right and left in a slow rhythm, his arms bent, snapping his fingers to the beat in his head. "How 'bout this?"

Wes smirked.

"Come on, Wes," Luther said. "This is the go-to dance for white people."

Wes shook his head, grinning. "You guys have fun. The club is definitely not for me."

"You still comin' to the barbecue, right?" Derrick asked.

"I'll be there," Wes said. "I do have to work. I might not get there until four. I hope that's okay."

"Party won't get goin' 'til then anyway," Derrick said.

"Old man's makin' you work on the Fourth of July?" Luther asked.

"It was my idea," Wes said. "With the Fourth on a Tuesday, it messes up the schedule for the rest of the week if we take off."

"Feel free to bring your dad," Derrick said.

"Thanks. I'll ask him. I'll see you guys."

Wes walked to his truck.

He removed two magnetic signs from the cab and slapped them on the doors. Wes drove against traffic to Joe's apartment. He parked in front of Building 10 and tapped on the horn. A minute later Joe emerged from his apartment in khaki shorts and a T-shirt. He held a small cooler in one hand and a newspaper in the other.

Joe sat in the passenger seat. "It's gonna be another hot one."

"Yeah," Wes replied, backing from the parking space. Wes drove out of the apartment complex. "Derrick's having a Fourth of July party. It doesn't start until four. You're invited if you wanna come."

"You goin'?"

"Yeah. You should come."

"I ain't got any other plans."

Wes drove across town. Joe read the newspaper.

"Anything interesting?" Wes asked.

"No. Just a bunch a bullshit. Politicians blamin' everyone but themselves for the real estate mess."

"It's a freaking disaster."

"I'm surprised it hasn't hurt our business," Joe said. "A lot a people losin' their homes."

"People want cheap housing now. That's apartments."

"And the rich pricks movin' in are used to someone takin' their trash."

Wes grinned. "Hey, we might be rich one day."

Joe smirked. "And I'll be a prick."

* * *

Wes carried six trash bags down the steps—three in each hand. His arms were veiny and muscular. His truck idled in front of the apartment building. Joe arranged trash bags in the truck bed to accommodate more. Wes strategically tossed in his six bags, adding to the heap. A woman in running shorts and a T-shirt stepped from a silver Toyota Corolla parked near his truck. Her legs were tan and toned, her brown hair in a ponytail.

She did a little hop-skip and bounded across the asphalt toward the mailboxes.

Wes ducked down behind the truck.

"What are you doin'?" Joe asked. "We're burnin' daylight."

Wes stayed crouched.

"Wes?" Joe walked around the truck. "What the hell are you doin'?"

Wes looked up at his dad. "See that girl by the mailbox?"

Joe turned his head and pointed. "That one?"

"Don't point."

"Why not?"

"It's a girl I used to work with at school. I had a huge crush on her."

"Then go talk to her."

Wes put his finger to his lips. "Shh, not so loud."

Joe turned his head again. "She's a cute girl. What the hell you waitin' for?"

"I'm picking up trash."

Joe frowned. "You work an honest job. You ain't got a damn thing to be ashamed of. Stand up."

Wes stood eye to eye with his father.

Joe said, "People in this life'll tear you down. Don't help 'em out."

"You're right."

Joe smiled and smacked Wes on the shoulder. "Damn right I'm right. I'm gonna take these to the Dumpster. At least say hi to the girl."

Joe drove the truck toward the Dumpsters. Daisy flipped through her mail as she walked toward the building. Wes was frozen on the sidewalk. She was headed his way. She would have to alter her course, or she would run right into him.

She was about ten feet away when she glanced up from her mail. She smiled that perfect smile. "Sorry, I almost ran into you."

Wes opened his mouth, but nothing came out.

She changed course, walking around him. She continued toward the building, away from Wes.

"Daisy," Wes called out.

She stopped and turned around.

Wes waved and walked toward her.

She tilted her head and narrowed her eyes. "Wes Shaw?"

He smiled. "Yep. How are you, Daisy?"

"Wow, I almost didn't recognize you."

Wes nodded. "It's been a while … three years."

"Time flies. What are you doing here?"

"I work here. Well, here and other apartment complexes." Wes pointed to his shirt.

She read his T-shirt. "You take care of the trash?"

"Yeah, for anyone who doesn't wanna make the trek to the Dumpsters. We have a fair amount of clients here."

"I think I saw your flyer."

"Are you still at Twain?"

"I am, but I may not be there for too much longer."

"Really?"

"I wrote a young adult series. I mean, I never expected the books to do anything." She grinned. "But they've been doing really well."

"That's great."

"Thanks."

"What's the title? I'd like to read them."

She shook her head. "I'm not sure you'd like them. They're definitely chick lit."

"I think I would." Wes's face felt hot. "Because you wrote them."

She blushed. "Just go on Amazon and search for Daisy Bennett."

Wes nodded. "I'll do that. Congratulations."

"Thanks." She glanced at the building steps. "I guess I should go. I try to write at least two thousand words a day."

"If, umm, if you ever wanted to go out for lunch or something, I'd like to take you."

She blushed again.

"I always liked you at school," Wes said. "I just think you're nice and pretty, and I'd like to get to know you better. That's all."

She put her hand to her chest. "That's really nice of you, but I kinda have a boyfriend." She winced. "I'm really sorry."

"I understand completely. I think it's important to be honest with people, even if you don't get the result you hoped for."

Joe drove the pickup toward them.

"That's an interesting perspective." She smiled.

"I'll see you, Daisy. Good luck with your books."

She stared at him for a moment. "Thanks."

He turned and stepped toward the passenger side of the pickup. The sign on the door read Esposito and Son Trash.

54

Mary and Perception Is Reality

"I can't believe you're bringing this up now," Mary said as she arranged side dishes on the center island.

"You have to tell them," Warren said.

Mary exhaled and took off her apron. She wore a sundress and chunky heels. "And you think now is appropriate?" She put her hands on her hips. "It's a party, Warren."

Warren shook his head, his face red. "By delaying the inevitable, we've given them no time to budget. Matt and Colleen may lose their homes. Don't you think Rich should know that we can't afford his tuition?"

"I delayed because I thought the market might come back."

Warren blew out a breath like a bull. "Which market? Housing prices are cratering, especially for luxury vacation homes, and we've lost a fortune in the stock market."

"And whose fault is that?"

"I wouldn't be worried if we didn't buy that five-million-dollar money pit that we can't rent."

"It's rented this weekend."

Warren clenched his jaw. "At half of what we figured on for a holiday weekend."

"We still have *your* income."

"My business is going down the fucking toilet."

"Since when?"

"Since the stock market tanked. People liquidate during a crash. I tell them that it's the worst possible time to sell, but they have bills. And you know what? We're just as bad. The past few months I've had to liquidate stocks from our retirement accounts just so you can pay the bills."

"Jesus, Warren, why didn't you tell me?"

"Maybe I was hoping the market would rebound too. We need to consider defaulting on the beach house."

Mary frowned. "Our guests will be here any minute. I really don't want to talk about this right now."

"They need to know." Warren pointed at Mary. "If you don't tell them, I will."

"Fine," Mary replied. "Can you at least make yourself useful and start on the burgers?"

Warren stomped to the fridge, each step reverberating through the hardwood. He grabbed the burgers and marched outside. Mary stepped to the bathroom and checked her hair and makeup. She finger-brushed her blond hair from her eyes. She stared into the mirror and sighed.

Warren's not the provider I thought he'd be. He had such potential. A successful company. Mary shook her head. *I need to talk to my divorce attorney. I also need to start moving money.*

The front door opened. "Mom, we're here," Matt said.

Mary exited the bathroom and walked to the foyer. Matt was there with Kyle.

Mary cocked her head. "Where's Allison and Connor?"

"They're not feeling well," Matt replied.

Mary pressed out her bottom lip. "That's too bad. I hope it's nothing serious."

"I think they'll be okay."

Mary smiled at Kyle. "Do you have a hug for Nana?"

Kyle held on to an iPad. He gave Mary a one-handed hug. "Can I go play my game?" Kyle asked Matt.

"Go ahead," Matt said, "but not when we sit down to eat."

Kyle went to the TV room.

Greg opened the front door and entered the foyer, with Abby holding his hand.

"Nana!" Abby said. She hugged Mary's legs.

"Hi, sweetheart," Mary said, bending down and wrapping her arms around the child.

"Hey, Mom," Greg said.

Mary looked up, smiling. "Hi, Greg."

"She loves her Nana."

Abby let go, and Mary looked her over. "She just looks adorable in this dress," Mary said.

Abby wore a red, white, and blue dress.

Greg smiled. "That's all Colleen."

Colleen waddled into the foyer, still tapping on her phone. She shoved her phone in her purse.

"My back is killing me," Colleen said, in lieu of a greeting, one hand rubbing her lower back, the other on her pregnant belly.

"Go sit down, honey," Mary said.

* * *

The dining room table was filled with empty dessert plates, each with remnants of icing. Except for Warren's. He had scraped up every last bit of sugar.

Warren leaned toward Mary. "They'll be leaving soon."

"Not now," Mary whispered.

"I have some bad news," Warren said.

Mary kicked his foot under the table. She looked at her children. "Colleen, Matthew, Richard, I need to speak with you in private."

They looked at each other quizzically.

"Happy?" she said to Warren.

"It has to be done," he whispered.

Mary led her kids outside on the deck.

"You three should sit down," Mary said.

Colleen grunted as she sat on the wooden bench. Rich sat next to her. Matt stood with his arms crossed.

"What's this about?" Matt asked.

"Sit," Mary said.

Matt sat next to Colleen.

Mary's mouth turned down, her eyes glassy.

"What is it, Mom?" Colleen asked. "You're scaring me."

"What I'm about to tell you has to stay between us. If it gets back to Warren that I told you this, I might lose everything."

Matt's eyes went wide. "What are you talking about?"

A tear slid down Mary's face, then a few more. "Warren's not the man I thought he was."

"What does that mean?" Rich asked.

Mary made no attempt to wipe away the tears. *They need to see them.* "Warren has a gambling problem."

"What do you mean, a gambling problem?" Matt asked. "Like betting on sports?"

Mary shook her head. "He gambles in the stock market. High-risk options. With the market falling, he's … he's lost everything." Mary covered her mouth, unable to stifle the sob.

"Oh, no," Colleen said, sitting up, suddenly aware of the ramifications.

"What do you mean, he's lost everything?" Matt said.

"I'll fix this, but, for now, we're broke." Mary sniffled. "I'm so sorry."

"So, no more help?" Colleen asked.

Mary shook her head. "I'm so sorry."

Matt stood. "Jesus Christ, Mom. We can't afford to make our mortgage without help. We could've stayed in Woodbridge."

Rich stood. "What about my tuition? My truck?"

Mary shook her head. "You'll have to ask your father and Sheryl for help."

Rich glowered at Mary. "They don't have any money."

"We have another baby coming," Colleen said.

"I know. I know," Mary said. "I'm fixing it."

Matt crossed his arms. "How are you gonna do that?"

"I'm meeting with a divorce attorney. I might salvage some money if we default on the beach house and the house here. I don't care if I have to live in a cardboard box. I won't let you kids down." Fresh tears streamed along Mary's cheeks.

"No," Matt said, glancing at his brother and sister. "Mom's gonna need that money. Divorce is expensive." Matt looked at Mary. "I won't put you on the street so I can live in a nice house. Allison and I will figure it out."

Colleen stood with a groan. "So will Greg and I."

Rich stood. "I hate college anyway."

They laughed, the tension broken.

"I love you kids," Mary said.

Mary's children wrapped her up in a group hug.

I win. Again.

Dear Reader,

I'm thrilled that you took precious time out of your life to read my book. Thank you! I hope you found it entertaining, engaging, and thought-provoking. If so, please consider writing a positive review on Amazon and Goodreads. Five-star reviews have a huge impact on future sales. The review doesn't need to be long and detailed, if you're more of a reader than a writer. As an author and a small businessman, competing against the big publishers, every reader, every review, and every referral is greatly appreciated.

If you're interested in receiving my novel *Against the Grain* for free, and/or reading my other titles for free or $0.99, go to the following link: http://www.PhilWBooks.com. You're probably thinking, *what's the catch?* There is no catch.

If you want to contact me, don't be bashful. I can be found at Phil@PhilWBooks.com. I do my best to respond to all emails.

Sincerely,
Phil M. Williams

Author's Note

What would life be like without a conscience? How would you treat others if you didn't care about hurting them, deceiving them, or exploiting them? This is the reality for 4 percent of the population. According to the FBI, approximately twenty-five to fifty active serial killers are in the United States. According to psychologists, there are approximately thirteen million sociopaths. It's unlikely that you've encountered a serial killer, but you probably have a handful of sociopaths who you interact with on a regular basis.

For the sociopath, life is a game, and you're just a pawn to manipulate. These people plot and scheme and destroy. You pick up the pieces and wonder, *what the heck happened?*

The serial killer thriller has been done and redone, used and reused to shock the reader with scenarios they are never likely to encounter. With *No Conscience*, I wanted to explore the more pervasive problem of sociopaths—a predator who every single one of us have encountered.

Gratitude

I'd like to thank my wife. She's my first reader and always will be. Without her support and unwavering belief in my skill as an author, I'm not sure I would have embarked on this career. I love you, Denise.

I'd also like to thank my editors. My developmental editor, Caroline Smailes, did a fantastic job finding the holes in my plot and suggesting remedies. As always, my line editor, Denise Barker (not to be confused with my wife, Denise Williams), did a fantastic job making sure the manuscript was error-free. I love her comments and feedback.

Thank you to Deborah Bradseth of Tugboat Design for her excellent cover art and formatting. She's the consummate professional. I look forward to many more beautiful covers in the future.

Thank you to my mother-in-law, Joy Ollinger, for her expert advice on all things medical. I originally had Nana choking in the hospital after the stroke. As a retired nurse, Joy knew why that was unlikely.

Made in the USA
Columbia, SC
25 July 2020